The 5.18 Mystery

The 5.18 Mystery

J. Jefferson Farjeon

COACHWHIP PUBLICATIONS
GREENVILLE, OHIO

The 5.18 Mystery, by J. Jefferson Farjeon
© 2025 Coachwhip Publications edition

First published 1929
J. Jefferson Farjeon, 1883-1955
CoachwhipBooks.com

ISBN 1-61646-610-3
ISBN-13 978-1-61646-610-7

1

Dramatis Personae

Railway stations are how you see them. Particularly, perhaps, if the station is Liverpool-street station. To the hurried, harried workers who are poured into it each morning from the north-east of London, and are poured out again without welcome or ceremony into prosaic, soulless offices, Liverpool-street is one of the necessary nightmares of existence, and the original designers did their best to breathe into the terminus an inherent ugliness. One day Epstein may discover in it a perfect subject for his irony. It haunts the final, fast-slipping hours of Sunday night, bursts into hideous fact on Monday morning, and belches its sullen streams of smoke and humanity all the week.

But just as an ugly man may grow noble to those who surprise him in an act of grace, or an ugly woman may be beautiful in the eyes of faith, so even Liverpool-street station can rise on occasions above its gloom, and appear an enchanted spot. It was an enchanted spot to a young man in a light grey suit who alighted from a taxi one August afternoon and walked on air to the booking-office. To him there was no ugliness. (He lived in the north-west of London, travelling to his work by bus.) The porters were not gaolers, but liberators. The smoke was not an oily and tarry vapour mixed with soot, but a film of mystery beyond which lay worlds of wonder and of easy conquest.

The engine shrieks were melody. The grubby grey platforms were golden roads of adventure. Even Edgar Wallace
on the bookstall, a numb and spiritless sight to those who
came every day from the north-east, was a thing of joy to
this contented young man who had come, on one day only,
from the north-west. Experience, like currency, must be
exchanged if we are to fight against our apathy.

There were many obvious reasons why Freddy Reeve
was in such a gay humour, and why he did not swear when
a little cockney bloke opened a long account with him by
accidentally stepping on his toe. (This was the first of
many offences that were ultimately to appear in that cockney's charge sheet.) One reason was that Freddy was drinking the initial draughts of holiday freedom. Another, that
he was wearing, for the first time in his life, a suit that
had dawned in Savile-row. Another, that the afternoon
was exceptionally sunny. Another, that he was responding
to a great decision, formulated that morning during the
process of shaving.

"Why shouldn't I go out for a dash of adventure?" he
had demanded of his lathered face in the mirror. "You
know—real adventure! The mountain would not go to
Mohammed, so what did Mohammed do? He marched
up to the bashful mountain, and said, 'Hey, we've got to
meet!' To-day I will adopt the Mohammedan principle.
I will seek beautiful maidens, and offer them cigarettes.
Gold-tipped ones. Russian Teofani. And if I come upon
any fire-spouting dragons, I will biff them on the nose.
Yes, I, Freddy Reeve, perfect gentleman, and hitherto of
no account!"

And so he had set forth, Savile-turned and gold-tipped,
to beckon adventure, all unconscious that adventure was
beckoning him, also, and was opening an enormous mouth
to swallow him up.

His very first act, on alighting from his taxi at Liverpool-street station, was a gesture of his mood. He did not join the lengthy, undistinguished queue that was pressing its way like a congested human snake towards the third-class booking office; he strolled towards the first-class booking office, which had no queue at all, and where ticket-purchasers remained separate individuals. He bought a first-class return to Cromer, paying the considerable sum of 57/10d for it. He pretended successfully that he was quite used to paying such sums for railway tickets, and he asked in a lordly tone what time the train left. Five-eighteen, wasn't it? Yes, five-eighteen, corroborated the booking clerk, treating him pleasantly as an equal. First-class passengers are never superior to booking clerks; they are merely not inferior. And while all this was going on, a large and expansive gentleman with white spats and gold-rimmed glasses drew up, waited patiently, and ultimately bought a ticket for Sheringham. He watched Freddy's departing figure with vague interest. The interest of each in the other would have been enormously increased had they known how closely their fates were to be interwoven during the next few hours.

Freddy strolled contentedly away and passed through the barrier of Platform Nine, and it was here that the little cockney bloke trod on his toe.

"Don't mention," smiled Freddy.

"Wasn't goin' ter," retorted the cockney, huffily. "Why doncher look where yer goin'?"

A nasty, cantankerous chap! But Freddy wasn't going to argue. He shook the cockney off—dismissed him, so he imagined, from his life—and continued his stroll along the glamorous station platform. A porter appeared, a rather sad-eyed, disillusioned fellow who no longer dreamed of retiring on his tips, and offered to find him a seat. But

Freddy declined his aid. He was going to find his own seat, and he had made up his mind that it should be an auspicious one. Not a seat beside an elderly business man, for instance, or opposite an old dame with a parrot.

Fortunately he had plenty of time for his selection. The big hand of the large station clock pointed to three minutes past the hour, and the first-class compartments were not yet filling up. So, having completed a preliminary barren tour of the train, he decided to visit a bookstall in order to give the empty compartments a chance to fructify. Freddy, as you shall know in good time, was a reputable fellow, with moral standards somewhat unusual for the age he lived in; but at the moment he was searching for adventure in a frankly blatant fashion, and, although he might not have admitted it in blunt terms, adventure in his present mood stood for an attractive girl who would not discourage modest conversational advances. That the modest conversational advances would lead to any thrillingly human episode was not seriously anticipated. The girl who would attract Freddy was hardly that sort of a girl, and Freddy was hardly that sort of a man. Still, out of pleasant little beginnings, greater things did sometimes arise, and . . .

"Hallo! There's that darned little cockney again," thought Freddy, as he approached the bookstall. "Nobody seems to love him!"

The comment was induced by the attitude of an agitated old lady whom he appeared to have jostled.

"Is it *necessary* for you to stick your elbow into me?" demanded the agitated old lady.

"Wots that?" replied the cockney bloke.

"Your elbow!" rasped the lady.

"Wot abart it?" retorted the cockney. "It's mine, ain't it?"

This argument being irrefutable, the old lady bought a paper quickly and hurried away. The cockney bloke looked after her, and rudely spat.

"Some people think they owns the bloomin' hearth," he observed, as he tossed a coin to the newsvendor. "Chuck us the Pink 'Un!"

As he received the periodical and turned to leave the stall, his eyes fell upon Freddy, and the sight did not render him any the more amiable. Scowling, he mumbled something uncomplimentary, and shuffled off, in the wake of the old lady.

"He thinks *he* owns the earth!" remarked the newsvendor.

"Quite a common delusion, when you've had a glass too much," replied Freddy.

And then he acted as though he owned the earth by purchasing half-a-dozen expensive magazines.

Armed with refined reading, he glanced again at the station clock—the big hand had advanced another three minutes—and as he did so an incident occurred that sent him into a ridiculous flutter. Out of the corner of his eye he saw the most beautiful girl in the whole of creation.

Of course, you will not believe this. It is not necessary that you should. The point is that Freddy believed it, and that from this moment his whole outlook on life changed. The value of existence became established in a blinding, illuminating flash. Hitherto, there had always been some doubt about it. The reason of existence was explained, together with the object of continuing it. This girl was what he, Freddy Reeve, had been born for. She was also, quite obviously, what Freddy Reeve would be ready to die for . . . now someone ran into him, causing him to swing round, and the next moment the most beautiful girl in the whole of creation had vanished.

For an instant, even on this splendid, sunny afternoon, Freddy almost saw red. Why was everybody jostling him? What was the idea? He stared at this latest offender, ready to let loose his most picturesque language. But the man was so gentle and so apologetic that the language died on Freddy's lips.

"I'm terribly sorry, sir," said the man. He had just regained a small brown bag he had dropped in the encounter. A very different fellow, this, from the blundering cockney. Bright-eyed, alert, and rather scrupulously neat in a dark brown suit. "I hope I haven't hurt you?"

"Not at all," muttered Freddy, refraining with difficulty from the sarcastic comment that he was getting used to it.

"I was running for my train," proceeded the man in the dark brown suit. "It goes at eighteen past—"

"Well, you've ten minutes still to catch it in," interposed Freddy.

"Ten minutes!" The speaker stared up at the station clock, then took out his watch and quickly replaced it. "I'm eight minutes fast! I'm afraid, sir, I ran into you all for nothing!"

He smiled and departed. Freddy frowned after him. He would have frowned more had he known that the man's watch was not fast, but was exactly right.

Dashed nuisance! The girl had disappeared utterly. But while he was sympathising with himself a vein of sanity returned, and he realised that if the girl was not travelling on his train he could hardly stay behind to track her to her lair, whereas if she was travelling on his train—Freddy's heart gave a little jump at the possibility—he merely had to keep his eyes open and he'd be about to see her again. He walked slowly to the barrier, and watched. He watched in vain. The big hand of the large station clock crawled across the minutes, and a quickening of life on the platform beyond the barrier indicated that the time of departure was nearly due. With a sigh, Freddy passed through the barrier for the second time, and strolled along the waiting train. At the far end, the engine was fretting steam and smoke. He walked two-thirds of the way to the engine. Then, all at once, he paused.

A small knot of people had begun to say good-bye to the occupant of a compartment. It was a first-class compartment. And the occupant had momentarily poked her head out of the open door to make some remark. Freddy recognised the hat immediately.

"Be good, Lydia!" called one of the group on the platform.

"Don't forget to send a wire," called another.

"By Jove, I envy you, Miss Leveridge," exclaimed a third. "Give my love to the golf links!"

And then Freddy joined the group, murmured, "Excuse me," caused the group to stand aside, and entered the compartment.

He was conscious of eyes upon him. Not only the eyes of the girl in the compartment, but of her friends outside. But after all, he told himself, he had a perfect right to enter any compartment he liked, and, by a stroke of good fortune, this was the first that had contained only one occupant. All the same, he felt horribly guilty for a few seconds, and made no attempt to meet any of the eyes that were, or seemed to be, covertly watching him.

And then a queer thing happened. A disconcerting thing. The girl suddenly left her seat, and went into the corridor. The corridor was on the side of the train farthest from the platform.

For a moment Freddy interpreted this as a direct snub. She had left the compartment because she did not want his society, and she would not come back again! The sight of her crocodile dressing-case, however, reassured him, as also did the fact that her friends outside made no movement to leave their spot; and, a few seconds afterwards the girl returned and resumed her seat.

"You *are* a worry," cried one of her friends outside. "Didn't I swear to you they'd put your golf-bag in the corridor?"

A few hours later this remark recurred to Freddy Reeve, and he decided that it was one of the smartest impromptu observations it had ever been his lot to hear.

2

A Minute of Time

The big hand of the station clock, crawling callously across the face, pointed to seventeen minutes past the hour. It had crawled round and round for countless hours, and countless weeks, and countless months, and although in its early days it may have experienced some temporal emotion, it had become numbed by now to the business of horology, and cared nothing for the fate of those who depended on it. It moved neither more swiftly for them, to speed a departure, nor more slowly for them, to ensure a departure. It behaved, in fact, in distinct contrast to those who shot anxious glances up at it, frowned at it, smiled at it, or swore at it. Let fools hurry! Time, of which the clock was a minion, knew better than that. It knew that the distance each would travel was already marked, and that such distance would be covered, but never exceeded, through an agency more potent than scurrying feet, or even puffing engines.

The book was written. Even the station clock could not alter one word of it. It merely turned the pages.

But who among those who had boarded the train, and who still had a minute to bask in the dubious joy of Liverpool-street station before the platform began to glide slowly backwards and away from them, would have agreed with the station clock? Do you agree with it? Do I?

Certainly a large and expansive gentleman with white spats and gold-rimmed glasses, whose acquaintance we have already briefly made, did not agree with it. Life, to this gentleman, was immensely interesting, immensely varied in its potentialities, and immensely easy (on occasions) to steer. The idea that a prehistoric monkey, missing a branch as it swung from tree to tree and descending on the surprised head of an ichthyosaurus, could have set in motion a train of events that had eventually caused a large and expansive gentleman, without the vestige of a tail, to be sitting in a first-class compartment of a Norfolk express, was a notion against which his entire egotistical soul would have rebelled. "What! Do you mean to tell me," he would have retorted to the station clock, "that if the monkey had not missed the branch, or if the head of the ichthyosaurus had not been there to catch him, I should be travelling up to Norfolk on a motor-bike?" To which the clock would have responded, "My dear ignoramus, if that monkey hadn't slipped—and it only slipped because two jelly-fish happened to bump into each other forty million years earlier—you wouldn't have been travelling anywhere at all. You wouldn't exist."

Only, of course, the station clock wouldn't really have been sufficiently interested to enter into so infantile an argument at all.

So the large and expansive gentleman stared out of his window with amiable belief in himself; and several times he smiled quietly as he stared. For instance, that little cockney bloke—he was quite amusing. Apparently, urged by some cantankerous instinct, or that extra glass he should have refrained from, he was pestering the life out of an agitated old woman. The old woman, it seemed, did not want the cockney bloke in her compartment. He had upset her. And the cockney bloke, on his side, wasn't going to be dictated to by anybody.

"I got a right to get in where I like," he barked.

"But this compartment's full!" retorted the agitated lady.

"Go on! It ain't," answered the cockney bloke. "I see a seat, and I'm goin' ter 'ave it."

And he shoved his way in.

It was at this point that the large and expansive gentleman gave one of his quiet smiles. A clergyman, sitting opposite, smiled back, encouraging and contributing to the world's happiness.

Then another little group interested the large and expansive gentleman. Unfortunately he could only see this little group out of the corner of his eye when he turned his head, because he was facing the engine and the little group was standing outside a compartment just a little to the rear. But he knew—for he had noted the group earlier, before taking his seat—that it comprised an exceedingly distinguished-looking gentleman (a gentleman, alas, even more distinguished-looking than himself, despite the white spats), two other men, and a woman. These latter, also, bore an air of social importance.

There had been one other member of the group, a remarkably attractive girl; but she had now entered her compartment, and preliminary good-byes were being exchanged. . . .

And now a sudden disturbance arose. At the moment, this disturbance merely amused the large and expansive gentleman. It seemed, in truth, to afford him some actual inner satisfaction. But at a later stage of the journey, when his mind reverted to it, the inner satisfaction was not so evident; and the station clock, had it cared to tackle him at this later stage, would have observed, "You see, my dear ignoramus, out of tiny causes come great and startling effects, to confound all our devisings!" . . .

The cause of the disturbance was the agitated old woman who, giving way to an attack of nerves, suddenly

seized her bags—there appeared to be two or three dozen
of them—and jumped out upon the platform. She was
literally garbed in small luggage, and even a French porter
might have stood and admired. An English porter, however, whose technique was merely a barrow, became almost
as agitated as the old lady herself, and sprang towards her.

"It's jest goin', mum!" he cried.

"Find me another seat!" gasped the old woman.

There was a seat two compartments nearer the engine.
She scrambled towards it, the porter threw open the door,
and she was shoved in.

But that was only the first half of the incident. The
second half was to come. It came a moment or two later
out of the compartment which the old lady had just vacated. It was the cockney bloke.

"Wot! Ain't I good enuff fer 'er?" he complained, to
the world. "Jest becos' I ain't bin ter Heton and 'Arrow
and Hoxford and Cambridge, ain't I good enuff ter sit by
anybody?" He stared round, aggressively, for acceptance of
the challenge. None came. He decided, therefore, to have
a tilt at Life itself.

"*Ain't* I?" he shouted. "We'll see!"

And, with only a few seconds to spare, he dived after
the old lady and plunged into her sanctuary.

"There seems to be some trouble," remarked the clergyman to the large and expansive gentleman. He frowned a
little, taking it personally, as though Religion were failing.

"Yes—a bit of socialism, I imagine," answered the large
gentleman. "Upon my soul, I don't know what the country's coming to!"

There was a tiny pause. The clergyman sought the correct rejoinder and found it.

"We think too much in terms of politics," he said gently. "If we devoted a little more attention to the spiritual
side of things, there would be only one Party."

The large gentleman tried not to feel sick.

And then a whistle sounded, the guard waved his green flag, and the 5.18 began to move. While an agitated old lady and a cockney bloke glared at each other. While a large, expansive gentleman and a clergyman smiled at each other. While a pretty girl and a young man glanced covertly at each other.

And while a bright-eyed, alert, and rather scrupulously neat little man in a dark brown suit, with a little brown bag beside him, sat thoughtfully regarding his finger-nails.

3

A GIRL'S FINGER

Judged by externals, there is possibly no less romantic stretch in the two hemispheres than that between Liver-pool-street station and Stratford. The train traveller is squeezed out of London through a scarred and blackened tube, and if he has no knowledge of the fair lands beyond, all he can do is to hug on to hope. Tunnels, homicidal in atmosphere, derelict platforms, walls with black shadows and black apertures in them, lead dismally through no-man's land to miles of dejected enterprise. Surely nothing is finished here, nothing completed to stay and hold one! The train is wise to hurry through! The man who started that large brick building may have set out with high ideals—but he gave up. Uncompleted, it stands as the tomb-stone of some despairing historian. Beyond is another building that has been completed. The world would be a little gayer had it not been. Some hopeful fellow was going to make a garden out of that patch of blackened green. Tin cans and cats have captured it. Do people really and truly live in that little hovel by the back windows of which we are passing? The windows are filthy. There is no sign of effort anywhere, nor of the reason for effort. But a pram is in the apology of a garden, symbolizing, even here, the miracle of continuity; and the engine belches derisive smoke at the pram as it passes.

But we make our own worlds, and our moods are actually the trains that convey us from one world to another. To Freddy Reeve, as he sat in his corner, separated by only a foot or two from the most beautiful girl in the universe, this land of tunnels and of torture was enchanted. He was not passing over tracks made by grim men's sweat, but over a road forged by fairies. What if it was a bit ugly outside the window? That only made this little sanctuary within all the more precious and delightful!

The minutes slipped by. Time went forward, while space went back. Then a sudden, ridiculous panic seized the young man.

"You're *wasting* it!" ran through his mind, riotously. "Are you going to sit here, doing nothing, all the journey? Do something! *Do something!*"

They had passed through Bethnal Green and Bow, however, before he collected himself sufficiently to open the attack. His weapon was almost pathetically simple.

"Do you mind if I smoke?" he enquired.

Fortunately for his request, it was not a smoking carriage.

"Not at all," answered the girl, promptly. Almost as though she had been expecting the request.

Freddy blinked. It was amazing. It was staggering. Not only was he in a compartment with the most beautiful girl in the world, but also with the most beautiful voice in the world. A low, rich voice. Later on, when he had cooled down a little and was in a mood for analysis, he decided that it was a whisky voice without the whisky. A voice that could make the three words, "Not at all," sound more wonderful than a Chopin sonata or a Tschaikowski symphony. . . .

Of course, Freddy was being an ass. He knew it. But he wasn't sorry for it. Better an ass with sensation than the Sphinx with none.

He brought out his cigarette-case. A silver one, and not too bad. He had given it a bit of a polish that morning, in order that it should justify the dozen gold-tipped children of Teofani that now resided in it. The gold tips looked a trifle ostentatious, he was afraid. They might need a bit of explaining—when one got to know one better. Meanwhile—well, hang it, they were travelling first-class!

He hesitated for an instant before his next step. Then, deciding that it was quite a natural next step, he looked at the girl enquiringly and held out the case.

"Will you have one?" he asked.

Now she hesitated, and for the first time their eyes met quite directly. Freddy felt as though he were suddenly being bathed in sunlight. No, better than sun. Something that penetrated beyond the skin, and caught the soul as well. "Lord, is this happening?" wondered Freddy. He was not taking it to him personally, or building on it. He was just amazed, genuinely amazed, that such a thing could be. The sun does not y rise out of the sea for the special glorification of the beholder, but the beholder is glorified. . . . He felt abashed, as well as amazed. He felt that he must continue to hold her eyes, quietly and coolly, or give himself away. He hoped there was no perspiration on his forehead. To have to wipe your forehead after being looked at for three seconds by a pretty girl would be a terrible admission of innocence. . . .

Yes, and why was she looking at him like this? Surely there was something personal in her expression? Something queerly enquiring? But perhaps the time merely *seemed* long to him, and actually . . .

"Thank you," said the girl. "But not just yet—perhaps a little later."

As she settled back in her corner, he pondered over the remark. She had not accepted the cigarette, but she had not snubbed him. On the contrary, she had definitely left

open the door which he had pushed ajar, and had invited
him to renew his own invitation presently. This not only
lent promise to the future, but sanctioned the present.
Until the future dawned, a permitted, unspoken intimacy
could exist between them.

But it was not this alone that intrigued Freddy Reeve
as, having used his new lighter (which, amazing thing,
worked), he leaned back in his own corner and puffed the
best cigarette of his career. Her response and the manner
of it, seemed in some queer, unexplainable way to fit into
that strange scrutiny of hers, that strange enquiry. If it
did, had it any important significance beyond his present
comprehension? Further, was his present comprehension
obtuse?

If it appears that Freddy was revolving these questions
somewhat elaborately, it must be remembered that he was
at the moment entirely obsessed by his subject, and that
nothing else had any consequence in the world. Not even
the half-dozen expensive magazines that lay on the seat
beside him. But another reason, as well, urged his meticu-
lous enquiry, a reason of which, at this early point, he was
scarcely aware.

Subconsciously, it was dawning upon him that the
journey of the 5.18 on this particular summer evening was
more than personally significant. Had you questioned him
about this as the train ran with a rattle through Stratford,
he would probably have stared at you blankly. The journey, at Stratford, was only ten minutes old. But tiny little
things had happened. Tiny little things that would never
be remembered again if they proved to be meaningless,
or if their meaning were never revealed, yet which, until
they were set aside by time or dealt with by circumstance,
raised minute queries at the back of the mind, setting up
a small area of irritation like a tickle, or a grain of grit in
the eye.

The agitated old woman and the cockney, for example. Quite trivial and unimportant by themselves. Yes, an insignificant piece of grit. But, just before the train had started, Freddy had been vaguely conscious of a continuation of the episode the inception of which he had witnessed at the bookstall, and had heard the old woman's voice raised on the platform, and, afterwards, the cockney bloke's. And then there was that fellow in the dark brown suit who had blundered into him at a most inconvenient moment, on the pretext that he was hurrying to catch a train that did not leave for ten minutes! Another tiny piece of grit. The encounter might almost have been designed to make Freddy lose sight of the girl! But he had found her again. Here she was, opposite him—though *she* had jumped up and left the compartment just before the journey began, giving him a nasty jar. . . . Another little piece of grit. . . .

He found himself dwelling on that hurried departure of the girl. He could not say why he dwelt upon it. The thing had been explained. She had gone to see about a piece of luggage. A golf-bag or something. Then why did he harp on the incident? Golf! He played golf, too. He eyed her hands through his cigarette smoke. Without knowing it, he had been eyeing those hands, lying in her lap, for quite awhile. Without knowing it, he was largely being prompted to his present enquiry by those hands. They fascinated him. The fingers were slender, and artistic, and capable. He was sure they could grip you firmly, or be very tender. Yes, he was sure of that. But they worried him, too. They worried him! Why did they worry him?

Now, all at once he became definitely conscious of the worry. Was the girl growing conscious of it, too? She stirred ever so slightly, and her eyes, which had been staring out of the window, shifted a little in his direction. Perhaps she had seen him in the glass of the window, through some trick of reflection. In any case, Freddy still stared. And

then his heart began to thump. He knew now why those
hands had worried him. He had just noticed something
about them. The discovery confused him, beat him. Although, of course . . .

Sometimes you may forget big things while little things
become indelibly photographed upon your mind.

You cannot say why. There it is. A counsel will question
you, and riddle you, and twist you inside out. He will de-
mand proof, which you cannot produce. Yet there lies your
knowledge, within yourself, and you know it is true even
if you have not a shred of evidence to support it.

What Freddy knew was that, when he had first seen the
girl who was now sitting opposite him, she had been wearing a ring on the third finger of her left hand. He had not
taken in the full significance of this at the time; he had
just been aware of it. Now, the finger was bare.

She had removed it! Why? For one absurd instant Freddy wondered masculinely whether *he* might be the cause.
Was she, after all, as ready to form a quick friendship
with him as he was with her? He recalled the unexpected
graciousness of her refusal of his cigarette. A girl who is
not wearing an engagement ring makes casual friends more
quickly than a girl whose finger proclaims that she is only
really interested in one man. But an instant later Freddy
was appalled at his thought. He felt that the only decent
thing to do would be to go down on his knees and apologise to her. That being impossible, he removed his eyes
from the ringless finger as a sort of penance.

The ringless finger remained in his thoughts, however,
if not in his vision, and he was soon compelled to steal
another glance at it.

The compartment began to spin. The finger was no
longer ringless. A single, lustrous ruby gleamed from it.
But the engagement ring he had first seen had contained
three diamonds!

"Excuse me," said the large and expansive gentleman from the corridor, "do I intrude?"

4

THREE'S NONE

An elderly gentleman who enters a railway compartment already occupied by two young people of opposite sex, and who asks whether he intrudes, is either astonishingly obtuse or astonishingly callous. Obviously, he intrudes. All the best elderly people know this.

But apparently the large and expansive gentleman in the white spats was not growing old really gracefully. Instead of taking the obvious for granted and beating a decent retreat, he sailed in from the corridor and beamed egotistically, while the young man swore at him silently. The girl, on the other hand, showed no sign of emotion whatever.

"I've really come here to *escape*," said the large gentleman, offering a quite voluntary confession. No one had asked him to explain himself, so perhaps he did feel some vague necessity. "There's a clergyman in my compartment who's—h'm—getting on my nerves."

An enquiry as to what the clergyman had done to get on a fellow traveller's nerves would have been polite, but the enquiry, which the newcomer seemed to expect, did not materialize. The only response was silence—a silence which sensitive natures would have interpreted as frigid. The large gentleman, however, was merely sensitive at the moment to clergymen. The laity did not worry him.

"Why *do* clergymen try to save your souls on railway journeys?" he demanded, as he sank into a corner seat next the corridor—the seat facing the engine, and, diagonally, the girl. Freddy wished he had taken the other seat, because now he could only see the intruder out of the corner of his eye, unless he turned directly to him, which he had no present intention of doing. Moreover the intruder himself did not have to turn to face the girl, to whom his observations were mainly addressed. Another cause for irritation. "I should have thought," proceeded the large gentleman, blandly, "that a railway journey was the last occasion on which a soul could be saved. Passengers are not, in my experience, proverbially gracious." Was this a little hit? "No, they are apt to be glum, or grumpy, or worried, or worrying. They either—h'm—talk too much, or they don't talk at all!" He laughed gently, as though to ease any personal implication. "If you want my opinion, I *like* conversation in a train—provided it's unclerical. But a fellow who tries to point out the joys of heaven while you are passing through London suburbs—well, what's one to say about him?"

The moment had been reached when further silence would be definitely rude. Had he been alone, Freddy would not have hesitated to be definitely rude. If he could love at first sight, he could also hate at first sight. But he did not want to appear definitely rude in the presence of the girl, and it suddenly occurred to him that if he betrayed too much resentment at this unwelcome intrusion his attitude might savour of presumption. After all, although the girl had been gracious, she had not sanctioned his public declaration that he wanted to be alone with her; and she had not as yet implied that she wanted to be alone with him.

So Freddy made a brave attempt to swallow his annoyance, and murmured a mild defence of clergymen.

"Dear me, have I put my foot in it?" exclaimed the large gentleman, insincerely contrite. "Perhaps you are studying for the Church?"

"Does my collar suggest it?" asked Freddy.

"Your collar? True! It doesn't," agreed the large gentleman. "Vicars in mufti—you don't come across 'em, do you? But, even if you did, I don't suppose you'd recognise them, would you? Any more than you recognise a sweep when he's clean. How little we can tell of each other from—h'm—outward appearances, eh?" He closed his eyes for a moment, to dwell on this illuminating reflection, then opened them abruptly snapped them open, as it were, and fastened them on the girl. "But perhaps your wife is religious?"

Now Freddy flared. The presumption of the fellow! . . . And the momentary glory of the presumption!

"I beg your pardon?" he barked.

"Dear me!" murmured the clumsy one. "Now I *have* put my foot in it!"

The girl saved the situation. Opening her lips at last, and smiling faintly, she remarked,

"*You're* not very good at outward appearances, are you?"

It was a neat if obvious comment, proving that she was not the kind of girl to be crushed by cumbersome conversation. Freddy admired the cool, unruffled spirit behind it. But it worried him, nevertheless, for her entry into the conversation had destroyed the screen of her silence, and now the large and expansive gentleman turned to her directly, determined that the screen should not be replaced.

"*Touché!*" he cried. "A thousand apologies! It was, as you suggest, extremely bad judgment. If you will forgive an elderly fellow for saying so, I ought to have known my error by our young friend's face. In the circumstances

I suggested, his expression would presumably have been much happier."

This was not merely cumbersome. It was insolent. Was this an insolence natural to the objectionable man, or was there anything behind it?

Even in the middle of his extreme annoyance, Freddy found his mind rattling along. He could not quite understand why, but the intruder was in some way stimulating him, setting up a sort of subtle challenge to which Freddy's instincts were responding. At the moment, the only object of the challenge seemed to be an attempt to ruffle Freddy. "Our young friend"! Impudent expression! The common device employed to exclude an enemy from a charmed circle on the score of juvenility—to stamp him as an immature outsider! But why *should* there be any attempt to ruffle Freddy? . . .

The girl herself was not ruffled. She controlled any indignation she may have felt, though her retort contained a little sting in it.

"Don't you think it would be better to return to your clergyman?" she asked.

"Conversationally, you mean?" blinked the large gentleman, quickly, and ran on, giving her no time to confirm or deny the interpretation. "I assure you, I couldn't return to him in any other form! Positively, such people kill all one's desire to go to heaven. One would have to meet them there. On the other hand, I always have had a curious objection to smoke."

He broke off. His eyes were now upon Freddy again. They frowned, and became definitely unfriendly.

"*You* are smoking, I see," he observed.

Was he trying to drive Freddy out of the compartment? Was *that* it? By Jove, if he was! . . .

"The lady doesn't object," replied Freddy, shortly.

"No—I'm sure she doesn't," nodded the large gentle-man. "But—h'm—I'm afraid *I* object!"

Yes! He was trying to drive Freddy out of the compart-ment!

"I don't smoke myself," he continued. "I have trouble with my throat, and smoke is bad for it. As a matter of fact, that was another reason why I left the next compart-ment. Our reverend friend was about to indulge in a pipe."

"And you allowed him to smoke?" challenged Freddy.

"I had no option," returned the large gentleman. "It was a smoking-compartment. This, I see, is not."

Freddy shrugged his shoulders, and began to extinguish his cigarette. He caught the girl's eye as he did so, and suddenly realised that she was watching him closely. She seemed to be interested in how he was taking all this. Siz-ing him up. . . .

"Must you put it out?" exclaimed the large gentleman suddenly.

"Why not?" replied Freddy. "I thought you asked me to."

"I asked you not to smoke—"

"Well?"

"*Here!* As I've said, the next compartment is a smoker. Pity to waste it."

The atmosphere tightened. Freddy became conscious that the girl was watching him more intently than ever, though she was leaning back in her corner, with her eyes half-closed. But half-closed eyes can improve one's focus. Her hands still lay in her lap. The ruby gleamed from a fold in her skirt.

"Or you could finish it in the corridor," suggested the large gentleman.

Freddy did not reply. He completed the operation of extinguishing the cigarette, and then threw it out of the window. (A loafer picked it up, and finished it for him.)

Well, that was that! What next, wondered Freddy? The
girl, her eyes still half-closed, had relaxed into a smile.
The smile lay on her lips as well as in her eyes. Was she
congratulating him on his little victory? Because it was a
victory. He had not moved from his seat, and he had not
lost his temper.

The next move came from the corridor. A vague smudge
grew and materialized into the man in the dark brown
suit. He looked a little pale and agitated, and as eyes were
turned upon him he paused and hesitated.

"I—I beg your pardon," he murmured.

"Is anything the matter?" asked the girl, quickly.

She was not leaning back in her corner now. Her smile
had melted into an expression of human sympathy. It was
easy to see that the man in the corridor was not well.

"I'm not feeling too good, miss," replied the man,
making an obvious effort. "If one of you had a drop of
brandy—?"

The girl turned, and looked at Freddy enquiringly. He
shook his head.

"Not a drop," he said.

"Have *you* any?" the girl then asked the large gentleman.

The large gentleman blinked, as though considering
the question. He must have known, yet it took him quite
a second to make up his mind; and during that second his
eyes roved rapidly first to the girl, then to Freddy, and
then round to the man in the dark brown suit.

"Feel groggy, eh?" queried the large gentleman.

"I'm taken like this sometimes," answered the ill one,
in a low, unsteady voice. "Been working rather hard. A
spot would just put me right—"

"Very well, I'll get it," interposed the large gentleman.
"It's in my bag—in the next compartment."

He rose, and the ill man moved aside, rearwards, to
give him room to pass out.

"Follow me," said the large gentleman.

But, when the large gentleman had passed out, the man in the brown suit did not follow him. Instead, he swayed towards the door and took hold of the framework for support.

"Hadn't you better bring him in?" whispered the girl, bending forward to Freddy. "I've got a small flask in my bag, after all—I'd forgotten it."

She spoke rapidly. Her voice, as well as the obvious urgency of the moment, urged Freddy to quick action. In a couple of seconds he had the man on a seat, and in another five the girl had produced a small, leather-bound flask, and was holding it to the man's lips.

"How did it happen?" asked Freddy, after the man had drunk.

"Just felt a bit giddy," mumbled the man. "I'm feeling better now. Be all right again in a moment."

"Shall I see if I can find a doctor on the train?" suggested Freddy.

"No, thank you," answered the man. "That's not necessary. I'm very sorry, giving you all this trouble." The trouble seemed to disturb him. "I wish you'd go and tell that other man not to worry any more. He's probably fishing about in his bag—"

"Oh, don't trouble about him," interrupted Freddy. "He won't mind."

"No, but I mind," retorted the man. The spirit was taking effect. "I hate putting people to all this bother for nothing."

"You'd better go," the girl murmured to Freddy, warningly. "I'll look after him till you come back."

Freddy hesitated, then obeyed. He determined, however, not to be long over his errand. Leaving the compartment, he turned into the next one, and found an altercation in progress.

"Do you think I don't know my own luggage?" the large gentleman was snapping.

"I'm sure, I'm very sorry," responded the clergyman. "But, you will admit, the two bags look alike, and I certainly thought you had got hold of mine."

"Bah!" muttered the large gentleman. He looked warm and exasperated. "All this delay—and a sick man in the next compartment needing the stuff—"

"But he doesn't need it now," interposed Freddy, throwing oil upon the troubled waters. "We found we had some, after all, and I've just come to tell you not to trouble."

The large gentleman, who had been on the point of unlocking his bag, paused in surprise. Then, abruptly, he pocketed his keys, and pushed the bag back under the seat, from where he had drawn it.

"H'm—a useless errand, eh?" he frowned; then suddenly smiled again. "Well, well, that's good. Let's get back and see how the poor fellow is getting along. Between you and me, sir," he added, studying Freddy's face, "I've an idea he's had as much as is good for him already!"

Meanwhile, the subject of their discussion was saying to the girl,

"No—not Chelmsford. He'll get in at either Ipswich or Norwich. And shortly afterwards—*it'll happen!*"

5

INTERLUDE

London's suburbs lay behind, a scarred memory. Romford had come and gone. The ugliness of progress had given way to pleasant pastures, and to cottages that began to take a little picturesque interest in themselves. Now the sun had something reasonable to glow on. But the memory of London still hurt a little. Its murky shadow still smudged, in fancy if not in fact, the western horizon, and it would be a few miles yet before one could shake oneself entirely free of it and emerge from its depressing influence. A small boy in the rear of the train poked his head perilously out of the window and stared back almost fearfully. He could not really believe that he was escaping from that smudge. Not until he had seen a lot more pleasant fields and pretty cottages—not until he had seen wide water, perhaps— would he be quite, quite sure that the smudge would not follow him and catch him up. He turned his head abruptly, to exchange the pain of looking backwards with the joy of looking forwards, the sweet winds of freedom swept into his face, and he got a piece of grit in his eye.

"There! Didn't I tell you not to put your head out of the window, Billy?" exclaimed his unsympathetic mother.

But we cannot stay and watch a mother screw up a corner of a handkerchief and poke it around the optic of a little boy she had not been given time and opportunity to understand; more vital things were happening in another compartment, where a man in a brown suit was recovering from a sudden dizziness, watched by three very interested people.

"He's better," said the girl.

The large gentleman, who had just reappeared with Freddy, nodded drily.

"So it appears," he observed, "so it appears. Your little flask," he added, with a glance at the flask in her hand, "has undoubtedly done the trick."

"Yes, I'd forgotten I had it," replied the girl.

"It was a pity," murmured the gentleman. "It would have spared me another interview with the clergyman. However, that's a small matter—h'm—a small matter. The chief thing is our friend here. Yes, he certainly looks better. These sudden dizzinesses—they soon pass, eh? How are you, old chap?"

He prodded the recovering man, almost playfully. The man jumped up, with a suddenness that made the prodder fall back a little.

"I'm quite all right," answered the man, rather flurriedly. "And I mustn't stay here any longer. I've been too much trouble, as it is. Very kind of everybody, I'm sure." He glanced round, gratefully and comprehensively. "And now I'll be getting back."

"Don't hurry," suggested Freddy.

But the man was already in the corridor. He was ill at ease among such distinguished company. He wanted, obviously, to return to his own social set. First-class compartments had not been designed for him, and he only fell into them when circumstances forced him to.

"Queer fellow," remarked the large gentleman, after he had departed. "Queer fellow. If I were a doctor, I should probably give him a little advice."

"What would your advice be?" enquired Freddy, curiously.

They were settling back into their seats. The girl was looking at a gold wrist watch attached to a neat black band round her wrist. It was thirteen to six. The journey had so far lasted twenty-nine minutes.

"A little less drink, and a little more appreciation of human kindliness," said the large and expansive gentleman. "It is our outlook on life that largely determines our hygienic condition. Don't you think so?"

Freddy was irritated by a moral observation behind which he detected no sincerity.

"Human kindliness," he grunted, "might put the poor fellow's condition down to hard work rather than hard drinking. To me, the chap looked thoroughly done up."

Was Freddy doing the other an injustice? An expression bordering on genuine concern spread over the large features.

"I wonder if you're right," muttered the gentleman. "I wonder—if you're right." He glanced towards the corridor. An idea had occurred to him. "Perhaps—h'm—perhaps it would be an act of human kindliness to follow him, and to see whether he is safely back in his compartment?"

The girl, from her corner, stirred slightly.

"I'd leave him alone," she said.

"But, come!" exclaimed the gentleman, now rising resolutely. "I have been accused of callousness! Well, not accused, perhaps, but it has been suggested to me by our young friend here. Although I rushed off for brandy, and had to dispute with a clergyman who seemed to think that my bag was his, and then came back on hearing that my assistance was not needed— and smiled—I am set down as a nasty, ungenerous person—no, don't interrupt me, sir! If not an ungenerous person, at least one who lacks human

kindliness! Well, well, I will make amends for my poten-
tial cruelty! I will go and find the patient—and I shall
not return until—h'm—until I am satisfied that all is as it
should be with him. All as it should be!"

He was in the corridor in a flash. When he liked, this
rather portly adult could move quite quickly. A fact that
was to be further demonstrated before the end of the journey. Freddy stared after him; then, abruptly turned to
the girl. At any rate, the galvanic departure of the large
gentleman gave them a minute or two without his undesir-
able company, and a tremendous urge to make some use of
this blessed minute or two swept over Freddy. He discovered that the girl was frowning.

"Funny fellow, isn't he?" said Freddy, boldly.

The frown remained, and she did not answer. Freddy
plunged on, deciding to be adventurously natural, and
either to establish himself or to destroy himself in her eyes
through some revelation of what he actually was.

"In fact," said Freddy, "I detest him."

What a thing to say! Well, never mind—he had said it,
and somehow he felt glad. His heart was thumping rather
loudly, though.

"Do you?" she replied.

His heart went on thumping. He was in the middle of
it now—establishing or destroying himself. It is a necessary process in all friendships, though not necessarily, of
course, in all railway intercourse. Her tone was non-com-
mittal. She was not yet accepting him. On the other hand,
she had not decided to exclude him. And she might easily
have decided to exclude him after such a remark!

"Don't you?" asked Freddy.

A tiny smile dawned. She appeared to be fighting
against it.

"One shouldn't discuss one's fellow-travellers," she reproved.

"You're thinking of guests," he retorted. "A man like at could never be our guest!"

"Aren't you taking a lot for granted?"

"Yes. An awful lot. I'm taking it for granted that you won't be offended at my utter boorishness. Too much for granted, perhaps. I beg your pardon."

The sound of the travelling train suddenly increased. Or, rather, it became concentrated, and forced itself upon one's notice. A long platform flashed by.

"Where was that?" exclaimed the girl, quickly.

He jerked his head round violently. If she had asked him to jump up on the luggage-rack, he would have done it. He was in a terrible, glorious state of subjection. With her beside him, he would have declared war on the world.

Perhaps it would not have been much harder to conquer the world than to conquer the speeding, inadequate letters on the departing platform. The platform was rushing backwards, trying hard not to let him know where it was. Lamp-posts, boards, darted by. "Never you mind!" they shouted, voicelessly. "Station names weren't written to be read!" He nearly broke his neck trying to decipher a virgin seat. Just because a pretty girl had told him to, and because civilisation would stop if he disappointed her . . .

"Brentwood!" he cried.

Then she laughed. She had noted his struggle. He untwisted his neck, brought it back to normal, and found himself laughing, too.

"Aren't stations idiots?" he grinned.

"Ridiculous," she smiled. And suddenly added, "There was no need to apologise."

The large gentleman reappeared in the corridor. He was returning. Confound it! . . . No, he wasn't returning! He . . .

"Well, that's a funny thing," said Freddy. "He's passed on!"

"He didn't even look in here," added the girl, also puzzled.

There was a little silence.

"P'r'aps he's as fed up with us as we are with him," suggested Freddy, "and prefers even religion!"

"More likely he's missed the compartment," replied the
girl.

But she was quite sure he had not missed the compartment. She was quite sure there was very little that
was missed by the large and expansive gentleman with the
conspicuous white spats. Freddy, watching her, wondered
why she did not look more pleased that the intruder—for,
hang it, he *was* an intruder!—had failed on this occasion
to intrude.

"I expect he'll be back in a minute," she murmured.

"I'd rather like to test our respective theories," returned
Freddy.

"How do you mean?"

"Well—I could easily find out whether he's gone the
clergyman."

"What would be the use of that?"

"Oh—I don't know."

"And then he might think it funny if he saw you."

"Don't see why he should. I could say I was enquiring
about that chap who was ill."

"Yes, that's true," she nodded, thoughtfully. "It would
be nice to know—how he was." He looked at her quickly,
arrested by some peculiar quality in her tone. As quickly,
she added, "No, I don't think you'd better. You might
bring him back."

"Whew! So I might," he answered.

Conversation flagged for a few moments. Her mind was
elsewhere. He stared out of the window, wishing he could
know where her mind was, so that he might join it. An

amazing journey, this! People bumping into each other, agitated old ladies and pursuing cockney blokes, large, artificial gentlemen with most unnatural conversation— the kind of conversation you might stick in a play, but that didn't ring quite true in a railway carriage—men taken with sudden dizziness—and, by Jove, that ring! He'd forgotten that! The diamond ring that became no ring at all, and then turned into a ruby ring. . . .

Then he caught sight of the girl's face. Not directly, but in momentary reflection through the window-glass. He caught it as a spasm of fear shot through it. . . .

Whew! There *was* something strange about this journey! Something *wrong!* Mighty wrong! And the large gentleman might be back at any moment!

"You all right?" Freddy heard himself saying.

He hardly knew he was saying it. His heart had spoken, entirely of its own accord. Simply hadn't consulted his brain, at all.

"Why, of course," she answered. "What made you ask?"

He was looking directly at her now. The fear had gone. It had merely been in the window-glass—and for that one instant.

"I—I don't know," he replied. "Just for a moment, I thought—" He turned back to the window, flushing slightly, and unable to face her. "Well—if there's anything I can do," he said, lamely.

Only a second passed before her reply, but it seemed an eternity.

"You *can* do something," she said, in a low, tense voice. "You can—you can give me that cigarette you offered me some time ago."

He turned to her, in astonishment. Her tone had suddenly altered. He felt convinced that she had not originally intended to ask him just for a cigarette.

And then Freddy Reeve understood the reason for that abrupt transformation. The large and expansive gentleman stood in the doorway.

Whether he had just arrived, or whether he had been there for several seconds, Freddy did not know. But he did know that there was a queer little glitter in his eye.

6

ON CHELMSFORD PLATFORM

And now a new spirit entered into Freddy Reeve. To the trivial little incidents that vaguely seemed like designs in a strange and sinister mosaic, two new factors had just been added. One was the flash of fear that had passed across the girl's face. The other was the hard little glitter in the large gentleman's eye. These made a new person of Freddy Reeve. They changed him from a young man in a holiday mood to a being of responsibility.

It need not be supposed that, even at this stage, Freddy had any definite idea of what lay before him, or of the astonishing events towards which the train was speeding him. He did not know that he would be needed. He did know, however, that he *might* be needed; the girl's own attitude and her interrupted request proved that; and, if he were needed, he intended that he should be on the spot.

But this intention was not in itself sufficient. It occurred to Freddy, in an illuminating flash, that his best prospects of assisting a girl who was menaced—yes, he had got as far as that in his mind, rightly or wrongly—was to disarm any suspicions that might be entertained about him by those who formed the menace. By the large and expansive gentleman, for instance. He must prepare himself for the battle not merely by watching the enemy's moves but by concealing his own. He must, in fact, cease to *appear* to be interested.

His first step towards this necessary deception was to smile at the unwelcome figure in the doorway. The unwelcome figure smiled back.

"Oh, so *here* you are!" exclaimed the large gentleman.

"Yes—did you lose the compartment?" replied Freddy. "I called as you went by just now, but you didn't hear me."

The large gentleman's eyebrows went up. This kindly interest seemed to surprise him.

"A tap on the shoulder would have been more sure of results," he said.

"I dare say," returned Freddy, easily, "only to tap you on the shoulder I should have had to go to the fag of getting up and running after you—and events seem to be proving that, when it comes to the point, sir, you have more—how did we put it?—human kindliness than I have! Besides, I thought you might have decided to tackle the clergyman again. Oh, and by the way," he went on, as his hand dived for his pocket, "I'm about to tax your human kindliness once more. This lady asked me for a cigarette just before you came in. I'm sure you won't mind her smoking, will you?"

He paused, rather breathlessly. Freddy did not often make long speeches, and the effort had taxed him somewhat, in spite of the apparent ease with which the words were poured out. It was really rather a good effort. He had been afraid, halfway through it, that he was appearing too friendly all of a sudden, but the introduction of the cigarette would, he hoped, explain that. He was being friendly to invite the large man's friendliness, so that no objection would be raised to the girl's request.

The large gentleman played up to the amiable atmosphere.

"Why, of course, I don't mind," he responded, good-humouredly. "With a lady—it's quite a different thing."

A little cumbersome, but it served. At the moment, nobody was searching for rough edges. Freddy brought out his case, opened it, and held it towards his *vis-à-vis*.

"Thank you," she said.

As she helped herself, Freddy wondered whether she were thanking him only for the cigarette. He had a strong sensation, based partly, perhaps, on hope, that she was thanking him for something she valued more—for the effort she divined behind his attitude.

"I suppose it's no good offering *you* one?" queried Freddy.

"Thank you, no," answered the large gentleman. "Smoking is one of the few vices I happen to be without."

"Well, I'm glad to know you've got some vices," smiled Freddy, as he produced his lighter. "You don't want to go to heaven, do you?"

The large gentleman showed that he could be quite as humble as Freddy.

"Ah—and meet the clergyman?" he exclaimed. "Ah! Quite so! A lower elevation will suit me admirably."

"Ditto, me," nodded Freddy. "And, as that's so, I think you'll have to relent and let me have a puff, too. You see, smoking is my *only* vice, and if I don't indulge it periodically, I'll be forced to join the clergyman." Having lit the girl's cigarette, he now lit his own. He had a pleasant sense that he was quietly scoring. "Tell me, how did you find the invalid?"

The question was asked casually, but Freddy divined that the reply would be of more than casual interest. Indeed, the large gentleman did pause before delivering it, as though to give it weight, or to enjoy any little suspense that might be attaching to it.

"The invalid?" he repeated, slowly. "Oh—the invalid's all right, I fancy. I imagine he's got over his—h'm—indisposition."

"You found him?" queried the girl.

"Yes. I found him. Two coaches off. He—h'm—toddled a long distance for his little drink."

"How was he?"

"When I last saw him, he was lying quietly in a corner, with his eyes closed."

There was another tiny pause.

"Asleep?" asked Freddy. He had a sense that he was asking the question for the girl.

Then the large gentleman altered his tactics, and suddenly gave generous information.

"One imagines so," he said. "Yes, probably asleep. And he must be a pretty heavy sleeper, too, I should think, or an adept in the art of simulation. There is a family of five in his compartment making as much noise as five families of fifty. If *I* had to travel under such conditions, upon my soul, I think I'd prefer a wheelbarrow!" He broke off abruptly. "Hallo. We're slowing up," he exclaimed. "This must be Chelmsford."

The train was definitely reducing speed. Freddy peered out of the window.

"Oh, we stop at Chelmsford, do we?" he queried.

"Yes," answered the girl. "And then at Ipswich and Norwich."

"Now, why," wondered Freddy, "did she volunteer that?"

The statement seemed to interest the large gentleman. He had risen from his seat, and was moving towards the door of their side—the door that would open on to Chelmsford platform. As he drew near the gid he turned to her, his head at an angle.

"Ipswich and Norwich," he repeated. "Are you sure we stop at Ipswich and Norwich? I had an idea we went straight through."

"Through Norwich?" she answered. "I believe all trains stop at Norwich. We shunt or something."

"So we do, so we do," nodded the large gentleman. "Of course. I'd forgotten. So we do."

The train came to a standstill. It was its first halt. Freddy looked at his watch. Six o'clock exactly.

"Hey!" called the large man, thrusting his head out of the window. His bulky form made an unprepossessing screen between the girl and Freddy. Nothing would have given Freddy greater pleasure than to tip it out. "Hey! Do we wait here long?"

"Couple o' minutes," said an Essex porter.

"Ah, then I've just time to dive and get a paper," murmured the large gentleman.

He swung the door open, and jumped down onto the platform. Freddy was surprised at his litheness. The white spats winked briskly away from them, towards the stall.

"Well?" murmured Freddy.

The girl glanced out of the window, towards the spats. They had stopped winking, rather abruptly. A rude cockney bloke was passing remarks about them.

"Gawd! There's a sight fer sore eyes," jeered the cockney.

He, too, had descended from the train for a stretch.

"What's that?" snapped the large gentleman.

"Some blokes 'ave ter mike a show at the bottom, cos they can't mike no show at the top," grinned the cockney.

"Don't be impudent, sir!" exclaimed the large gentleman, and proceeded indignantly on his way.

The cockney bloke applied the closure in his usual characteristic fashion. He spat after the departing spats. And an agitated old lady, watching him from the window of the compartment he had just vacated, shuddered violently, and began an excited dissertation against socialism.

The girl bent forward. Her head was close to Freddy's. For one short, glorious moment, he felt her breath upon his cheek.

"I don't know whether you'd be interested to have a look at the patient?" she said, very quietly. "Two coaches forward. You could get a glimpse from the platform. . . . Will you give me another light? My cigarette's gone out."

He gave her the light. He guessed that the spats were returning. As she leaned back in her corner—he felt cold as she did so—he slipped out onto the platform, turned enginewards, and shouted.

"Hi! Boy!" he cried.

A lad with a tray of chocolates was in the distance. Freddy bounded towards him, spent sixpence, and then slowly returned.

He returned through a little, excited knot of five people. They had just shot themselves out of their compartment, and small luggage was shooting out after them. They were very agitated.

"I swear they tole me it stopped at Colchester!" declared a flustered girl.

"Them porters, they never tell yer anything right," rasped another indignant personage. "Nice thing, if we'd been carried on to Hipswich!"

Recollection returned to Freddy. The large gentleman had mentioned five loquacious passengers in the compartment occupied by the man in the dark brown suit. These must be the five people. And the man in the dark brown suit must now be in the compartment alone.

He glanced up, through the window.

It was only a quick, casual glance. The large gentleman was standing watching him. But the glance was sufficient to show Freddy that the man in the dark brown suit was indeed alone in his corner, that his eyes were still closed, and that he looked very ill indeed.

7

The Tunnel

Three-quarters of an hour after leaving Liverpool-street station, the 5.18 glided out of Chelmsford and continued its way north-eastwards. In another three-quarters of an hour it would become temporarily obscured in a tunnel to emerge at Ipswich.

To the majority of the passengers on that train, the forty-mile stretch was uneventful. They continued reading their papers, or snoozing, or gazing out of their windows at the pleasant, sun-bathed land without being emotionally stimulated, though one enthusiastic statistician did attempt to create a little sensation by counting the telegraph poles, with watch in hand, and announcing to an apathetic audience that they were travelling a mile a minute; and in another compartment, a little boy whose eye was still smarting slightly from a piece of grit and whose small soul smarted even more from a maternal lecture, abruptly forgot his woe as the train unexpectedly ran by a wide, wonderful mud-bordered channel of water beyond Manningtree.

In a select minority of other compartments, however, more vital emotions stirred the occupants; and, in one, vital things happened. This was the compartment in which, silent and alone, the man in the dark brown suit lay back in his corner with closed eyes.

For a minute or two his eyes remained closed, while Chelmsford dropped behind like a friend who has been hailed, exploited, and shed. Then his eyes slowly opened, and fixed themselves on the emptiness of the seats opposite. When he had closed his eyes these seats had been occupied. So had been the seats beside him. Now he was entirely by himself, which may have accounted for his somewhat odd behaviour.

He sat up suddenly. His eyes still stared ahead of him, but they had lost their indolence, and seemed now to be studying matters beyond the limited area that confined him—matters beyond the cushioned partition on which his eyes were seemingly fixed. He rose, swayed slightly, and then sat down again. A frown, in which were traces of savageness, came to his lips. Had a psychologist passed along the corridor and spent a second on him, the deduction would have been that the man in the dark brown suit was unwell in spirit as well as in body.

No one passed along the corridor, however. The man looked, indeed, to make sure of it, twisting his head round suddenly for the purpose. Then, getting a grip on himself, he put his hand into his breast-pocket and drew out a well-worn cigarette-case.

The cigarette he extracted was not a gold-tipped Teofani. It was a cork-tipped Craven. He lit it slowly and leisurely, seeming to enjoy the deliberation. Then, for a few moments, he puffed.

Odd, the soothing effect of a cigarette! Odd, and undeniable. It brings you back to normal out of your distress, joining you once more to the pleasant security of things. One does not smoke, as a rule, through the agonies of life. One smokes in pleasant company, over tea, in the intervals at a theatre, after work, during the miracle of convalescence. Frayed edges are smoothed by the gently coiling smoke, the illusion of dominance returns to one. Yes, very soothing . . . very soothing indeed. . . .

This particular cigarette was so soothing that for awhile the smoker gave himself up to it utterly, failing to notice that a pleasant-featured young man, in a holiday suit considerably gayer than his own, passed along the corridor and paused for just one instant to dart a glance at him. Perhaps there was no special reason why the smoker should have been watching for so ordinary a sight. At the same time, he was usually quite observant, and on this afternoon had particular need to be so. Indeed, a few seconds after the pleasant young man had gone by, the necessity for observation recurred to the smoker, and he settled himself in his corner in such a position that he could now watch the corridor and note anything of interest that happened there.

Thus, he noted the return of the pleasant young man, and the pleasant young man, noticing that he had been noted, stopped to poke his head in.

"Hallo!" he smiled. "Feeling more yourself again?"

"Yes, thanks," said the smoker.

"Well, I can't say too much for your looks," observed the man in the corridor. "I got a glimpse of you from the platform at Chelmsford, and I almost thought you'd gone off again."

"Just dizziness," murmured the other. "That's all."

There was a little silence. Then the pleasant young man went on, easily.

"But I spotted you smoking just now as I passed by trying to find the dining-car—of course choosing the wrong direction!—so guessed you were all right once more. You know—we were quite concerned about you."

"Exceedingly good of you."

"Not a bit. You don't know how rocky you looked. Gave the lady in my compartment quite a turn."

"Eh?"

"Yes. As a matter of fact, she wanted me to find out how you were, so I said I'd look you up while ordering my table for dinner."

There was another little silence. The eyes of the man in the brown suit became thoughtful.

"Eh—*she* sent you along, did she?" he asked.

"Yes. Er—want to send back any message in reply to her kind enquiries?"

"You can tell her I'm—all right."

"Splendid! I know that'll please her!"

"Yes, and you can tell her," the man added, suddenly, "that I really think it's wonderfully kind of everybody to go to so much trouble about me. I'm sure I don't know why they should. Why, that other gentleman came along a little while ago, you know, and he—"

"Talk of the devil!" boomed the other gentleman, appearing with startling abruptness. "Here he is, to enquire after you again! Getting along quite all right now, eh? Feeling as fit as a fiddle?"

If the newcomer intended to have a cheering effect, he failed signally. His insistent geniality appeared to dry up any genial currents that were flowing between the other two. The man in the dark brown suit mumbled some vague and unimportant reply. The man in the gay grey suit murmured, "Well, cheerio!" And the party dissolved. Now the man in the brown suit was alone once more, with his cigarette and his thoughts.

The train sped on. Every now and again the man's eyes began to close, and each time he pulled himself up with a jerk. He appeared to be fighting a return to his lethargy. The battle continued for nearly twenty minutes; he had almost lost, and was nearly asleep when the train rushed through Colchester. Then he came to with an unusually violent jerk. Somebody had popped his head in at the doorway.

The somebody was the cockney bloke, and he saw the drowsy man before the drowsy man opened his eyes and saw him. In fact, he had stood in the doorway regarding the drowsy man for some fifteen seconds with serious interest; but now the seriousness departed from his face, and he smiled.

"'Avin' forty of 'em, are yer?" he observed. "Well, I don't blime yer. *I* don't go on trine journeys fer me 'ealth."

The man in the brown suit did not respond. You do not necessarily encourage a loquacious cockney. This particular cockney, however, did not require encouragement.

"Gawd, yer orter see *my* carridgeful!" he exclaimed, jerking a dirty thumb over a threadbare shoulder. "Fair lot o' cheeses they are! Think the bloomin' world was mide fer 'em! Think chaps like me ain't got no right ter hegsist! Well, wot I ses is, let 'em wite till we gits a Labour Government with a four 'undred majority. Fust thing it'll do'll be ter tike people like that ter the top of Mount Heverest and drop 'em in a pond!" He stared round the compartment approvingly. "Yer luckier in 'ere, mate! Plenty o' room. No old lidies screamin' at yer not ter touch 'em! Mikes yer want er touch 'em, that sort o' thing, don't it? Well, I reckon I'll come in 'ere fer a rest—if you've no hobjeckshun?"

The man in the brown suit made an effort.

"I've no objection," he said. "Only there aren't any ponds at Mount Everest."

"Owjer know?" retorted the cockney. "Ever bin there?" Then he chuckled, completed his entry into the compartment, and sat down. "Bit of a 'umerist, aintcher? Well—so'm I. When I was a nipper and begins ter think—fancy chap like me thinkin'!—I ses ter meself, 'Look 'ere, life's funny or 'orrible, you gotter decide.' So I decides as it's funny, see? I'm funny. Yer're funny. This 'ole bloomin' trine's funny." He grinned in a queer, humourless fashion for one of the world's wits. "'Ave a garsper?"

The man in the brown suit shook his head.

"Go on," urged the cockney. "Yer looks a bit peaky, mate. Smoke and fergit it!"

"No, thank you," replied the other. "I've smoked too much already."

The cockney regarded him sharply.

"'Ave yer?" he observed. "Well—ter my thinkin'—one more is jest wot yer wants."

But the man in the brown suit did not agree. He declined, with firmness, and indicated a desire to go to sleep again. He even closed his eyes, rather rudely. This time, however, he managed to keep one of the eyes half open.

"Orl right—if yer won't, yer won't," remarked the cockney bloke, as he fumbled with a packet of gold-flakes. "But one more than yer meant is the rule I goes by. If yer say yer goin' ter smoke three fags, yet needs four. . . . Bit of a draught 'ere. Think I'll come yer side." He rose, and changed his seat to one considerably nearer his companion. "And if yer say yer goin' ter 'ave seven glasses o' beer, yer needs height. I've 'ad *nine!*"

He laughed. The man in the brown suit frowned, and opened his eyes complainingly.

"Don't think me unsociable," he grunted, "but I'm not feeling well! If you want somebody to talk to, you'd better go back to your old ladies!"

"Orl right, no need ter git 'uffy," responded the cockney, now frowning also. "Feller can hopen 'is marth, carn't 'e?"

A silence followed. The man in the brown suit closed his eyes again. The cockney bloke smoked.

Suddenly the cockney's gaze became riveted on the floor. He appeared to be regarding nothing more interesting than a cigarette stump, and a cigarette stump is not a particular arresting object, as a rule. But this was an unusually long stump; in fact, only a small portion of the cigarette appeared to have been smoked; and, of course, stumps of this length do sometimes interest cockneys.

It was lying a little way under the seat on which he sat. He only saw it because he happened to be bending forward, with his head down. The smoker had evidently dropped the cigarette, after only a few puffs, and it had rolled to the spot where it now lay. All at once, the cockney dropped his own stump from his lips.

"'Allo—wot's me marth doin'?" he muttered to imself. "Blimy, if I ain't dozin' orf, too!"

He stooped, to regain the end of a perfect goldflake. He also regained the longer cigarette-end. It was of a brand not so popular.

Was the man in the brown suit watching him? The cockney slowly straightened up. He had replaced the goldflake between his lips, but his second capture remained concealed in his hand. He turned towards his companion.

The eyes seemed to be closed. Quietly, the cockney slipped the second cigarette stump away in his pocket. Then he stared beyond his companion out of the window.

"Nice bit o' mud, that," he commented.

"Eh?" blinked the man in the brown suit, opening his eyes abruptly.

"I ses, nice bit o' mud, that," repeated the cockney. "Jest gorn through Manningtree, mate. Looks like the sea, don't it? But, o' corse, it *ain't*. It's one o' them hestewaryries. It won't be long now afore we're at Hipswich. You gettin' aht there?"

"No," answered the other.

"Ain't yer?" murmured the cockney bloke, and suddenly grew thoughtful.

"No, I'm not!" snapped the man in the brown suit, very irritably. "You don't know when you're not wanted, do you?"

"'Allo!" exclaimed the cockney, huffily. "Now *you're* goin' up the spout, are yer?"

The country is interesting between Manningtree and Ipswich. There are undulations; and a sense of shipping and the sea, created by a glimpse of the wide estuary of the Stour rolling muddily to Harwich, remains with one after the glimpse is over. But neither the man in the brown suit nor the cockney seemed to find any attraction in the prospect. The former lay snuggled in his corner, fighting desperately against the sleep he was feigning, while the latter smoked his second goldflake and stared moodily ahead of him.

Then, all at once, the atmosphere in the compartment changed. The cockney threw away his cigarette, and his teeth closed rather tightly behind his unattractive lips.

"We'll be at Hipswich in a minit," he said.

You could listen to the remark or not, as you liked. The cockney didn't mind. He rose, and stepped to the window. The window of the door that would be next to Ipswich platform "in a minit." The window was half open. He loosened the strap, and opened it fully. He poked his head out.

"'Allo," he said. "We're comin' ter the tunnel."

The small black hole grew in size, rushed towards them, reached them, and swallowed them up. The cockney bloke brought his head in.

"Now we're 'ere," he remarked. "When we come aht of it, we'll be at Hipswich. Ah—but you ain't gettin' aht at Hipswich, are yer?"

The train ran through the blackness of the tunnel. It reached Ipswich. And, as it slowed down, the cockney bloke sat in the compartment alone, lighting his third cigarette.

8

Dinner for Two

There is a five-minute wait at Ipswich. That is, if you are lucky and your train is on time. Between 6.51 and 6.56 you may leave your compartment and stroll about a spacious platform like a liberated entity, transforming ugliness into beauty and drawing a charm from cold stone that is securely hidden from the local porters. You may even enjoy a dashing cup of coffee, ordered breathlessly at 6.52, delivered at 6.53, drunk at 6.54, and paid for at 6.55 with a minute still in your pocket. This is merely one of the delights that many a passenger has experienced at Ipswich, the port of call, on his way to find sea breezes.

This evening, however, the train was a little late, and the coffee enthusiasts thought twice. One of them did make a rather surprising dash. This was the clergyman. But he grew agitated at the last moment, changed his mind, and returned to his compartment unslaked, with the sensation of one who has prepared his spirit for a hot bath and then discovered the maid has not kept the fire up.

"No luck, sir?" beamed the large gentleman, watching him return from the adjacent compartment.

"I believe I'd have had time," replied the clergyman, rather fretfully. "Someone told me we were just off!"

"Bad luck," said the large gentleman. "But, haven't you noticed, railway officials *always* tell you you are just off? They seem to object strongly to any other theory."

The clergyman was too unhappy to discuss the psychology of porters, and he disappeared back into his compartment hoping that the train would start immediately, so that he could be quite sure he would have lost it if he had stopped for his coffee. The train callously refused to oblige, however, and remained static for another couple of minutes. Meanwhile, the large gentleman, who was on the platform a few yards from his base, continued to watch the hurrying people, and to miss none.

Inside the compartment which he had lately left, someone else watched the hurrying people, and missed none. The girl was just as interested as he was, and just as well able to camouflage her interest. But if anyone possessing enough importance to justify that interest boarded the 5.18 before it began the next stage of its journey, this must have occurred at the very front or the very rear of the train. There was no sign of any distinguished personage in the central portion.

"Are you dining after Ipswich, Miss Leveridge?" asked Freddy suddenly, a minute before the train started.

She turned to him in surprise, but her eyes were back on the platform the next instant.

"How do you know my name?" she asked quietly.

"Your friends who saw you off used it," he answered.

"And that gives *you* permission?"

"Not a bit. But I'm beginning to do things without permission, I'm afraid. I've done something far more audacious than use your name."

"I suppose I'm expected to ask what it is?"

"I've booked a table for two in the dining-car," said Freddy. "How's that for absolute, unadulterated coolness?"

"It is absolutely and unadulteratedly cool," she agreed, though without censure.

"It was also rather thoughtful," remarked Freddy, now eyeing the platform with her, and noticing that the back of the large gentleman was beginning to stir. "When I went to arrange for my own seat—and to bring you a further report of the poor fellow you were interested in—I discovered that nearly all the seats were booked. In fact, there was only one small table left. Well—I booked it."

"It was nice of you. But passengers don't always take dinner on the train, you know."

"I know they don't."

"And I might already have booked my seat."

"I know you might. But none was booked in the name of Leveridge."

She shot him another glance. Her expression was rather quizzical.

"You seem to do things rather thoroughly," she commented.

"I'm not sure—I haven't introduced myself yet," he responded. "My name is Frederic Reeve."

"Thank you. And now, I suppose, I *must* dine with you?"

The large back was turning round.

"Only if it fits in with your purpose," he answered quickly, dropping his voice. "Naturally—there's no other obligation whatever."

Now the back had turned right round, and the large gentleman was slowly coming towards them. The girl's voice was as low as his, and her lips hardly moved, as she murmured,

"I'm not sure—but I *will* dine with you, if it fits in with my purpose. Go on ahead, when the train starts. Don't wait. . . ."

The large gentleman climbed in. He had a vaguely resigned look about him. Perhaps it was train boredom.

"Four minutes to seven," he remarked a few seconds later, as a porter bawled, "Stand away there!" "Another whole hour to Norwich! We stop at Norwich, I think you said?" he added, turning to the girl.

"Yes," she nodded. "Just before eight."

"You know your timetable well! Do we stop anywhere between?"

"I don't think so."

"H'm—plenty of time to fill up."

"Well, *I'm* going to fill up the time by dining," exclaimed Freddy, rising abruptly. "And I'm glad I had the forethought to book my seat. It was the last one."

He dived out into the corridor, while the large gentleman looked a little concerned.

"The last seat, eh?" he muttered. "Then that does *me!* I'd hoped—hallo!" he broke off. "He's gone the wrong way again!"

"Yes—he doesn't seem to have much brain, does he?" said the girl, with a little contemptuous frown. "I hope they don't put me at his table."

The large gentleman looked at her curiously. "You've booked your own seat, then?"

"Yes."

"Ah! H'm. Well, let us hope your fears will not be justified."

"Thank you. I'm not going in just yet, though."

"Not just yet," repeated the large gentleman, absently. "Not just yet." He abruptly pulled himself together. "Well, well, it's the fortune of war, I expect. I shall have to go without any dinner at all! Not even a luncheon basket. . . . But let me seize upon one crumb of comfort. I can at least occupy our young friend's seat while he is away." He moved to the corner opposite the girl, and smiled. "Perhaps, as you say you are not going in to dinner for a few minutes, you will—h'm—relieve my monotony a little, and chat with a bored old man?" He smiled elaborately, displaying a very creditable set of teeth, as though to combat the theory that he was really an old man; but possibly the teeth were a little too creditable to believe. "Please smoke again, if you want to. And have one of mine." He produced a case, surprisingly. "Yes, yes, I know what you are thinking. I said I did not smoke. Well, I fear our young friend incited that little fib. It was not strictly true. I do smoke occasionally—h'm—just occasionally."

He snapped the case open, and held it out to her. The contents were of the same brand as that of the cigarette discovered by the cockney bloke under the seat.

9

Corridor Happenings

Of course, Freddy had repeated his error of taking the wrong turning on purpose. He wanted to have another glance at the man in the dark brown suit before he took his seat in the dining-car, and he was perfectly willing to increase his reputation for having no bump of locality. There are plenty of people who almost invariably turn left when they should turn right. Even a soldier has been rumoured to do it.

The compartment in which he had seen the man in the brown suit was a couple of coaches away, towards the front. As he passed through the second of the narrow isthmuses that connect one coach with another, a figure blundered into him.

"Cantcher ever look where yer goin'?" demanded the figure.

"Good Lord!" exclaimed Freddy, recognising the cockney bloke. "I think it's your turn to apologise this time!"

"G'arn!" grunted the cockney, and shoved himself by.

An amazingly rude fellow! Seemed to make a special point of it!

Freddy proceeded on his short journey. Ah—here was the compartment. He poked his head in. It was empty.

"Hallo! He's gone!" thought Freddy.

He was vaguely surprised. He did not know exactly why he was surprised. The man might have got out at Ipswich. . . .

"Yes, but I don't remember seeing him get out at Ipswich," reflected Freddy. "I remember looking towards his carriage when we stopped. The door didn't open. No one got out."

No, he *hadn't* got out. There was his little brown bag. The man must still be on the train.

"Silly ass, I am!" murmured Freddy, the next moment. "If anybody came along and looked for me in my compartment, they wouldn't find me, would they? 'Cos why? 'Cos I'm going to have dinner in the dining-car. That's where the chap is. In the dining-car."

Just the same, the man in the brown suit didn't look like a fellow who would pay 4/6 for his dinner. A packet of sandwiches in a newspaper was more in his line. . . . Hallo, and there *was* a newspaper that looked as though it had contained sandwiches in it!

He took a step towards it. Yes—distinctly crumby! But the crumbiness of the newspaper was not what held Freddy Reeve's attention as he stared at it. The newspaper contained something considerably more arresting. A picture of Miss Lydia Leveridge, the girl with whom he was expecting in a few moments to be taking dinner!

"Don't believe it, my son," he advised himself. "Something's wrong with you! Coincidences like this simply don't *happen!* Close your eyes, like a good boy, and then open them again, and the picture will fade away!"

He tried it. It is astonishing how many people do try it, even when they know there is not the remotest chance that the device will work. He closed his eyes. He still saw the face of Lydia Leveridge. Dark brown hair peeping from beneath a *chic* little hat. Wonderful complexion—possibly

not entirely hers. Never mind! Call it a triumphant blend
of artistry and health, designed not to dupe man, but
to make him joyous in its sight. Lips almost terrifyingly
desirable—to Freddy Reeve, at any rate, in the final throes
of subjection. Brilliant eyes, that pierced you with arrows
of light. Yes, he saw it all, though his own eyes were closed;
and in the darkness of his lids the solution dawned upon
him. Of course—he'd got it, now! He saw Lydia Leveridge
everywhere. And he would go on seeing her everywhere for
the remainder of his life. That, obviously, was the explanation!

He opened his eyes. The picture still smiled up at him
from the newspaper. . . . That, obviously, was *not* the
explanation.

The picture was in a society column. He peered closer,
and read beneath:

"Miss Lydia Leveridge, one of this year's debutantes,
and daughter of Sir Henry Leveridge—" Sir Henry Leveridge? Something familiar about that name. "—is travelling to-day to Sheringham, Norfolk—" Sheringham! Dash
it! Freddy's ticket was to Cromer! Still, the two places
weren't many miles apart. . . . "—where she is spending
the week-end with Lord and Lady Treadmouth, to whose
son she recently became engaged—"

Freddy took a deep breath. So—she was engaged! True,
he had already seen the engagement ring; he had seen two
engagement rings, in fact; but he had also seen her without any engagement ring at all, and the circumstances had
been so odd that he had subconsciously held on to hope.
Girls who wish to flirt dispense with engagement rings;
girls who do not wish to flirt might conceivably put them
on! But here, in callous printers' ink, was the grim irrefutable proof. Seven little words that blocked the road to
Glory!

"Of course, Freddy—you're a fool," he said aloud. "How on earth could you think—?"

Yes, he was a fool. It was utter madness that he should think! There are times, however, when even the sanest among us—and Freddy Reeves was far from that—becomes a fool and believes that he can balance on a moonbeam. Old folk as well as young folk. And the old folk are the greatest fools of all, because when *they* fall they really and truly hurt themselves, and receive no sympathy as they struggle to rise and regain their normal pose.

Freddy regained his normal pose quickly and creditably. He felt as though somebody had suddenly clawed his heart out and had mockingly inserted a stone, but he wasn't going to cry about it. This was just his personal, private affair—the abrupt shattering of a dream that had formed itself without his sanction, and almost without his knowledge, until the pieces lay around him. Meanwhile, *everything* hadn't gone. If he no longer had the right to love her, he still had the right to serve her. And is there any higher expression of love than service? Or any expression, to our human desires, less satisfying?

"Now, then—let me think," murmured Freddy. "A man . . . A man in a brown suit. That's what I'm here for. Man in a brown suit."

He hugged on to the thought. It brought him back to the world of activity, and activity was his necessity. The man in the brown suit wasn't here, and he hadn't got out at Ipswich—Ipswich, a place Freddy had passed through millions of years ago, when the heart was young!—because, though he wasn't here, his bag was here. And therefore he must have gone into the dining car. Yes, Freddy remembered it all now. That was where his deduction had arrived at. The dining-car. All right. Very well. He would go and have a look in the dining-car, satisfy himself that the man was contentedly eating, and then take his own seat. Yes, that was the jolly old idea!

He left the empty compartment hurriedly, with a guilty sensation that he had stayed there too long. As a matter of fact, he had stayed there for far less time than he had imagined. Hurrying back, he passed the compartment in the next coach in which the cockney bloke was beginning to agitate the old woman again (what an oddly neurotic creature she was!), and then, in the coach beyond that, his own compartment. He slackened speed here for the fraction of an instant, so that he could mumble something incoherent about "having gone the wrong way again like the idiot he was," and also so that he could flash a glance at the occupants. The glance did not add to his composure. It occurred at the moment when the large and expansive gentleman was holding out his cigarette-case to the girl.

"Blighter!" muttered Freddy.

But he did not stop. It would not have helped, and he was not in the mood to do any fencing just then. He proceeded along the corridor and entered the first-class dining-car. He did not stop here, either, though the courteous official from whom he had booked his seats gave him a welcoming smile and waved towards a table. "In a minute," murmured Freddy, and passed out of the car and by the kitchen where the railway chef, in spotless white and with a tall white hat that appeared to have been made out of a mammoth napkin, was turning out dishes at sixty miles an hour. Beyond, again, was the third-class dining-car.

Now Freddy paused, and gazed around. He was searching for a familiar face above a dark brown suit. There were plenty of dark brown suits in the car, but only one familiar face, and that he could not see because it was his own.

"Have you booked a seat, sir?" enquired a voice.

"No, not here," replied Freddy. "I was looking for a friend."

Another young man, sitting at a table near him, over-
heard the remark, and smiled at the lady opposite. He had
found one.

Freddy turned, and retraced his steps. The good-natured
chef, his face steaming, threw him a smile as he went by;
it was the fourth time the chef had seen this peripatetic
passenger. Freddy smiled back. Even in the midst of grave
matters, life holds its pleasant trivialities; without them,
life would be grave indeed. Another smile greeted Freddy
in the first-class dining-car. It was the car attendant, whose
duty it was to make passengers happier travelling by train
than by motor-coach, and who achieved his object.

"This is your table, sir," he said.

"Thank you," replied Freddy.

He sat down, choosing the seat facing the engine. By
this means he was able to keep his eye on the entrance
to the car through which Miss Leveridge would appear,
or through which he hoped she would appear. The table
was small and scrupulously neat, but even more than by
its neatness was he pleased by the fact that it was farthest
from the entrance. This meant that it was also farthest
from the large and expansive gentleman, and that when
Miss Leveridge joined Freddy the unpleasant individual
she would just have left would have the maximum distance
to travel should he decide to come along during the meal
and make himself a nuisance.

"Consommé? Cream Portugaise?" enquired the waiter.

"I'll wait a minute or two," answered Freddy, nodding
towards the empty seat opposite.

"Very good, sir," responded the waiter, and hurried
away to pacify an irritable diner who had asked for brown
bread, who had not yet received brown bread, who wanted
to know the reason why.

Freddy fought again a wretched anxiety that was beginning to settle on him. He visualized the third-class

compartment in which he had come across the picture of Miss Leveridge, and wondered whether it were still empty. Wondered whether, at this moment, the newspaper still lay open upon the seat, and whether the little brown bag still occupied a corner of the luggage-rack. But even more anxiously he wondered what was happening in his own compartment. Miss Leveridge had promised to join him if it fitted in with her purpose. What was her purpose? And what incident did she anticipate that might prevent her from joining him? Was the large and expansive gentleman connected with this incident? . . .

"Ah! An empty seat!"

Freddy looked up quickly as a hungry passenger dived for the vacant place.

"I'm sorry, sir, but that's taken," exclaimed Freddy, quickly.

"Yes, I know it is," retorted the passenger, acting on the principle that you can get anything if you go for it hard enough, and that possession is nine points of the law. "I've taken it."

About to blaze up, Freddy changed his mind and summoned official aid. One didn't want a scene, he reflected.

"Waiter," he called, "will you please tell this gentleman that the seat he is in is reserved?"

The waiter looked worried. He had just had rather a bad time over a piece of brown bread. However, the honour of the London and North Eastern Railway had to be maintained and its traditions for square dealing upheld, so he turned to the intruder and said, deferentially,

"The seat is booked, sir."

"And how long does it remain booked?" demanded the intruder. "A week?"

"No, just a few minutes," said a quiet voice behind him. "Do you mind?"

The intruder turned his head, flushed, and jumped up. He went through life rudely, but there are always a chosen few to whom you cannot be rude. Lydia Leveridge was one of them.

10

From the Soup to the Fish

"What are you thinking of?" asked Miss Leveridge in the middle of the Cream Portugaise.

"That's rather a risky question," replied Freddy.

"If it is," she answered, after a moment's thought, "I'm taking the risk."

"I see," said Freddy. "But what about my risk?" She waited for him to explain. "If I answer you seriously, you may have intended me to answer you frivolously—and if I answer you frivolously you may have meant me to answer you seriously. Give me a lead!"

She smiled. "That's terribly cautious, Mr. Reeve," she remarked. "Try answering me truthfully, and then I'll know your mood."

"Seems to me I'm not the only cautious one," he retorted. "Mustn't I know *your* mood? However, you asked first, so here goes. I was wondering whether to follow this with grilled turbot or to go straight on to the chicken sauté."

Her smile faded.

"Now I know," she said. "Will you pass me the pepper?"

"No, you don't," grunted Freddy, contritely. "Of course, I wasn't thinking of that. Tell me that you seriously want to know what I was thinking of, and I'll shoot. As a matter of fact, I expect you've got a glimmering already."

"I think I have got a glimmering already," she admitted, "and it's because of that I asked. I want to know—very much—what's in your mind."

"Right," murmured Freddy. "There's a lot in my mind." He glanced towards the entrance to the car. The view was wholly harmonious. "And it'll take a little time to unload it," he added, suddenly.

"We've got several courses," she reminded him. "We can spin them out by not missing the grilled turbot."

Freddy's heart warmed. She could be frivolous, too! A sudden longing swept over him to discard all solemn thinking, and to enjoy the moment in the gay, holiday spirit which had been his when he first boarded the train. A *tête-à-tête* meal with a glorious girl like this! Half-an-hour of jolly, pleasant chatter. A compliment or two, innocent and impulsive. Smiles with the turbot, laughter with the chicken sauté, and the compliments over the apple tart. The sun danced very prettily across their table. Such a dream might not happen twice in a life-time!

But then he realised that she was treating him to a better side of herself than that. Mere society would have been a small compliment. Moreover, would he have appreciated her quite so much if she had been over-ready to assuage his selfish thirst for her smiles? He had a perfect right to fall in love with her, so long as he did not trouble her by betraying the fact. On the other hand, she had no right to show any special personal interest in him. He glanced at her finger. The ruby flashed back at him.

"Well—I was thinking of a lot of things," he said, "and I'd rather like to spread them out before you, if I may. You see, I'm wondering whether they are separate matters, or whether they're all a part of the same sum. P'r'aps you can help me?"

"Perhaps I can," she nodded. "I'd like to hear them all. There's no chance of your boring me."

"There you are, to begin with!" went on Freddy. "The very fact that you *want* to hear them seems to knit them together! I say, Miss Leveridge—*is* anything mighty queer happening on this train, or am I an idiot? I don't mean just a little queer—I mean *mighty* queer?"

"If it is," she responded, "it might be wise not to raise one's voice."

She had kept her own voice low throughout. Freddy looked a little guilty, and lowered his.

"I'll take that as my answer," he said, and paused while the waiter whisked away their plates. Then he went on, "I expect you saw me take the wrong turning again, when I left our compartment to go to the dining-car?"

"Yes," nodded Miss Leveridge. "And I guessed why."

"It was to have another look at our friend, of course— the fellow who was ill."

"How did you find him?"

"I didn't find him." She shot him a quick glance. "He wasn't there."

She offered no comment, but her expression tightened almost imperceptibly. As she said nothing, he continued:

"No, he wasn't there, Miss Leveridge. Now, under ordinary circumstances, that would not have been of much importance. But then I'm taking it that these *aren't* ordinary circumstances. Am I right? Of course, he might have got out at Ipswich. But, in that case, I think I'd have seen him get out. I'd have seen him on the platform. And, anyway, his bag hadn't gone. It was still on the rack."

"He may be dining, like us," she exclaimed, suddenly.

"I'm afraid not," he returned. "I thought of that, too, you see, and I went into the third-class diner."

"And he wasn't there?"

"No."

Another idea occurred to her.

"He may have been in one of the corridors, smoking," she suggested. "He may have gone back by now."

"Would you like me to find out?"

"Yes—I would!"

"It's important then?"

"The poor fellow's ill."

He had not got her full confidence yet, then! Her anxiety was obviously greater than the most humane passenger would be likely to evince in a total stranger who had had a fit of dizziness, but she still refused to admit that she was urged by more than ordinary, impersonal compassion. Freddy rose, a little disappointedly, and a waiter approaching with grilled turbot raised his eyebrows enquiringly.

"Back in a minute," said Freddy to the waiter. "I left something in my compartment."

His compartment was in the adjoining coach, but in his hurry he over-ran it. He did not stop until he had reached the second coach beyond it. Then he paused, and looked into the compartment where the man in the brown suit had sat. It was still empty.

About to return, he entered the compartment, and gazed round. At first, nothing struck him. Then he was vaguely worried by a change. Something was different—some little detail—but he could not put his finger upon it. The newspaper was still there. The brown bag was still there. . . . The brown bag . . . something about the brown bag . . .

"It's been moved!" flashed the thought.

Yes, it had certainly been moved. Before it had been on the rack, in the corner. Now it was a foot or two from the corner. Oh, well—what of it? This was ridiculous! He was straining at details. . . .

But the bag worried him. Since he had last been here, somebody had entered the compartment, had made it his business—or her business?—to move the bag, and had then left the compartment again. If this somebody had been the owner of the bag, then why had he left the compartment a second time? There might be a quite simple reason; on the other hand, there might not; and, backed by Miss Leveridge's own anxiety, Freddy was in a mood to look on the dark side of things. Suppose the somebody who had moved the bag had *not* been its owner? Would he have moved it without opening it? And, if he had opened it, what was the reason?

A simple brown bag, yet how intensely interesting! How intensely tempting! . . .

And then Freddy did a very unorthodox and audacious thing. He suddenly advanced to the rack, stretched up his hand, and brought the bag down. "If anybody comes," he reflected, as he opened it, "how am I going to explain myself? What on earth shall I say?"

He had no idea. He also had no time to devise one. distant later the bag was open, and he was regarding the contents.

The bag was full of bright little leather note-books. Each note-book was fitted with a neat little pencil, and on the covers were the words:

"Write us down to-day, for to-morrow we are forgotten!"

Travellers' samples, evidently. The man in the dark brown suit was a commercial. A little card, lying loose on the top, provided further evidence of the man's vocation. The inscription ran:

MESSRS. RACE & SPENDLOW
Wholesale Dealers

Representative:
Mr. W. G. Biddock

Well—that was that. The contents of the bag did not convey very much, and after staring at them fixedly for a moment or two, Freddy suddenly closed the bag with a snap and replaced it on the rack. He replaced it in the exact position in which he had found it.

An odd thought struck him, coming out of nowhere. His finger-marks were now invisibly imprinted on the bag! Did this matter? It is remarkable how guilty an innocent man can feel if, actuated by the best of motives, he goes off the conventional rails a little. Freddy actually took out his pocket handkerchief to wipe the bag. Then he paused.

"Upon my soul, you *are* an idiot!" he told himself. "Do you really suppose you are going to be hanged by the neck because you've opened a bag containing leather note-books?" He did not realise that people have been hanged on substance seemingly as slight. "Besides, you prize ass, if you wipe off your fingerprints, you'll be wiping off somebody else's, as well!"

So he put his handkerchief back in his pocket, and turned to go.

But something else detained him. The newspaper. Was it, after all, as he had left it?

No, it was not. The pages containing Miss Leveridge's picture had been uppermost. Now, another page was uppermost. That must have subconsciously worried him, too, when he had entered the compartment, and given him a sense of transformation. The somebody who had looked inside the bag before him had also handled the newspaper.

Freddy, also, handled the newspaper. Hardly knowing why, he turned the sheet over. Perhaps he wanted another glimpse of the attractive portrait, even though the more attractive reality was waiting for him at that moment. . . . He turned two sheets over . . . three . . .

"Well—I'm dashed!" he murmured.

The sheet containing Miss Leveridge's picture was gone!

Bag opened—picture gone. Bag opened—picture gone. The words danced idiotically through his brain, significant at one moment, meaningless at the next, but inexplicable all the time. Then other words joined in the dance. Man in compartment—man not in compartment—man not anywhere. Bag opened. Picture gone. Man not anywhere.

He gave it up. He left the compartment, this time forgetting to replace the newspaper as he had found it. But, once again, unseen fingers seemed to dart out and grip him, as though loth to let him go. The compartment was trying to talk to him, but he could not hear the message.

"My God!" he murmured suddenly.

He was back in the compartment in a trice. He bent down, and looked under the seats. Something glinted dully at him. It was the heating-pipe.

He rose and wiped his forehead. To his surprise, and also annoyance, it was very moist. The heating-pipe had not been responsible. Nor, surely, could have been the little discoveries he had made. Freddy had done his bit by Edgar Wallace, and thought his forehead was immune. He did not know that, when great emotion has been stirred, its aftermath often lingers awhile, like smoke that has been belched into a tunnel and hangs there till it thins itself out and dissipates. The engine has rushed by, but the smoke still chokes you. . . .

Freddy certainly did feel a little choked as he went into the corridor again. During the past two hours he had gone through many emotions and no fulfilment. That takes it out of one. Also, he had looked under a seat for a body. That also takes it out of one. The window of the door in the corridor was wide open, and a refreshing breeze poured through. Impulsively, Freddy put his head out of the window, and drew in great draughts.

Everything was very peaceful beyond the window. A genial river flowed along, and the fields were full of pleasant undulations. A child, watching the train from one of the fields, raised her hand and waved. Freddy waved back. . . .

Good Lord! What was happening? Something had lurched into his back—his legs were like ton weights—and now they seemed to have no weight at all! They were being raised . . . his body was being tilted outwards. . . .

Freddy kicked. He kicked hugely and violently. The fields outside the window were pleasant, but he had no wish to join them. In two seconds he had slithered his body sideways and had shaken off that sudden propulsion. Now his head was back inside the corridor again, breathless and blazing. . . .

He stared up and down the corridor. He was alone.

She passed his compartment on his way back to the dining-car, Freddy heard himself hailed.

"Hallo!" came the bland voice of the large gentleman.
"I thought you were at dinner?"

Freddy reflected rapidly. He could not tell the truth;
on the other hand, to suggest that he had left the dining-car for his compartment and had once more lost his
way would be lying beyond belief. Besides, what could
he have come to his compartment for? He had his cigarettes, his lighter, and his handkerchief on him, and in
the moment following the large gentleman's exclamation
he could not think of anything else that might logically
have brought him back. . . . Then an interesting solution
occurred to him. Its interest intrigued him, its simplicity
appealed to him. Why not, after all, *tell* the truth? Up to
a point, of course. It is the little truth that successfully
hides the big lie.

"Technically speaking, I *am* at dinner," answered Freddy.
"I am eating fish. But I suddenly got worried about that
seedy fellow—the fellow who came here for the brandy,
you know—and thought I'd just pop along and have another look at him."

"Exceedingly nice of you," commented the large gentleman. "I hope you found him all right?"

"Well, as a matter of fact," smiled Freddy, "I didn't find him all right or all wrong. I didn't find him at all."

"Really?" exclaimed the large gentleman. "I wonder what's happened to him?"

"Oh, I expect he's having dinner," replied Freddy, airily, "and now I must get back to mine."

He nodded, and passed on. The clergyman, standing in the corridor, stood aside for him.

"Excuse me," said the clergyman, "but do you know our next stop?"

"Yes, Norwich," answered Freddy.

"Norwich," repeated the clergyman, thoughtfully. "Not till Norwich, eh?"

Freddy did not prolong the conversation. He had one immediate desire in life, and one only. To get back to Lydia Leveridge. And a second or two later he was walking along the aisle of the dining-car, his eyes on her neat and attractive back. While he looked at her, the car attendant looked at him, and turned with a quick nod to one of the lesser waiters. The lesser waiter whisked himself away and then whisked himself back again, accompanied this time by grilled turbot and potatoes.

It is a common habit to complain of meals on trains. In fact, you can scarcely call yourself a patriotic Englishman if you fail to do so. Tradition, lumping the restaurant-car with the climate and the income tax man, has set its seal upon it with the inscription, "You may grumble here," and full advantage is taken of this amiable permission. But a few, who have grumbled on the continent, are silent and stupidly grateful in the restaurant-cars of the homeland, and unless you strike a really bad day—when the chef with the napkin on his head has a tooth-ache, perhaps, and would be happier with a napkin round his face, or when the car attendant meant to back a victorious hundred-to-one horse and forgot to—you will have no excuse for your complaints on the 5.18. Certainly, Freddy had no excuse. He expected to sit down to cold fish. Instead, through railway vigilance, the fish purred up warmly at him. He could not have been treated with more smiling consideration if he had been on his honeymoon. . . .

"You've been a long time," said Miss Leveridge.

"Yes," answered Freddy. "Several interesting little things detained me." Should he tell them all to her? The interesting little attempt on his life, for example? "The first was the discovery that our friend was still absent from his compartment."

"I was afraid he would be," murmured the girl.

"Do you know why he should be?"

"How should I know?"

"I wasn't asking that," frowned Freddy. "I was asking *if* you knew. However, I won't insist on your confidences. I'll see if I can earn them." His eyes were on his plate at the moment, and he missed the grateful glance she threw at him.

"What other little things detained you?" she asked.

"Well—the man's brown bag was one of them."

"Why, wasn't it there?"

"Oh, yes, it was there. But it had been moved." His eyes were still on his plate, almost as though he were deliberately giving her a chance to register her emotions without the necessity of his seeing them; and thus he did not see that her anxiety was growing. He may have sensed it, however. "The bag was still on the rack, but in a different position."

"I suppose you're sure of that?"

"It was obvious."

"The train might have jerked it—moved it a little—"

"It couldn't have moved it two or three feet, Miss Leveridge. No, somebody had shifted its position. And I had an idea that the somebody might have had a peep in the bag. So I took the liberty of peeping into it myself."

Surprise now joined her anxiety. A new look entered her eyes, born of a realisation that this young man had greater possibilities of definite action than she had imagined. The opening of a bag without any dishonest purpose may seem a trivial matter. It formed the measure, however, of Freddy Reeve's interest, and suggested that, if he were pressed, he might go to greater lengths. . . . It was impossible to gather from Miss Leveridge's expression whether her new realisation pleased her or not.

"Wasn't that rather risky?" she asked.

"I dare say it was," he replied. "P'r'aps I'm in a mood to take risks. Anyway, I opened the bag, and found a lot of note-books inside. Just note-books. Nothing very exciting about them, eh?"

"No. Were they all you found?"

"There was a card in the bag. It said 'Messrs. Race & Spendlow, Wholesale Dealers.' And then his name was on it, as their representative—at least, I suppose it was his name. W. G. Biddock. Commercial traveller, apparently."

"He looked rather like one," she said.

"He looked very like one," Freddy agreed, and paused.

Their plates were whisked away. Chicken Sauté appeared.

"Any other little thing?" asked Miss Leveridge.

"Yes. Another rather queer little thing," said Freddy, now frankly watching her. "When I first went into the compartment—I mean, the first time I went there and found it empty—there was a newspaper on the seat. It contained a photograph—of you."

She smiled at him.

"I don't think that's quite as queer as it seems," she remarked. "I have the misfortune to be known in Society a little, and I suppose some editor thought his public would like to see my face."

Freddy smiled, too. When she spoke lightly, everything eased out. But he refused to be diverted. She was fencing with him, and before the meal ended he wanted to disarm her or receive her thrust.

"Rather a coincidence that your picture should be on this particular train," he commented.

"I don't see that," she retorted. "People who get photographed are constantly travelling on trains with their pictures."

"Yes, that's true. But—well, was it queer, or wasn't it, that when I returned to the compartment just now, the newspaper was still on the seat, but your picture had been taken out of it—that's to say, the page that had your picture?"

"Most ungallant; your theory of queerness!" she responded. "You won't admit the possibility of an unknown admirer who comes upon the picture, falls in love with it, and tears it out so that he can wear it next his heart!"

She spoke quickly, and smiled more brightly than ever. Here was frivolity, with a vengeance! Yes, but with too much of a vengeance. One didn't know if one quite trusted it! If she were still fencing, this might be rather a wild thrust to hide her anxiety.

"I quite admit the possibility that someone might fall in love with your picture—since you raise the point," answered Freddy, after a little pause. "I might even have thought of that possibility myself. But, however ungallant you may think me, I'm going to stick to my theory of queerness in this instance, because—well—you remember that I was going to tell you of some other queer little things before I left you just now. The disappearance of our Mr. Biddock was only one of them. Another is an amazingly unpleasant cockney. He seems to be deliberately unpleasant, and I don't believe he's half as drunk as he pretends he is. Another is the detestable gent who has invaded our carriage. He *is* detestable. If you want to know the truth, I loathe him! Another is—is the feeling—of course, you can always correct me if I'm wrong—that you know him, or something about him—and that he's got some game or other on—"

"Am I in the game?" she interposed, now very cool and composed again.

"How do I know? Is it my business anyway? I'm perfectly conscious, Miss Leveridge, that I'm behaving like an ass and probably saying things I shouldn't . . . shall I stop?"

"No, I'd like you to finish," she responded. "I'd like to hear the rest."

"I wonder if you would?" he murmured, doubtfully. "I think p'r'aps I'd better stop, after all."

"Why? Is the rest about *me?*"

"Most of it is."

"I give you permission."

"Whatever it is?"

"Yes."

"All right, Miss Leveridge. Here goes!" He looked at her finger. She followed his glance. "Have I said anything, or haven't I?"

"Yes, you've said something, Mr. Reeve," she answered, slowly. "You've said it rather cleverly." She held her left hand out, and regarded it reflectively. "But, you know, a girl sometimes changes the position of her rings."

"But when she's engaged—"

"How do you know I'm engaged."

"You forget. That paragraph."

"Oh, yes. Of course. Well—when a girl is engaged—?"

"She's rather proud of her engagement ring, and keeps it on," said Freddy, a little lamely.

"Well, mine's on," replied Miss Leveridge.

"Yes. I saw you put it on," nodded Freddy.

"I know. Your glance reminded me that I hadn't got it on," she said. "Is that all about the engagement ring? If there's anything more, I want to know it." Her voice grew more insistent. "It's necessary for me to know it."

"Necessary?" he repeated, in surprise.

"Yes. Very necessary. Please go on."

"All right. It struck me as odd that, when I first saw you in the train, before it started, you were wearing a diamond ring. Now it's a ruby one. And—I don't see the diamond one."

"I see," she murmured. "Yes—that might strike you as odd. Not by itself, perhaps. But when added to all the other things." She withdrew her hand. It disappeared in her lap, while she turned her head and gazed out of the window. She gazed out for a full minute. Freddy felt that the fencing was at an end, and that he would soon know where he stood—with her, at any rate. Had he disarmed her—or was he about to receive her thrust?

She turned her head towards him again.

"And that's all?" she queried.

"Nearly all," he answered.

"Nearly all! Then there's something more?"

"Yes. But not concerning you."

"Let me hear it."

"No. I'm going to keep this to myself. If I tell this to anyone, it'll be to the guard. . . . What's the matter?"

She was staring at him now in consternation. For an instant he thought that something had happened to him—that he bore some traces on his person of the encounter in the corridor, when some person unknown had tried to shove him out of the window. He even glanced at himself. But her voice suddenly brought his eyes back to her again.

"Listen, Mr. Reeve," she said, striving to control her anxiety. "You've been very nice to me on this journey, and I appreciate all you've done. You've got to believe that.

But do you want to do something more for me—something that will be of greater value than all the rest put together?"

"Of course, I do," said Freddy, simply.

"Thank you. Well, it's this. Forget all that's happened. Don't say a word about it to the guard or anyone. If you do," she added, as she saw his trouble and his hesitation, "you may be injuring me more than you can possibly dream of!"

12

Calm Before Storm

The fencing was over. She had delivered her thrust. Or, rather, she had thrown herself upon his mercy.

Freddy would like to have answered her at once. He hated to let her think that he could hesitate in granting any request she made, and particularly a request which was made so earnestly and which involved an issue that was vitally personal to her. Yet he did hesitate. He could not help himself. He hesitated because he wondered whether she really knew how best to protect her own interests, and whether the granting of her request would genuinely form that protection. He wondered further. He wondered whether she would have made the request at all had she known that, a few moments previously, somebody had tried to shove Freddy out of a window!

Perhaps he ought to tell her about that? It was on the tip of his tongue to do so. But two considerations caused him to suppress the impulse. The first was that he did not want to frighten her, and the second was that, since she was trying to impose restrictions on him regarding certain matters they both knew about, he might have a freer hand if he kept this particular knowledge to himself. A freer hand to make use of the knowledge, if the occasion arose, in her own ultimate interests.

For Freddy was convinced of one thing about that attack upon him. It had been made by somebody who feared he was acquiring too much information. . . .

Well, if his lips were to be sealed by a promise, of what use would be this information? For an unpleasant instant it flashed through Freddy's mind that both the girl sitting opposite him and the person who had attacked him in the corridor were united by the common desire to ensure his silence—though their means of attempting to obtain that silence were considerably different!

These thoughts passed through the mind of Freddy Reeve while Lydia Leveridge waited with ill-concealed anxiety for his reply.

"I could only do half of what you ask me," he said, at last.

"Half?" she repeated, not understanding.

"Yes. The half that asks me not to say anything about the things we've been discussing to the guard or anyone else. But you also asked me to forget the things, you know. Do you think it's possible for me to that?"

"Perhaps not, Mr. Reeve. Perhaps I didn't mean that particular half to be taken quite so literally."

"But the other half—"

"Was meant quite literally."

"You mean that if I tell anybody I may really injure you—literally?"

"Yes."

"That my knowledge—slight though it is—is a danger to you?"

Now she hesitated for an instant. Her voice was not very happy when she responded, "Yes." It may have been the weakness in her voice that caused her to add, almost defiantly, "More than you have any idea of."

"Miss Leveridge," said Freddy, earnestly, "you mustn't misunderstand me if I ask you a few more questions, and

maybe I've a reason you don't know anything about—"
He saw the new anxiety in her eye, but he refused to be
influenced by it. "—but I've got to know a bit more of how
things stand before I give that promise. This danger—I'm
to hear nothing more about it?"

"If I ask you to forget things," she responded, nervily,
"is it reasonable to expect me to tell you more?"

"Then there's more to tell?"

Now she looked at him directly.

"That's obvious," she said.

"Yes, it is," he agreed; and went on, ruthlessly, "I suppose the danger is to you, personally?"

"Oh, dear!" she murmured, with a little desperate
shrug. *"Can't* you let it drop?"

"It isn't, for instance, to—your fiancé?"

"My—*fiancé?*" Her mouth opened wide. Two rows of
perfect teeth expressed her astonishment. Then, suddenly,
the teeth snapped together again, and she almost laughed.

"It has nothing to do with my fiancé," she told him.
And, later, he recalled the remark.

"One more question," said Freddy. "This. We're talking,
so far, of things that have happened. Well, nothing much
has happened—"

"Then why worry about it?" she interposed, seizing on
the point.

"—yet," proceeded Freddy. "As you say, why worry about
it? I might put the same question, mightn't I? Why should
you worry about it if I were to mention what we've been
talking about to—well, say, the gentleman who is sharing
our compartment—or the cantankerous cockney—or Mr.
Biddock, if I find him?"

"Oh, do stop!" muttered Miss Leveridge. "I've already
admitted it's serious!"

"Or the guard," suggested Freddy, bending forward so
that his mouth was close to her. "Would it be a danger

to you if I went to the guard and said, 'Look here? I'm
a bit worried. A man who was in this train seems to be
missing—do you suppose he could have fallen out of a
window?'" Miss Leveridge, whose eyes had been on his,
abruptly turned away, and transferred her gaze to the scen-
ery outside. "Of course, he may not have fallen out of a
window. I'm only just suggesting it. Probably old Biddock has emigrated to another part of the train altogether,
and is trying to sell somebody one of his note-books! But
what's worrying me is this. If I give you my promise, what
happens if all these tiny things suddenly burst out into
one big thing—and you're the centre of it? Am I to say
nothing then? Am I to do nothing?"

"Nothing," she replied. "Absolutely nothing."

Freddy sighed. Roast sirloin of beef appeared. Food
seemed immensely unimportant.

"I promise I won't do anything you'll have cause to regret," he said.

"Thank you," she answered. "But how will you know
what would cause me regret?"

"How does one know the sun is a ball of fire?" he retorted. "One doesn't know. One just thinks it is. But one
can bank on a damn good guess."

"Then the way to guess right, in this case, will be to
guess that the sun is made of green cheese," she responded.
"In other words, not to judge by appearances. If there's
any trouble on this train and you don't present a blind
eye to it—in fact, if you don't decide to act as though you
weren't there—you may be bringing a sorrow into my life
that I will never get over. A sorrow too terrible to think of.
I'm telling you this because, after all, I think that knowledge will help me more than your promise. I understand
you—and I'm trying to make you understand me. And now
let's eat and be jolly. Because, after this meal, we're not
going to see each other any more. You're going to be the

best friend I ever had, and take up your residence in another compartment."

"No, not that!" interposed Freddy. "The rest, I dare say. But you *don't* understand me if you think I'm going to change my compartment!"

His tone was definite. Miss Leveridge realised for the first time that there was something determined about his chin. She decided—for the time being, at any rate—to let matters rest.

A silence fell upon them. It was almost with a sense of relief that Freddy heard the brown bread enthusiast complain that he had ordered salad and that he was still waiting for salad. There was something refreshing in the contemplation of Life's definite little troubles that could be easily adjusted, and there was something humorous in the contemplation of those who could be obsessed by such trivialities. The irritable diner looked almost as green as the lettuce he was waiting for.

"But there *is* your salad, sir?" the waiter pointed out.

"Eh? Is this mine?" exclaimed the irritable one, glaring at the dish. It had been there five minutes, and he had thought it was his neighbour's.

How easy life would be, and how much irritation we should be spared, if we had a little more faith! The disagreeable diner had made up his mind that he would be left waiting, and, in the munition factory of his soul, had prepared his indignation in advance.

"I suppose you know Sheringham well?" said Freddy, breaking the silence conversationally.

"How did you know I was going to Sheringham?" asked Miss Leveridge.

"It was in the paragraph about you."

"Oh, of course! Are you going there, too?"

"No. To Cromer." He imagined that he was. "Ever been there?"

"Yes, once."

"Is it a decent sort of a place?"

"I liked it. There are no n—s or penny-in-the-slot machines."

Freddy grinned suddenly.

"I say," he said. "We're not too good at small talk, are we?"

"We might be more brilliant," she agreed.

"Then let's have a shot," he exclaimed. "Let's joke, like the old French aristocrats on the scaffold! P'r'aps we'll come out stronger over the vanilla ices! I've never felt that roast beef was really inspiring."

"That may explain why the English aristocrats were not so witty as the French aristocrats," she suggested.

"By Jove, we're improving!" laughed Freddy. "It's a little late in the day, but how about some French wine to keep the good work up? I suppose you know something about wines? I'm rather a duffer at them." He glanced at the Wine List. "Let's squander four-and-six on some French Moselle!"

"No, thank you," she answered.

"Waiter," he called. "A half-bottle of Moseloro Royal Cabinet, please."

"1910? Very good, sir," said the waiter.

She shook her head at him reprovingly, and observed that he shouldn't have done it.

"Do you know, Miss Leveridge," he responded, "I definitely think that I *should* have done it! Brilliant small talk is what you and I need. Otherwise I'm afraid we'll talk of larger subjects!"

"In that case, you may be right," she conceded. "But I shall contribute my two-and-threepence."

The wine arrived, and the ices. And, afterwards, black coffee. Judged externally, the end of the meal was certainly less strained than the beginning. The waiter made the excusable mistake of charging them both on the same bill. Miss Leveridge rectified the error by laying down seven-and-sevenpence.

"And now, I suppose, we'd better get back," she said, gravity suddenly returning to her.

"Unless you'd rather stay on here," answered Freddy unhopefully. "That's the advantage of taking the second dinner. There's no one to follow you."

"No, I'm going back," she replied. "I suppose it's too much to ask *you* to stay on here?"

"Much too much."

They rose. The car attendant paused in his hurrying to smile at them. If the meal had not been frictionless, it was not his fault.

"How soon do we reach Norwich?" asked the girl, suddenly.

"We're due in five minutes, madam," said the attendant; "7.55. But we're a little behind time."

She asked a second question, after an almost imperceptible pause:

"Do we wait there long?"

"About four minutes."

"Thank you."

Meanwhile—

The large and expansive gentleman sat in his compartment, with a little frown on his face, twiddling his thumbs. The agitated old lady sat in her compartment bolt upright, trying not to notice the existence of the cockney bloke. The cockney bloke sat opposite her in the same compartment, sniffing, mumbling, and leering. The clergyman sat in his compartment, dozing. And the fellow in the dark brown suit, who travelled for Messrs. Race & Spendlow, wholesale dealers—well, no one seemed to know where he was.

Perhaps no one would have been more interested to know where he was than a thick-set, stocky man, with a face like a horse, who was pacing up and down a Norwich platform waiting for the 7.55 to draw in.

13

THE PASSENGER FOR NORWICH

Norwich station is not the most beautiful station in England. Although it is only a score of miles from the sea, it seems to have inherited some of the gloom of its ancestor, Liverpool-street, and the gloom is accentuated towards the end of a day when the sun is ceasing its attempts to cheer it. On this particular day the sun ceased rather earlier than usual, having slipped down into a heavy, brooding bank of clouds before its time. Darkness was spreading too swiftly over Norfolk.

But the man with the horsy face who paced the platform waiting for the overdue 7.55 (which was the Norwich name for the 5.18; a train's name changes all along the route) was not oppressed by the gathering darkness. On the contrary, he welcomed it. It suited both his mood and his purpose. Even the lateness of the train, which annoyed other prospective passengers, seemed to soothe him; for the later the time when the train arrived, the darker it would be at the moment of its arrival.

"Aren't trains *ever* punctual?" demanded a fussy old man, who believed in his rights and who lived in his wrongs.

"A little dislocation on the line, sir, I expect," replied a porter, trying to be consoling.

"Eight o'clock already!" grumbled the fussy old man. "And not even signalled! No wonder people are beginning to patronise motor-coaches!"

The porter did his best to combat the menace.

"There was a haccident to one of 'em last Tooseday," he remarked. "Two killed."

The fussy old man turned away, annoyed. He did not object to the two people being killed, but he did object to this weakening of his argument.

The horsy man, in converse with another porter, was more affable.

"Looks a bit stormy," he observed.

"Ay, sir, it do," agreed the porter. "It won't do no good to the corn."

"Farmers are never satisfied," smiled the horsy man. "I thought they wanted a bit of rain."

"Ah, not fer t' harvest," explained the porter. "My sister, she be married to a farmer, so I know. Beats it down, you see. Interferes wi' t' harvest proper, rain do."

As though in answer to his fraternal apprehensions, a low mutter came from the horizon. Thunder was joining with the clouds in making the swift gloaming oppressive.

The horsy man looked at his watch. It was two minutes past eight. He decided that he had had enough of agriculture and continued his stroll up and down the platform. In one of his turns he bumped into the fussy man.

"Ten minutes late!" rasped the fussy man. "At this rate it'll be nearly half-past nine before I get to Sheringham."

The horsy man regarded him amusedly.

"Trains were sent to try our tempers," he remarked. "Perhaps there's been an accident."

"Accident!" exclaimed the fussy one. The theory impressed him. "D'you think so?"

"I'm sure *I* can't say," answered the horsy man. "But accidents do happen to trains sometimes, don't they? And when they do, it's best not to be on them."

"Accident!" repeated the fussy one. "Well, of course—that's always possible." But the next moment this theory was knocked on the head. "Ah! There! It's signalled!" he cried, divided between indignation and delight. "It's actually condescending to arrive! No wonder the Americans laugh at us!"

Thirteen minutes late, the London express rumbled into the station. As it came to a standstill, the fussy man ran alongside and dived into a compartment. It was the compartment occupied by the cockney bloke and the agitated lady.

The horsy man took more time. He finished a cigarette he had been smoking, tossed it away, and strolled towards the first-class section. A bland head came out of a window at him.

"No room in here," remarked the bland head.

It belonged to the large and expansive gentleman of our acquaintance.

There were only two other occupants of the compartment, and they glanced at each other. Three may be a crowd, but it does not fill a railway carriage. The horsy man certainly did not think so, because he suddenly paused, although up till then he had not given any special attention to this particular compartment.

"There seems to me to be plenty of room," said the horsy man.

"Perhaps I spoke spiritually," replied the large gentleman, defending himself rather impudently.

"What's that mean?" frowned the horsy man.

He did not seem to like the attitude of the large gentleman. He had practically been told he was not wanted. That decided him that he would have to be suffered.

"Excuse me," he said, and pushed himself in.

Now the large gentleman frowned. *He* did not seem to like the attitude of the horsy man. But in the middle of their frowning there came one tiny instant—scarcely more than the flicker of an instant—when they appeared to soften towards each other. Something twitched between them, and was gone.

"Train's late in," commented the horsy man, addressing his remark pointedly to the younger members of the compartment. Obviously he was not going out of his way to make himself pleasant to the large gentleman who had tried to keep him out.

"Yes, nearly a quarter of an hour," answered Freddy.

"Trouble on the line?" suggested the horsy man.

"We had a bit of a wait outside Norwich," said Freddy. "The signals were against us or something."

"I see," grunted the horsy man. "Looks a bit stormy."

"Very," replied Freddy.

The conversation appeared to bore the large gentleman. He alighted, and stood outside for a few seconds, gazing along the platform.

All at once he turned his head, and gazed the other way. Something had attracted him. And it wasn't the thunder, although the horizon had begun to mutter again. He stood motionless, with head twisted, and then re-entered the compartment. Now he was smiling.

"Yes, and it *sounds* a bit stormy, too," he said. "It wouldn't surprise me if there isn't a little storm on this train before long!"

"Why, what's up?" asked Freddy.

He was annoyed with himself the next moment for asking, although his question was a perfectly natural one in the circumstances. He felt, however, that the large gentleman had expected his question, and had angled for it, and Freddy did not like doing anything the large gentleman expected. Particularly in the present electrical atmosphere . . . for it was electrical. . . .

"It's that frightened old lady," explained the large gentleman. "As I was standing outside just now I heard

her suddenly start up again. She'll have hysterics in a minute, I'll wager a fiver!"

The horsy man's curiosity now got the better of him.

"What's she worrying about?" he enquired.

The large gentleman turned to him, beaming.

"She has a nasty, unkempt cockney on her mind," he replied. "I think there was some little trouble between them
at Liverpool-street, though I don't know what it was. She
tried to avoid his carriage, anyway, and when she changed
compartments he hopped after her. He seems to have been
plaguing her life ever since."

"Well, of course he hopped after her," said the horsy
man. "When people show they don't want you, it's what
you do, isn't it? Human nature!"

"Ah! True," murmured the large gentleman. "True!"

Freddy smiled to himself. He didn't like the horsy man
much more than the large gentleman; there was something
sinister about him, particularly about his eyes; yet Freddy
was glad to find him scoring. It was comforting to find
anybody who was at loggerheads with the large gentleman.

"Yes, it's human nature," repeated the horsy man, rub-
bing the point in.

"Third-class human nature," said the large gentleman,
with a little cough.

"Are you trying to be rude to me?" demanded the horsy
man, suddenly sitting up angrily. Yes—his eyes were very
queer. . . .

"My dear sir," retorted the large gentleman, "please
don't forget there is a lady present."

"It's easier to forget there is a gentleman present,"
snapped the horsy man.

Freddy found himself a little less pleased with the argument. It occurred to him suddenly that it was not an
ordinary sort of an argument. It seemed to be an argument

between two people who had made up their minds to
argue. However irritable you feel, do you go about snapping strangers' heads off like that? And, if these two men
had made up their minds to argue . . .

"Hallo! We're going backwards!" exclaimed the large
gentleman, as the train began to move.

"If we had gone forwards," answered the horsy man,
"we would be in the station restaurant by now."

"Eh?"

"Passing through the buns."

"Excuse me, sir," exclaimed the large gentleman, his
eyes blazing, "but do you think you are funny?"

"I don't feel in the least funny," retorted the horsy man.
"I am merely interested in the idea that a train should
smash down the buffers, run into a restaurant, and scatter
ham sandwiches."

A little giggle came from the corner opposite Freddy.
The moment had beaten Miss Leveridge. Lord! thought
Freddy. "Now *she's* getting hysterical!"

The atmosphere became more electric. He found himself viewing details as though they were unnaturally illuminated. The details made a distorted picture in his mind,
a sort of futuristic jumble in which there was neither per-
spective nor coherence. Little things grew large, while
more important things dwindled. Freddy felt himself in
the grip of psychological indigestion.

He dwelt, for instance, with disproportionate intensity
on a vein on the forehead of the horsy gentleman. He
became curiously conscious that he was riding now with
his back to the engine, and that the corridor on his right
would henceforth open on the platform instead of on to
the track. The point of Miss Leveridge's right shoe attracted and held him. It was beating softly up and down, in a
quiet, unobserved, nervous tattoo. He could see it out of
the corner of his eye. Did she know she was doing it? And

was it of any significance, anyway? And then the horsy man was . . . something about him was forcing itself upon his notice, something he could not understand, but that was adding to the electrical, distorted atmosphere, and seeking to claim him.

All at once Freddy discovered what was worrying him about the horsy man. Beneath sandy, shaggy eyebrows, two little points of light were watching him. They had been watching him all the while, for years, and it was these two little points of boring brilliance that were upsetting time and space. Even while the mind that directed the lights appeared to be elsewhere, and the lips were engaged in sullen controversy, the eyes were searching him, destroying him. . . .

Miss Leveridge's shoe continued to tap. He shifted his gaze, and stared at it hard. He concentrated on it. He thought, consciously, of the slender beauty of the ankle it encased, of the graceful line of the calf above it, of the sweetness of feminine beauty. Unashamedly he dwelt on these things, because he needed to dwell on them. They were the channel through which he was escaping from a double tunnel that ended in two compelling points of light.

"Would you like a cigarette, Miss Leveridge?"

He heard himself ask the question, surprised that his voice was still his to control. She looked at him. Now the eyes beneath the shaggy, sandy eyebrows ceased to press on him. They lost their significance. But his forehead was damp. He wondered whether Miss Leveridge noticed it. . . .

"Thank you. Yes—I think I would."

He gave her a cigarette from his case, rejoicing in the simple operation and in his freedom to perform it. A minute ago, he doubted whether his hands would have responded to his will. God bless that little foot that had saved him from making a fool of himself!

As she bent forward to accept his light, she murmured, "It's hot in here, isn't it?"

Was she excusing him for the damp on his forehead?

"Very," he said. And added, impulsively, "Why don't you come out in the corridor and smoke there with me?"

"No, I'll stay here," she answered. "But I wish *you'd* go and smoke in the corridor?"

He looked at her squarely, and replied in a low voice.

"Sorry, Miss Leveridge, but nothing doing."

He wished she had smiled. But she did not. She just returned his look gravely, and then leaned back in her corner, to gaze out of the window once more at the darkening landscape.

The thunder rumbled more loudly. A streak of lightning made the compartment unnaturally radiant for an instant, and was gone in the same instant. The train was rushing towards the storm, and the storm was rushing towards the train.

Freddy wondered where they were. He had lost count of time, and did not know how long it was since they had left Norwich, or how many stations they had passed.

"Where are we?" he asked abruptly.

A shriek of terror answered him. Someone was pulling the communication cord.

14

THE LAST OF THE 5.18

The moments that followed that scream and the pulling of the communication cord were moments of chaotic confusion, and in recalling them afterwards Freddy was never able to place them consecutively. The train decreased its speed suddenly and violently. There was a rushing sound of brakes, drowned in an abrupt clap of thunder. People jumped to their feet. People pressed to doorways and filled corridors. People hurried along, jostling each other, while to the original shriek were added other shrieks from folk who were in no personal danger, but who imagined they were.

The corridor most closely packed was that immediately outside the compartment in which were the agitated old lady, the cockney bloke, and the fussy old fellow who had joined them at Norwich. They were now the sole occupants of the compartment, and it was the agitated lady who had emitted the original scream and who had pulled the communication cord, apparently waking the fussy old man out of a doze. The cockney bloke, when anxious heads were thrust in upon them, was scowling angrily.

The woman continued to scream. She was beside herself.

"What's the matter?" cried the corridor.

But the lady was not in a condition for a few moments to explain. All she could do was to point to the cockney, and continue her hysterics.

The fussy old man, now very wide awake, tried to calm her. As the cockney said nothing, the corridor appealed to him.

"Nerves, as far as I can make out," muttered the fussy man. "Just nerves! Bless my soul, what does one do in such cases? Can't somebody—?"

The hysterical lady interrupted him. All at once, she had rediscovered the gift of speech.

"That man there—he went for me!" she gasped. "I knew he would! He went for me!"

Now the cockney found his tongue, also.

"I didn't do nothink o' the sort!" he bawled back. "She orter see a doctor, she ort! Bin like that orl along, she 'as, hactin' as if I was a hogre—"

"I tell you, he went for me!" repeated the old lady, weeping. "I don't know if he was after my bag, but if you ask *me* I think he's mad! I know his sort! I knew as soon as I saw him. He's been at me ever since we started—"

"Calm down, mum, calm down!" came a voice from the corridor, as the guard pushed his way in. "Just take it easy for a bit. Nothing's goin' to harm you." He turned to the fussy old man. "Is there anything in what the lady says, sir?"

"I've told you there isn't!" retorted the fussy old man, definitely. "If a thing like that had happened, d'you suppose I wouldn't have noticed it?"

"There y'are," exclaimed the cockney bloke, triumphantly. "Takin' away a feller's character jest becos' 'e ain't wearin' a top 'at!"

The guard looked puzzled. He was willing to accept the testimony of the fussy old man, but the cockney did not invite much trust.

"What made you think he was going for you, mum?" he asked, frowning. "It's a serious thing to stop a train, you know—"

"Yus, and it's a serious thing ter tike away a feller's character," added the cockney, with a scowl.

"You raised your hand to strike me!" cried the agitated woman, pointing an accusing finger at him. "And it wasn't the first time!"

"Did you see him?" enquired the guard, of the fussy man.

"How many more times have I got to say, 'No'?" barked the fussy man. "He certainly bent forward to pick up a paper that was on the seat beside her, but that was all. Maybe she was half asleep, having a sort of nightmare, and—bless my soul! *I* don't know!"

Another figure pushed its way into the carriage. It was the clergyman.

"Calm yourself, madam," he said, gently. "Whatever you may have feared, there is no cause to fear now, as you must see. I'll stay here with you for a little, if it will help. And meanwhile, guard," he added, turning to the official, "don't you think you'd better carry on?"

"Yes, I do!" grunted the guard. "But of course—it's a serious thing, pulling the communication cord—"

"Oh, I wouldn't worry about that," said the clergyman, soothingly. "Something upset the lady. Imagination, if you like. I think the railway company will save itself a lot of unnecessary trouble by taking a lenient view. Anyhow, you can safely leave the lady in my hands for the time being. Other passengers' interests have to be considered."

"That's right, sir," nodded the guard, only too glad to have some of the responsibility taken from his shoulders. "I'm sure I've no wish to add to trouble. And p'r'aps the passengers had better get back to their seats now everything's over." . . .

Freddy was among the passengers who now turned to go back. When the original shriek had occurred, he had sprung to his feet with the rest, and he had a vague memory of having left the compartment, of having returned

to it, and of having left it again, this time with Miss
Leveridge immediately behind him. Then the human
stream had swallowed him up, and shoved him forward.
He assumed that the three other occupants of his compartment had been shoved forward also.

But when he now turned, he suddenly became conscious that the others had not been shoved forward, or
that, at any rate, they were nowhere visible around him. A
moment of vague disturbance was followed by another of
swift panic. Shoving his way along, he reached his compartment and ran in.

It was empty. And the door at the further end was open.

A groan escaped him. He was at the open door before he knew it. In the distance, beyond the low embankment, shadows flitted among the dimnesses of bushes, and
a tiny, shifting light gleamed somewhere. The train began
to move. . . .

But Freddy Reeve was not on it. He had jumped out
onto the track.

He stumbled as his feet touched the ground. In the
rush of the moment, and in the deception of the dusk,
he misjudged the distance and alighted heavily. By the
time he had picked himself up the train was slipping from
him, a long, illuminated caterpillar, bearing away a familiar world. This track he now stood on was a new world.
It was a world that lacked routine and the indolent ease
of confined spaces. A world that put a fellow on his own,
forcing him to shape the moments. The train was wedded
to a timetable, but the track was timeless.

Freddy did not think of these things. He sensed them.
His thoughts were concentrated on those flitting shadows,
which even in this short lapse had become more vague and
distant. Gathering himself together, he dashed forward
and slithered down the embankment. A bush received him,
and pushed his head back violently, as though indignant at

this unexpected visitation just when it was settling down for the night.

"Steady," Freddy warned himself. "Take a breath! Don't play the goat!"

He recovered himself for the second time. The first time the track had struck up at him; the second, the bush had pushed out at him. He was disturbed by all this inanimate enmity. Even the thunder seemed to be rolling at him ironically, telling him what a fool he was.

And, after all, who but a fool would leave a comfortable train on a stormy night to chase shadows? It was a gratuitous chase, for even while he dived round the bush and was clawed by another he recalled the girl's injunction: "If there's any trouble on this train and you don't present a blind eye to it—in fact, if you don't decide to act as though you weren't there—you may be bringing a sorrow into my life that I will never get over. A sorrow too terrible to think of!"

In his mind he replied to her, as he found a break in the bushes,

"You're asking a human impossibility! Anyway, if I *do* bring sorrow into your life, one thing's damn certain—I'll share it!"

Now he was beyond the bushes, and a rough path lay before him. He could barely see it, and was unable to judge its length because of velvety interceptions; but at the end of it, and running at right angles to it, was a faintly gleaming road. To get to the road you apparently had to go down into the velvet patches and then rise up out of them.

He plunged forward. No shadowy figures were visible now. Were they lost in the velvet patches, or had they reached the road? He quelled an impulse to shout. That would have been ridiculous, but under such stress as Freddy was suffering even the sanest people often do the most ridiculous things. If he had shouted he would merely have revealed to the pursued ones that they were being pursued. He would have lost his sole weapon—the weapon of surprise. . . .

"Lord—there they are!" he gasped.

The shadows had reached the road. He increased his speed, and went head over heels into one of the velvet patches. Long, dank grass, sodden with rain. When he had risen, the shadows were no longer on the road, but through the wildness of the elements he heard an engine throbbing. A shaft of white light flicked for a moment into the sky, then went out. The throbbing of the engine grew fainter and fainter; then that went out, too.

"Don't worry—you'll get 'em," said Freddy.

Up a bit, down a bit, round a tree, through more velvet patches . . . and now, at last, he had gained his Mecca—the good, hard surface of the road. It was comforting to find the solid ground beneath his feet again, but he was disappointed that the road did not look a little lighter. It had gleamed more brightly when he had been striving to reach it than it gleamed now he was actually on it. It knew life and its ways, that road!

Well—what next? Only one thing, of course. He must go along the road after the car. How was he going to catch the car? He hadn't the remotest idea! All he knew was that he was going to catch it. And, that being definitely so, the first step was to follow it.

He ran as fast as he could. Anyone seeing him would scarcely have wondered. The rain was beating down and the thunder was pealing at intervals, to be succeeded by instants of blinding brilliance. Who would not run as Freddy was running through such a storm?

The ground squelched under his feet. He fought against a sensation of hopelessness. Keep on—that's the idea! Keep on! Something'll turn up!

There came one of the moments of blinding brilliance. In fairy fashion it illuminated a little streak of road far away, glimpsed through distant trees. A car was on the road. It was clear and distinct, as though viewed through the wrong end of a telescope. A closed car. Red. . . .

Gone! The world became black again.

In less than thirty seconds, another peal of thunder, and another blinding flash. Freddy stared ahead, with glazed eyes. The streak of road was revealed again, with the car still on it. It was the same streak of road. How did the car come to be still on it? . . .

"God!" thought Freddy, his heart bounding. "It's stopped! Something's happened!"

He was already running as fast as he possibly could. When he reached the car, if he ever did, he would be capable of doing only one thing, and that was to fall down in a dead faint. But you can't think of little things like that, can you? You've just got to go on and on, haven't you? Just sticking to it, you know—and trusting to something—and just sticking to it. . . .

"Freddy," said his second self, very clearly and distinctly, "you're done."

"You confounded idiot," gasped his first self, "you're as fresh as a daisy."

"Freddy," insisted his second self, "don't you know when you're done? Can't you hear your heart trying to burst? Can't you hear your ears throbbing? And doesn't a sort of blackness seem to be creeping over all your senses? In a second you'll be blotto—"

"I *wish* you'd shut up!" pleaded his first self, tearfully. "You wait—something'll happen—you wait!"

A third voice joined in the conference.

"Gawd, guv'nor!" it said. "Yew bean't in 'arf a 'urry, yew bean't!"

The speaker was a workman with a bicycle.

15

The Meeting in the Road

The workman was not on the bicycle. If he had been the
course of events would have worked out very differently.
He was in a shed by the side of the road, sheltering from
the storm, and the bicycle was leaning against a wheelbarrow in the doorway.

"Better come in 'ere, mate," said the workman, as Freddy paused.

Freddy had no intention of going in there. Not to stay,
at any rate. He had paused for quite another reason—a
reason unprincipled and unscrupulous. Here was the very
thing he wanted; the thing that might make all the difference between life and death; but if he stopped to explain,
it was hardly likely that a common, unimaginative workman would accept his story, and the moment of precious
opportunity would pass.

Opportunity, aided and abetted by his emotional mood,
undoubtedly favoured him. In a calmer humour he would
have thought twice, or three or four times, before seriously contemplating the move that now seemed so grotesquely
obvious. There was the bicycle, its front wheel protruding
invitingly from the doorway like the nozzle of a friendly
animal asking to be stroked. Behind it, with more interest
in his own dryness than the bicycle's, stood the workman.
He had been in the act of lighting a pipe when Freddy had

appeared, and he was now proceeding with that momentarily interrupted occupation. The match was struck, and
both hands were engaged—one in holding the match, and
the other in making a screen against the draught. When
you are fully prepared for an emergency, you can easily
drop a match and grab a fellow's collar or hit him on the
nose. But when you receive a sudden surprise it takes you a
second or two in which to recover, and during that second
or two a war may be won or a life may be lost—or saved.

While these considerations flashed through Freddy's
brain, another insistent thought raced round and round,
trailing a thread that spun itself into the pattern of a back-
ground. "It's only a loan—I'll see that the chap gains by
it," ran the thought. "I'll see that the chap gains by it—it's
only a loan."

Then it happened, all in a single instant. Freddy's hand
shot out and grasped the handle-bar. The bicycle came
forward like a lamb. (Freddy was vaguely surprised that
it did not struggle.) The workman's eyes popped, and his
mouth flew open. He was not a quick-witted workman,
though, as subsequent events proved, he could make up
for his mental deficiencies by doggedness. His eyes had
not ceased to pop, or his mouth to remain open, before
both Freddy and the bicycle were out in the road, the
latter beneath the former.

"Hi!" bawled the workman, waking up suddenly out of
his bad dream.

What! This nice young feller . . . ?

"Hi!" he bawled again, louder.

Freddy heard the first "Hi!" but not the second. Distance and thunder drowned it.

The bicycle, by good luck, was not too highly geared,
for Freddy's calves were not in the best condition. His
legs whirled round in a frantic, grotesque frenzy, and they

could have whirled no more frenziedly had three roaring lions been after him. As a matter of fact, one roaring work-man was after him, but he was soon left a long way behind.

How far ahead was the motor-car? Freddy had no notion. Though the lightning still flashed the portion of the road on which the car had stood was no longer visible; it had merely been visible before through a chance break in the deep vista of foliage. It might have been a couple of miles away as the crow flew, and that couple of miles might be four as the road wriggled. Desperately Freddy pedalled on, straining is eyes on the road ahead, and striving to pierce the gloom beyond the little illuminated arc of the bicycle lamp.

As stretch after stretch and turn after turn were nego-tiated without any sign of the red car, a sense of futility began to settle on the pursued pursuer. Suppose—as was likely—the car was now on its way again? How could he possibly hope to catch it up? And when it had disappeared absolutely into the void, where would he be able to look for a clue that might lead him to its destination? The fact that he was himself being chased by a man who had a clear case against him did not add to Freddy's comfort. He was hero and villain rolled into one! Which of the two was going to survive?

Into his despair entered a consciousness of moisture. He felt his wet clothes against his body. When hope begins to leave, everything unpleasant enters and makes itself felt or seen or heard. The man who is grasping his ideal does not hear the grinding roar of the traffic, he can stare at a crude advertisement on the hoarding of somebody's pills without noticing it, and he can forget the pangs of a tooth-ache; but as the ideal slips from his grasp, the traffic and the pills and the tooth-ache all come crowding down upon him. Hope is the slender palisade constructed by our anxious minds to keep out realism. . . .

But suddenly, once again, Freddy's hope returned. It came sweeping back in an almost overwhelming rush. It was the maddest sort of hope, because even though the red car was now actually before his eyes—still standing stationary fifty yards along the lane—what sort of a fight could the spent man possibly expect to put up against it?

He did not think of that. All he thought of was that there stood the car, and that within the car was all that mattered in a dark world that had become suddenly and dangerously glorious! He would pedal on, increasing his speed over this final stretch, leap off the bicycle—and *hit!*

If steel has any sensation, that bicycle must have experienced considerable surprise that a half-dead man could urge it on to even greater speed. But the speed was not maintained. As a figure emerged from the shadow of the car, the brakes were abruptly applied. Even in his distorted mood, Freddy retained some instinct of self-preservation. After all, if he did not preserve himself, of what use would his self be to Lydia Leveridge?

The reason for the sudden decrease in speed was a revolver. The figure was levelling it at Freddy's breast.

"If you do not stop and dismount at once," said the figure, "I'm afraid I shall have to shoot you."

Freddy would have recognised the voice, if he had not already recognised the form, of the large and expansive gentleman.

"I mean it," said this unpleasant individual.

The very quietness of the tone made it all the more compelling. Automatically, Freddy slowed down, popped, and dismounted. The revolver was now six feet from his heart.

"Good," smiled the large gentleman.

"You'll change your tone in a minute," retorted Freddy.

"Do you think so?" asked the large gentleman, gently ironical.

"I'm sure so," asserted Freddy.

The large gentleman regarded, almost with compassion, the panting fellow who still had enough spirit to threaten him. Freddy wondered if he were playing for time. But then so was Freddy! Thirty seconds of conversation—and, of course, the car would not proceed without the large gentleman—would give Freddy back quite a useful amount of breath.

"Oh—so you're sure so, eh?" repeated the large gentleman, smoothly.

"Absolutely," nodded Freddy. "You don't know me yet."

"Perhaps I don't want to."

"The choice isn't going to be yours. By the way, do you know yourself? I mean, do you know yourself for a contemptible, degraded cur, for a damnable blackguard, and a miserable swine?" The revolver wavered a little. Could a man who was all that be also sensitive? "Why, you haven't even any pluck, really. If you hadn't got that revolver—"

"But I *have* got that revolver," interposed the large gentleman. "And I'm afraid, if you're rude, it will have to say something to you. It can talk even more than you can, my young friend."

"But not more than you," retorted Freddy. "You're pretty well made up of talking, aren't you?"

The large gentleman did not reply immediately. He appeared, like a hare, to be seeing both ways. In front of him was a troublesome young man, and behind was a troublesome car. The trouble with the car had nearly been dealt with; a figure was working with desperate haste on a front wheel. In a few seconds, there would only be the young man to account for. Then the interrupted journey could be resumed.

"If I do no more than talk," observed the large gentleman, with some shrewdness, "why are you worrying about me?"

"I didn't say that was all you did."

"Oh! And what else do I do?"

"You kidnap people."

"Kidnap?" The speaker looked shocked. "My young friend, you have been reading detective novels! Kidnap? Bless my soul! Or perhaps you go to the talkies?"

Freddy took a deep breath. He suddenly realised that the time being gained was of more value now to his opponent than to himself. He had recovered sufficiently from his spent condition to be able to deal a useful blow, if he chose the right moment and the right place for it, but should this conversation go on much longer the car would be ready to depart . . . yes, and that workman might turn up! Then Freddy would have another adversary to deal with. It was not likely that he could enlist the enraged workman on his own side in a few hurried seconds; far more probably, the astute large gentleman would take advantage of the opportunity to enlist the enraged work-man on *his* side! Then Freddy's position would be absolutely hopeless, and the workman would be justified in believing that, having begun with a bicycle, the "thief" was now trying to hold up a car! If only he could reach the girl . . . who was probably lying in the car, gagged or unconscious. . . .

"My dear young friend," the large gentleman observed, softly, "listen to me. All this is nonsense. Utter, utter non-sense. I am either a kidnapper or not a kidnapper. If I am not a kidnapper—don't move, please—then you are wasting your time. And if I am a kidnapper, well, then it's hardly likely I am pointing this revolver at you just for fun."

"You *are* a kidnapper," answered Freddy, "but that doesn't argue that you have the pluck to be a murderer, too."

"Pluck—?"

"Yes, pluck! You see, if you shoot me, you'll swing for it."

"Even if I shoot you in self-defence?"

"You'd never be able to prove that!"

"No?" And now the large gentleman became very astute indeed. "May I ask—just as a matter of curiosity, my young friend—where you got hold of that bicycle?"

"What do you mean?" frowned Freddy. "It was lent to me."

"Lent? You are sure?"

That settled it. The enraged workman must not be given time to appear and deny that the bicycle had been lent! It would provide the large gentleman a splendid excuse for delivering his bullet. Already, while watching Freddy with one eye, the large gentleman was sweeping the road behind Freddy with the other.

"And then, of course," went on the large gentleman, slowly . . . was he seeing something? . . . "I might not kill you. I might just shoot you in the leg. Yes, even a man of my timid propensities might do that. You don't swing for a leg, do you? I imagine the penalty for that is merely . . ."

His voice trailed off. The road behind Freddy was interesting him more and more. . . . He was seeing something there. . . . For an instant, he appeared more interested in what he saw behind Freddy than in Freddy himself.

Freddy seized the instant. He let the bicycle go, ducked, dived and struck. His fist met flesh. It was a wonderful instant. Unfortunately, however, it was as brief, if also as dazzling, as the lightning that played around them. The second figure came hurtling from the car.

"Here's for now—and next time'll be the *last* time!" Freddy heard in his ear.

Then followed the most vivid of all the lightning flashes. Or was it lightning? If it was, it struck him. Blazing gold was succeeded by velvet blackness. A sort of moving blackness, which slid and shifted kaleidoscopically, making shapeless forms. Only one form wasn't quite shapeless. It was a vista. A vista of complete darkness, through which some queer object could be discerned. An object that grew smaller and smaller up the vista—an object that contained a heart—Freddy's heart—smaller and smaller—farther and farther—farther and farther . . .

16

The Transitions of a Workman

Freddy opened his eyes to find the workman glaring down at him. Beside him lay the bicycle. There was no sign of the motor-car.

"So thair yew be!" panted the workman, malevolently.

"Yes, here I am," murmured Freddy.

"Ay, an' I've caught yew!"

"It looks like it."

"Ay, it do! A nice one, yew be! If yew wasn't down on t' road this minute, tha's where I'd put yew—"

"Yes, well, don't let's argue about it," interrupted Freddy, sitting up. "Somebody else hit me first and saved you the trouble, didn't they? What I've got to do is to explain to you, in the shortest time possible, that I'm not a thief—"

"Not a thief?"

"Am I talking, or are you?" snapped Freddy. His nerves were in a bad state, and he had to dominate or be dominated. "Of course, I'm not a thief! I took your bicycle to try and catch the motor-car that's just gone off—"

"Ay, I saw it," nodded the workman. "Yew was tryin' to steal that, too, I reckon!"

"Of course, I was!" rasped Freddy. "That's what I have pockets for. I steal a bicycle and slip it in one pocket, and

then I just take a motor-car and slip it in another. Don't
be an ass! Can't you see I'm dead earnest—"

"I can see ye're earnest," interrupted the workman,
"and yew ought to be dead."

Freddy swallowed, rose slowly—he was merely bruised
and groggy—and began again.

"Listen," he said. "How much do you want for your
bicycle?"

The workman frowned, and regarded him very suspi-
ciously.

"Yew be tryin' to bribe me, now! Is that it?" he demanded.

"If I offer to buy your bicycle, is that bribery?" cried
Freddy. "Doesn't that merely prove how much I need it?
I tell you, I took your wretched machine to try and catch
some rascals in a car. They've got a girl with them—they've
kidnapped her." The workman's eyes were growing big.
"Kidnapped, do you hear? *Now,* then—how much will you
take for your bicycle?"

The workman decided to test this surprising young fellow. A good offer would substantiate the story.

"We-ell—I give three pound fer it," he said, slowly.

He had bought it second-hand for two. Freddy offered
him four. This was beyond the arithmetic and the psychology of the workman.

"Go on!" he muttered.

"I'm longing to!" retorted Freddy, diving for his pock-
et-book.

The workman's mood began to change. He discovered
himself regarding Freddy from a new angle.

"Wot's this about a gell?" he demanded.

"I've told you. She's being kidnapped."

"'Oo 'as?"

"Eh?"

"Wot for?"

"That doesn't matter—"

"Ah, but it does," asserted the workman, growing interested, and threatening to be constructive. "S'pose she be elopin', and it be 'er faither? That bean't a kidnap. That be legal, that be. There yew are!"

"But it isn't her father, man!" exclaimed Freddy. "Here—take these notes and stop talking!"

"'Ow did it 'appen?"

Freddy thrust the notes into the workman's hands, and seized the bicycle.

"Whoa!" cried the workman. "Three's all I said." He had a conscience. "It bean't noo. And, then—corse, if it be like wot yew say—"

"Good-bye," shouted Freddy.

But the workman caught hold of the saddle-pin and detained him.

"Where yew goin'?" he asked.

"Good Lord! Where d'you suppose?" shouted Freddy.

"Where's that?"

"After them!"

"Where be *they* goin'?"

Freddy groaned. Not merely on account of the question, but on account of its relevance. Where *were* they going?

"If yew don't know where they be goin', it's no use t' foller 'em," the workman pointed out. "There be a rare lot o' turnin's about 'ere. A rare lot. 'Ow old would she be—?"

"Heavens, man—!"

"'Cos it seems to me the best thing'd be to get a description out. That be the way of it. Age, twen'y. 'Air black. Eyes blue. Put it in the paipers, sir. That be the best way. No good followin' 'em on a night like this on a bike like that not knowin' where they're goin'."

"What's the matter with you?" cried Freddy. For a moment he wondered whether this workman were in league

with the gang, and had been detailed to watch and detain
him. "You've got the money, and I want the bicycle! Let
go, or in another second I'll—"

"What be that?" asked the workman. "Down in the
road there?"

Freddy followed the workman's gaze. A small piece of
paper was being beaten by the rain into the long grass.
Ordinarily, the sight would not have excited anyone, but
this little scrap gleamed up significantly, seeming to say,
"Doesn't my newness interest you? Do I look as if I have
been here a week? Am I not worth picking up—even if you
are in a bit of a hurry?"

Freddy made a dive for the paper. The workman still
held on to the saddle-pin of the bicycle. The paper was a
mere fragment, a portion torn from a larger sheet or from
an envelope, and at first it appeared to be blank. But all
at once Freddy spied some faint writing upon it. Pencil
writing, nearly obliterated by the rain.

"There's something here!" he exclaimed, excitedly. He
brought the paper under the bicycle lamp and studied it.
"A name! Damn it—I can only make out a few of the letters. 'Sham.' Something 'sham.' Does that convey anything
to you, eh? Something 'sham'!"

"North Walsham," suggested the workman.

"By Jove!" cried Freddy. Then his face fell. "No—it's
not as long as that. What about 'Walsham,' without the
'North'?"

But the workman shook his head. He implied that nobody with a sound brain would delete the "North" from
"Walsham."

"They might, if they wrote the name in a hurry,"
argued Freddy.

"Then 'ow'd you know it weren't South Walsham?"
answered the workman.

"Well, perhaps it *is* South Walsham!" tried Freddy, beginning to lose his sense of logic.

"But this bean't the road to South Walsham," observed the workman. "And it bean't the road to North Walsham, neither."

"Confound! Isn't there any other 'sham' in the neighbourhood?"

"Yew see, they'd 'ave to go under the railway arch—"

"Yes, yes. And what's beyond the railway arch?"

"Ah, there's a rare lot o' turnin's, sir. Tha's wot I say. Corse, if yew bear round to the right, there's Aylsham—"

"Aylsham!"

Freddy pored over the faint writing while the workman rambled on:

"Ay, they could make Aylsham, they could. Ay, they could do that. Or there's Coltishall. Would it be a couple of ells instead of a nem? Or there's 'Orstead—"

"How far is Aylsham from here?" interrupted Freddy.

"Might be eight mile," replied the workman. "Might be ten."

"Right! I'll try it!"

He seized the bicycle again.

The workman hadn't quite finished yet, however.

"Look 'ere," he said. "This gel—bein' kidnapped, yew say?"

"How many more times!"

"And she chucks that bit o' paiper out o' the winder to give yew a 'int, like?"

"That's my idea!"

"All right. Yew needn't buy my old iron, I reckon. It's a loan." He thrust the notes back into Freddy's pocket. "When yew finished with it, sir, yew can let me know where yew leave it. Name and address be in the saddle-bag."

Even though it wasted two more seconds, Freddy turned and wrung the workman's hand.

"By Jove, you're a sport!" he cried.

"No, I bean't," replied the workman, "on'y I got a sister of me own, see?"

17

FLASHES IN THE DARK

To the accompaniment of thunder and lightning, Freddy
Reeve did some constructive thinking.

That drenching, sodden ride through the dark moist
lanes to Aylsham was the first opportunity he had had
since the pulling of the communication cord for clear
thought. Everything afterwards had been a confusing jumble, and even when he had left the train and had set out in
this amazing chase he had not been free to reflect on the
position. He had been obsessed by one immediate object,
and one only—the catching of the motor-car. Now, on this
fresh stage in the journey, he had leisure to reflect while
he pedalled.

He found himself trying to form a picture. He wanted
to see the picture clearly, or as clearly as the artist who
had not yet finished his work would let him. Until he
could see the picture he did not know where he belonged
in it, if indeed he belonged in it at all. He himself was
merely one of the queerly shaped pieces waiting to be fitted into the jig-saw.

His mind reverted to the beginning of the journey, when
he had strolled on to No. 9 Platform of Liverpool-street
station in a holiday mood to catch the 5.18. That had been
about four hours ago. . . .

"Good Lord—*not* quite four hours ago!" he reflected.

Astonishing reflection. Could so much have happened in so short a time?

Yes, but what *had* happened? Well, one thing that had happened was the pulling of the communication cord. . . . The pulling of the communication cord. Ah—what about that, now?

"Now, why did the old lady pull it?" Freddy demanded of himself.

Her explanation had been that the cockney bloke had "gone for her." That didn't seem too likely. In fact, the cockney bloke had denied it. Well, of course, he would deny it. . . .

"Whew!" muttered Freddy. "What a flash!"

Crashing thunder answered him. Let's see! Where was he? Oh, yes. The cockney bloke *would* deny it. But, favouring the cockney bloke's denial was the evidence of the jumpy old josser in the corner. Now, why should the jumpy josser back up the cockney bloke unless he were also backing up the truth? And why would the cockney bloke be such a fool as to try and molest an old woman with the jumpy josser looking on? Perhaps the jumpy josser had been dozing? Well, then he could have admitted it, couldn't he? But he had definitely stated . . .

"Yes, but why shouldn't the jumpy josser be in league with the cockney bloke? thought Freddy. "By Jove—this rain—"

Now, then! Jumpy josser and cockney bloke are working together. Good! What's their object? Say, theft. Maybe they'd got on to it that the old woman's bag contained something valuable. Cockney shadows her at Liverpool-street, jumpy old josser joins them at Norwich. . . . Why? To supply evidence in favour of the cockney bloke, if things go wrong. Good! Getting there! Ah, but what about this? If the cockney bloke was going to steal the old woman's bag, why didn't he lie low? Why did he start worrying the agitated dame even before the 5.18 started?

"Doesn't fit," grunted Freddy. "Begin again."

All right! *Why* did the cockney bloke worry the old lady more than three hours before he tried to rob her? He seemed to be making a dead set at her. Trying to frighten her. Thieves don't work like that, surely? He got her so frightened that it was almost a wonder she didn't pull the communication cord before. . . .

As a flash illuminated the darkness of the lane, another flash illuminated the darkness of Freddy's mind. "No one who had seen her agitation was really surprised to find that she had pulled the communication cord," he thought. "I know *I* wasn't. *I wasn't supposed to be!*" The whole thing had appeared to be a natural incident, born of the woman's agitation! The agitation had been worked up in advance to explain it! It had been worked up so that the cockney bloke's guilt would not be required to explain it . . . so that, when the train resumed its way, all three occupants of the compartment would be exonerated—exonerated, at least, of any crime for which any of them could be detained—and the whole thing could be ascribed to hysteria. A solution which the jumpy old josser had himself suggested!

"Which means," murmured Freddy, "that the old lady was in it, too, from the start! Which means that she was never really frightened of the cockney bloke at all."

Which meant that there was no coincidence about the pulling of the communication cord. It was pulled so that the train should stop, so that attention would be concentrated on a compartment where nothing important was happening, and so that attention should be diverted from another compartment where something important *was* happening!

"Yes, but look here!" muttered Freddy. "If that's so, it means something else, too. It means that the agitated old lady, the cockney bloke, the jumpy josser, the large gentleman, and the horsy fellow, are *all* working together! Five of 'em! Whew!"

It really was rather a solemn thought. Not only did it imply that the game was a particularly big one to involve so many players and such an elaborate, carefully thought-out plot, but that the enemy army was of considerable size. Why, there might be more than five. . . .

"The clergyman!" exclaimed Freddy, aloud. "P'r'aps *he's* No. 6?"

And another one. The man in the brown suit. The man who had disappeared. No. 7!

After that, the most bewildering thought of all swept over him, giving him a sensation of utter hopelessness. Lydia Leveridge, the girl who spirited away rings and produced others, whose photograph was in a newspaper at one moment and deliberately torn out the next, the girl who had been kidnapped, but who had told him that he was not to interfere because his protection would be a menace . . . where did *she* fit in?

Beneath the rain on his forehead another moisture began to settle. It was perspiration. A wretched thought had entered Freddy's mind. Was Lydia Leveridge herself a member of this gang? Was she—No. 8?

"Listen, Freddy," he argued, seriously. "There's one thing you've left clear out, my boy. Her *eyes*. Could any girl with such honest eyes have a dishonest purpose?"

He felt better. A tree went down twenty yards from him. He hardly heard it.

Still, his intention to report to the police at Aylsham was weakened. He could not be quite certain yet that the police would help Miss Leveridge's interests. If his own interest was a menace, how much larger a menace might be the interest of a whole police force!

He lost count of time. It was a journey punctuated mainly by his thoughts. Only long afterwards did he clearly recall three incidents upon the road of a more practical nature. One was an attempt to climb a signpost to read it. Another was a small boy of whom he unsuccessfully enquired the way. The small boy had apparently never heard of Aylsham in his life, although he was standing within three miles of it, nor did he seem to have heard of motor-cars or bicycles. He had been born with his mouth open, and would die with it unclosed. And the third incident was a side-slip, which took a piece out of a pair of Savile-row trousers; and also took three shillings away from the commercial value of a workman's bicycle.

Never mind! What did it matter? He was near his destination now. In a few minutes he would be there. . . .

"Hi!" he called suddenly, as a figure grew out of the blackness. "Is this right for Aylsham?"

Not until just after he had asked the question did he realise that it had been addressed to the back of a clergyman.

18

The Window's Secret

Freddy Reeve had cursed the storm many times during the past hour, but now he suddenly blessed it, for its discord had drowned his question and the clergyman made no sign of having heard it.

But the storm alone did not account for the clergyman's inattention to the needs of a stranger. He was himself absorbed in some problem; his back remained still. It was not the stillness of indolence or lethargy, but of intense interest. Every nerve in it appeared, from its queer, statuesque pose, to be tense.

What was he doing here? How had he got here? Why was his head bent slightly forward, and what was the object of this close, straining attentiveness? Fresh mysteries to solve! Fresh blanks in the bewildering picture Freddy was struggling to develop in his mind. Quietly, and keeping as much distance as possible between them, Freddy dismounted, and stood in the shelter of some over-hanging foliage, watching. The over-hanging foliage dripped on him, and leaked into his collar. He was quite unconscious of it. His neck and his collar were thoroughly acclimatised to moisture.

As he stood watching the clergyman's back, other things grew out of the blackness. A wall. A door in the wall. The simple outline of a roof. Some dead windows—and one faintly alive. Yes, there was a light behind that window-blind. A dim light. The clergyman's gaze seemed to be fixed upon it.

But Freddy's gaze became more interested in the door. He had had a sense that the door had been ajar when he had first come upon the clergyman, although he could not account for this sense. Often our brains take in things before we ourselves become aware of them; some of the things remain forever hidden from our consciousness, as though the brain enjoyed its ironic independence, refusing to share all its secrets with its jailer; but other things are yielded up to our knowledge later—a year later, a day later, a minute later. They are like people whom one suddenly finds in a room, but whom one has not seen enter. And so Freddy knew that the door of the cottage at which the clergyman was staring had been open a few seconds earlier. And that it was now closed.

The clergyman was standing very near the door. Perhaps he had closed it? Or perhaps it was somebody who was now behind the half-dead window? In that case why did the clergyman remain here? Why did he not go away like any ordinary visitor? . . .

Ah! He *was* moving now! He was moving slowly towards the left—towards the side of the cottage. He paused by the window for an instant. Then he moved on again, reached the corner of the cottage, and slipped round the side.

Freddy shifted his position, quickly leaning his machine against the hedge, and slipped forward a little. He was not going to miss the clergyman's actions! Now he could see the clergyman round the side of the cottage— could see that he had paused again, and that he was staring at another window. This window was also glimmering. Evidently it was a side-window of the same room, but it differed from the other window in two important particulars. No blind was down, and the window was open.

For fully half-a-minute (which is a longer time in actuality than it is in print) the clergyman stared in at the open window. Something inside appeared to fascinate him. Then he turned away, and faced the spot where Freddy stood. Freddy had no idea whether he could be seen or not, and it was impossible in the darkness to get any glimpse of the clergyman's expression. He was certainly looking towards Freddy, and he was certainly standing motionless again; but as likely as not he was engaged in thought rather than observation. As a matter of fact, the clergyman was not seeing Freddy. He was seeing quite other things.

Then the lightning took a hand. It flashed dazzlingly, and then flashed again before its instantaneous revelation had had time to fade. The lane, the woods, the cottage, the sky became blindingly white; and so did the two figures that stood facing each other, the one by the cottage, the other just across the road. Each was a luminous statue, suddenly created out of nothing. A moment later they returned to nothing, and the thunder roared over their memory.

But it could not wipe out the memory, even though the blackness that follows lightning is greater than the blackness that precedes it. Each statue knew that the other existed. . . .

"Good evening," said the clergyman.

The ridiculous commonplaceness of the salutation got Freddy on the raw.

"Do you think so?" he retorted.

"No, I don't," answered the clergyman. "You are quite right. It is a terrible evening."

"Are you referring to the storm?"

"Why, of course! What else?"

Freddy advanced a few steps. So did the clergyman. Freddy wished he had been ten years older, or that the clergyman had been ten years younger. He was oppressed by a sense of inequality, but this might not have been due entirely to the clergyman's greater age and experience. The clergyman was also the drier of the two. Though his coat was wet, his vest was not sodden.

"May I know how you got here?" asked Freddy, rather cumbrously.

If the clergyman considered the question cumbrous, he did not betray the fact.

"Well, it's quite an interesting story," he replied, readily enough. "I'll tell it to you—if you'll return the compliment. I'm rather inclined to think," he added, "that my own curiosity is more justified than yours."

"What do you mean? When I last saw you—"

"I was in a train. The 5.18 from Liverpool-street, to be exact. But so were you. And I didn't see *you* get out at the station."

Freddy was quite sure the other was fencing with him.

"Did you get out at a station, then?" he enquired.

"Certainly, I did. I got out at the station just beyond the spot where the train was pulled up—you remember? That frightened lady! Yes—I got out there. Did *you?*"

"No, I didn't," admitted Freddy.

"Then you must see the cause of my perplexity," remarked the clergyman. "If you had got out at a station beyond mine, I don't see how you could possibly have got back here in this time!" He paused for a second, and turned his head as though to glance at the window again; but if that had been his intention he thought better of it. "So may I have your story first?"

Freddy did not want to give his story first. The clergyman noted his hesitation.

"Well, well, what does the order matter, after all?" observed the clergyman. "Here is my story—and quite a simple one, as you will see. After the extraordinary incident of the communication cord—by the way, shall we draw a little closer to this wall?—there is some protection here—the train soon stopped again at the next station. There was quite an exodus, although the station was only a small one. I got out myself, and I found on the platform the three occupants of the compartment where all the fuss had taken place."

"That was rather a coincidence, wasn't it?" commented Freddy.

They were now both by the wall, but Freddy was keeping two or three feet between himself and his companion. The separating space would not help him much if a revolver were suddenly produced, but at any rate it guarded against an unexpected blow.

"Yes, I thought so myself at the time," nodded the clergyman. "And as I was still rather unhappy about the poor lady, I decided to keep an eye on her for a few minutes. You see, I thought that rough fellow might resume his unwelcome attentions. You would have done the same in my place, I think?"

"Very likely," said Freddy.

"But imagine my surprise," went on the clergyman, "when I heard the lady and the rough fellow both accepting an invitation, made by the third of their party—you remember that rather fussy old man?—he asked them if he could give them a lift in car. He had one waiting near the station, he said. That was rather odd, wasn't it?"

"Very," agreed Freddy, maintaining his watchfulness.

"Yes, it was! I undoubtedly thought so. I supposed that the old man was actuated by the Christian motive of trying to save two fellow human beings from two separate storms—one, the storm above, and the other, the storm within. A reconciliation, eh?"

"It was also rather odd," suggested Freddy, "that they were all going in the same direction!"

"Once again, my own thought!" cried the clergyman. "Though, as to that, I myself shared in this particular oddity. For they were going to Aylsham—and so was I! At least," he added, after a slight pause, "it was in my direction."

"Did they offer you a lift, too?" enquired Freddy.

"No," smiled the clergyman. "I asked for it. They couldn't well refuse—who could, on a night like this?—but they didn't seem too happy. No—they weren't too happy. They did not want my company."

Freddy regarded the clergyman a little more closely. Was he genuine? Or was all this a colossal bluff?

"We had a quick, uncomfortable journey," resumed the clergyman. "We sat on top of each other in a small Citroen. And at last, when they deposited me—just a little way from here—I wasn't sorry." He stopped speaking, and now there was a longer pause. Freddy wondered whether this was the end of me story.

"Is that all?" he asked.

"No—not quite," said the clergyman; and now he was watching Freddy quite as closely as Freddy was watching him. "I was deposited a little way from here. As I have said. On the outskirts of Aylsham. I thought I would rather end my journey on foot—yes, even in the storm. And—while doing so—I came to this cottage."

Another silence. Freddy broke it by enquiring,

"Do you live here?"

"No."

"I thought you seemed interested in it?"

"I was interested in it. And—since we are exchanging confidences—at least, I hope to have yours shortly—I may say, sir, that I am still interested in it. Are you?"

"Immensely."

"Why?"

"Perhaps because you are."

"I see," mused the clergyman, faintly ironical. "A re-flected interest?"

"Yes. And I think I've some excuse, if I may say so," said Freddy, deciding not to be cowed.

"But I've not asked for any excuse," protested the clergy-man, with disarming generosity.

"Just the same, I'll tell it to you," replied Freddy. "I've been standing here quite a few minutes, you know. I even asked you a question, only you didn't hear it. You were too busy staring in at that window. Do you mind if I have a look?"

The clergyman shook his head gravely.

"Not in the least," he said. "As a matter of fact, I was going to suggest it."

He stood aside. Freddy moved to the open window at the side of the cottage. He looked through.

He looked into a small, simple parlour, dimly illumi-nated by a lamp turned low. On the ground, prone and motionless, lay a figure. It was the figure of the fussy old man who had driven the clergyman to Aylsham.

19

Outside the Cottage

"So now," said the clergyman, quietly, "you can understand the source of my interest."

Freddy swung round. Although he had only been speaking to the clergyman a second or two before, the voice startled him. Shock plays ducks and drakes with time, and he had momentarily forgotten the clergyman's existence.

"And you may also understand," added the clergyman, "why I am interested in you, also?"

"You don't suppose I have anything to do with this?" exclaimed Freddy, quickly.

"I don't suppose anything," replied the clergyman. "Supposition is dangerous. But I have explained one half of the coincidence of this meeting. Will you explain the other?"

"While a man lies in there—"

"Dead?"

Freddy stared at the clergyman. He wondered whether he *did* know the source of the clergyman's interest—completely. Then he turned again, and looked through the open window.

The fussy old man was lying on his face. The inadequate lamp stood on a table not far away. A red cloth that covered the table was slightly ruffled. A chair was overturned.

"There seems, you will note, to have been a struggle," said the clergyman. "Perhaps, if I had been a little sooner—or if you had—it might have been prevented. But am I not to hear your story?"

Freddy hesitated, then turned to the clergyman again.

"My story's almost as unbelievable as—as that sight in there."

"Well," murmured the clergyman, "I'm ready to be credulous."

"At present, you know nothing of all this?"

"Beyond what I've told you? How should I?"

"You don't know, for instance, that this is a kidnapping case?"

"It seems to me more like a murder case," frowned the clergyman. "Still, of course, the two can hang together. Did somebody kidnap this poor man? No, but that would be impossible, for half-an-hour ago he was driving me in his car. Perhaps he was one of the kidnappers?"

"There's little doubt about it."

"I can hardly believe he was trying to kidnap the old lady or—"

"Listen," interposed Freddy, deciding that he would have to tell a part of his story, and wondering why he was not anxious to tell the whole of it. Of course, it was natural in the circumstances that he should be suspicious of everybody, just as it was natural that the clergyman should be suspicious of him; but the world was not entirely peopled by villains, and the clergyman's tale had sounded plausible enough. "Here are the bare facts," said Freddy. "There's no time or need for details. The pulling of the communication cord was a blind. Those three people were merely stopping the train so that the actual kidnappers could get to work—and they must have been pretty sick when you asked to join them in their car—"

"They weren't overjoyed," nodded the clergyman. "But I still don't understand—"

"Wait a moment, and you will. In another compartment was a girl. Besides her were myself and two other men. For reasons I needn't go into I'd been suspicious for a long while, and if I'd kept my wits about me I'd never have left my compartment at all. But I was duped by that old lady's scream, like the rest, and when I got back I found my carriage empty, and the door open. The men had gone off with the girl—"

"But this is terrible!" exclaimed the clergyman. "You mean to say—? Well, what did *you* do?"

"Me? What would anybody have done? I went after them. They got away in a car, and thanks to an accident—and also to a bicycle I borrowed—there it is, against a hedge across the road—I caught them up."

"Well done!" cried the clergyman.

"I'm afraid it *wasn't* so well done afterwards," replied Freddy. "I was threatened with a revolver, and got knocked out—"

"What! They shot at you?" interposed the clergyman. "The ruffians!"

"No, it wasn't a bullet that knocked me out. It was a fist. When I came to I thought I was done, but I found a piece of paper on the ground with a name faintly written on it. We had some trouble to decipher it, because the rain—"

"We?" interposed the clergyman, his eyes opening wide.

"Eh? Oh, of course! Lord, one can't mention everything! The other was the workman from whom I'd—borrowed the bicycle. Anyway, that part of it doesn't matter. The point is that we translated the name into Aylsham, and that I came along here as fast as I could. And I met you—and here we are!"

"Could I see the paper?" asked the clergyman.

Freddy fished it out of his pocket, and showed it to him. The clergyman studied it closely, then handed it back.

"And your theory about the paper is that this girl had managed to throw it out of the window of the car? Is that it?" enquired the clergyman.

"It is," nodded Freddy. "And, somehow or other, that dead fellow in there seems to confirm my theory."

"Then you must have yet another theory," suggested the clergyman. "I myself do not exactly see the connection."

"Why, but surely, it's clear?" retorted Freddy. "Can't you piece together what's happened? It must have been arranged between them that, after the kidnapping, they would all meet here, at Aylsham. Naturally your friends didn't want you with them! After they dropped you, they came on to this cottage—met the others—and fell out among themselves. And now they've gone on again—leaving one of the party behind!"

"Who will tell no tale," murmured the clergyman. "It's incredible—incredible! Tell me. You're full of theories. How do you suppose the girl knew they were going to Aylsham?"

"One can only guess at that," answered Freddy. "I'm sure I don't know."

"Then let *me* make a suggestion, for a change! Perhaps she wasn't quite as helpless in the car as her captors thought she was. Pretended to have fainted or something—and kept her ears open and her eyes closed!"

"Yes, that's certainly possible," agreed Freddy. "But what we ought to do, sir, is to look forward and not backward. We've got two jobs now, it seems. Firstly, to notify the police about this dead man. And second, to go after the girl—"

"Go after the girl?" interrupted the clergyman. "How can you do that now? It will be easy to notify the police, but I don't see how you can follow the girl any more!"

"P'r'aps I don't, either," said Freddy, "but I'm going to do it, just the same. If I have to move heaven and earth, I'm going to do it!"

The clergyman took a step nearer to Freddy, and studied his face closely. He seemed to be trying to size the enthusiast up. His expression had become suddenly personal.

"Take my advice, my friend," he said, "and leave this to the police."

"Sorry, sir," answered Freddy, "but nothing doing."

"You will only run into danger."

"You don't really suppose that's going to stop me? I didn't leave the train for fun."

"No, perhaps not. Still—when there's nothing to be gained—"

"There's everything to be gained!"

"Oh, well, I see I cannot prevent you," sighed the clergyman. "But what do you propose to do?"

"Well—what are *you* going to do?"

"Me? I shall notify the police, of course, as I should have done before now if I hadn't met you."

"Right. And I'll stick around here. P'r'aps I'll find something in that cottage."

"Yes. Maybe you will. On the whole, perhaps it's quite a good plan, after all, to divide forces. You will be here when the police arrive, and can report anything you find. I suppose, in the circumstances, I may borrow your bicycle?"

The request was a natural one, but it brought a little frown to Freddy's face. His bicycle—or, rather, the workman's—was his white charger! How would he fare without it? While he hesitated, the clergyman was crossing the road.

"This will save me considerable time," observed the clergyman, "and we've wasted too much already, I fear."

"Yes—but, look here—suppose I need it while you're away?" called Freddy.

The clergyman did not seem to hear him. He was already bringing the machine away from the hedge.

"Wait a minute!" exclaimed Freddy. "I may need the bicycle myself."

The clergyman shook his head, gently admonishing. "Remember the words of Sir Philip Sidney, at the battle of Zutven," he smiled. "'Thy need is greater than mine!' Then it was a glass of water. Now it is bicycle. But, in each case, the personal sacrifice was the cause of humanity."

The clergyman was now on the bicycle. He had jumped upon it in a most unclerical fashion.

"Wait a moment!" cried Freddy, springing forward.

"No, we mustn't wait any more moments," the clergyman called back.

He waved his hand, and, as he did so, the storm played another of its little tricks. It illuminated the hand, giving Freddy his first clear sight of it. There was blood upon it.

20

INSIDE THE COTTAGE

The normal thing to do if you possess normal courage and find a man with a blood-stained hand trying to escape from you is to chase him. There were, however, several reasons why Freddy Reeve did not chase the clergyman.

The first was that he had done a good deal of fruitless chasing during the past hour, and he was not too optimistic regarding his remaining store of wind. The second was that the sight of the blood-stained hand had momentarily stunned him. If the clergyman's hand was stained with blood, he had presumably been involved in the tragedy in the parlour. If he had been involved in that tragedy, he had been putting up big bluff all along. Yet, if he had been bluffing Freddy, and had also killed the man who lay on the parlour floor, for which side in the mystifying conflict was fighting? Was he perhaps a third point in the triangle—the friend of no one and the enemy of all? All at once Freddy recalled his sensation that the cottage door had been slightly open when he had first upon the scene, and that almost immediately afterwards it had been closed. Had the clergyman himself closed it while coming out?

A third reason why Freddy did not chase the clergyman was supplied by the clergyman's own nimbleness. He had sprung upon the bicycle in a most determined manner, and after that ominous wave had departed with considerable rapidness.

But a fourth reason, and the reason that overwhelmed the other three and made them insignificant, came from the cottage itself. It was a groan.

It was this groan that most definitely assisted the clergyman to make his get-away. "Your eyes have just been intrigued by the sight of a blood-stained hand," the groan seemed to say to the listener; "here is something now for your ears!" Certainly, Freddy's ears had been startled as greatly as his eyes had been. Either a dead man had groaned—or there was somebody else in the cottage as well as the dead man.

"Come on! This won't do!" muttered Freddy.

He shook himself out of his lethargy, and dived back to the window. He stared through the window at the familiar, gruesome picture: it was familiar because of the indelible impression it had made. There was no sign of any second presence. The sole inmate of the room still lay stretched out upon the floor. . . .

"Ah—but there are *other* rooms!" thought Freddy.

Of course! The groan might have come from another room! Well, in that case, the other rooms must be investigated.

Swift action came upon the thought. In a trice Freddy had slipped round the angle of the wall and had reached the front-door. He tried it. Closed fast; and, without a key, impossible to open from the outside.

"Damn!" muttered Freddy. "That means the blessed window!"

Somehow he hated the idea of the window. You can enter through a doorway in an attitude of dignity and defence. Your fist can be ready to strike. Your fingers can be ready to clutch. There is a sense of legality at your back, and, if you are caught in some fruitless or mistaken enterprise,

you can make your explanation in the recognised upright
position. But how different if you are caught while climbing through a window! You are in no position to defend
yourself physically or morally. You cannot say, "I only just
came in to borrow a book." You can be lugged in or shoved
out, or the window can be brought down upon your back.
True, unless the room is in darkness, you can see most of
it before you enter, while you cannot see through a door.
But there are window-curtains. . . .

There were window-curtains on either side of the little
parlour window. They were surprisingly and disconcert-
ingly generous for so humble a chamber, and flowed wide-
ly to the floor. The portions peering at Freddy, deep red
sentries on either side of him, were damp with the rain
that had entered. It was odd that the window should be
open on a night like this! Who had opened it? Had someone else entered through it before Freddy, raising himself cautiously as Freddy was doing, slipping one leg over
the ledge, pausing, peering, and hesitating? If someone
else had, had it been that figure lying on the floor . . .
or the clergyman . . . or somebody quite different, whose
acquaintance Freddy was about to make?

One of the dark red sentinels billowed at him. It
touched his left toe, which was over the window-sash,
and appeared as though it were going to grasp it. The toe
kicked out, and melted violently into innocuous moisture.
The curtain crumpled back, indignant at this onslaught,
like a man hit below the belt.

"Come on," said Freddy to his right foot, which still
seemed to prefer the storm outside.

The foot obeyed and swung itself over. Now Freddy was
sitting on the ledge, his two legs a few inches from the
floor. Three yards away, on the same floor, was the prone
figure. He gazed at it for an instant, then jumped in, and
as he did so the other curtain billowed at him.

"Ah!" cried Freddy, and dealt it a swinging blow. His fist met no resistance. The window-curtains did not think much of Freddy.

He did not think much of himself. He was beginning to crack up under the strain of the past few hours. Perhaps he had some excuse. His clothes were sopping. He had raced hard. He had been threatened with a pistol, and knocked out by a fist. He was desperately in love. He was desperately anxious. And in this small cottage with him were a dead person and some other person not yet dead, but perhaps dying.

Well, the dead could wait, but the dying couldn't. This reflection stimulated him. He searched the little room quickly and thoroughly, looking behind two tail-backed armchairs, behind the deceptive curtains, and under the table with the ruffled cover. Nothing. Then he crossed to the door, which was ajar. He took hold of the door-knob cautiously, then jerked it towards him.

A dark passage lay outside. Instinctively he groped for his lighter. Happily the rain had not diminished its slender chances of utility. The wick caught at the third attempt. The dark passage woke up disagreeably. There was nobody in the passage. The two most arresting objects were a flight of stairs and a door across the hall. He decided on the door first.

He threw the door open, crying "Who's there?" His voice sounded foolish, yet was somehow companionable. No other voice answered him. He found himself peering into an empty kitchen.

He spent ten seconds exploring the kitchen. Then he emerged, closed the door, and ran up the stairs. It is best to run up stairs in such circumstances. If you don't, you may not get up at all. There is one disadvantage, however, of your heroic dash. Your cigarette-lighter goes out.

Freddy's went out. He stood at the top of the stairs in utter darkness—utter, that is, save for the faint glow that slanted through a crack in the parlour door below—and in the darkness came the groan again.

He did not know from where the groan came. The acoustics were confusing, for the sky was groaning outside the cottage as well as some human being within. As he was relighting his cigarette-lighter (a blessedly easy operation this time; the wick was still warm), a streak of lightning flashed through a skylight, revealing the upper landing with white intensity. In that flash Freddy saw two doors. The groaning thing was evidently behind one of them.

Now the too-brilliant lightning was replaced by the glow of the cigarette-lighter which was not brilliant enough. Still, there was no time to worry over faults in illumination. He seized the knob of one of the doors and turned it. A bed-room flickered into vision. The bed—it was an ominous moment when he turned his eyes towards it—was empty. There was nobody under it.

Now, the second door. This was ajar. All he had to do was to give it a push. On the point of doing so, he paused. Something stirred inside. . . .

Well, that mustn't stop him! Wasn't his very purpose to find someone? It could not be the girl, of course—the groan had been a masculine groan, otherwise there would not have been even these momentary delays in the search—but whoever it was had to be traced and faced. What a nuisance he felt so groggy! That blow he'd received had evidently been harder than he had imagined, and his wretched, clammy clothes . . .

He pushed the door open. Two eyes gleamed at him. They gleamed from the bed. Green eyes, with large pupils.

"Damn cat!" gulped Freddy, almost hysterically.

And then he heard the groan a third time, and now, owing to a temporary lull in the storm, he knew where it

came from. It came from immediately below—from the
parlour in which the dead man lay.

A sudden, new theory swept into his mind. It startled
him, and entirely upset his focus on events. *Was* the man
downstairs dead?

As the question chased through his brain, he turned and
ran down the stairs again, while the cat closed its eyes and
continued to dream of mice. He reached the little hallway,
shoved the parlour door open a little, and listened. A low
mutter sounded from within.

At first Freddy could not hear the words. They were
tangled and unintelligible. After a second or two, however,
the mutterer became more coherent, and on the point of
entering the room, the listener paused. The words were interesting. It seemed a pity to interfere with their flow. . . .

"Thought you were clever, didn't you?" muttered the
voice. The last time Freddy had heard that voice had been
in a third-class compartment of a train that was whirling
happy folk to holidayland! Where were those folk now?
Some were strolling on the beach, enjoying their first
deep draughts of ozone while the black sea slid, white-
edged, towards their feet and then away again, in the end-
less rhythm of nature. Some were on a pier. Some were
more practical, and were unpacking. And one, a small boy
tucked up in a boarding-house bed, was defying sleep vig-
orously, lest he should miss all the jolly little sounds that
came in at his open window-—so different from East End
traffic!—and the jolly little smells that came in, too, and
the quiet voices below the window, and the quick little
trot of a mule that suddenly went by on some mystic, noc-
turnal adventure, and the sea . . . the sea . . . the sea . . .

"Yes, but you were a bit *too* clever, Mr. Clergyman-I-
don't-think! And when you come to, I've got something
more to give you. But of course, I'll wait till you come to,

because you don't hit a man when he's down, do you? Ha, ha! Never hit a man when he's down!"

Ironic laughter followed. Then a silence. Then muttering began again.

"Eh? Hallo! Where are you? Now, then—don't move! If you do you'll only get another one—and the second time you're hit on the same place you feel it twice as hard! Bah! What a get-up! If I'd been by myself I'd have spotted you at once, and you'd never have got your little lift. Well, it's a pity for you you didn't stay satisfied with your little lift! Fools! All fools! Now, then—d'you hear? Stop still! . . . Coming along here, and expecting to find out where we were taking her . . ."

Freddy's fingers tightened. His heart missed a beat. There was another silence. A longer one. Would the fellow never continue? Ah . . .

"Here! What are you up to?" The voice in the parlour rose to a shout. "Hey? Where've you got to? By God, now you're for it! . . . Keep away! Keep away! All right, then. If you won't . . . Drop that! Drop that. . . . Let go—let go! God, I'll break your back!"

Now another sound came from the room. Something had raised itself, and fallen again. There was a choking gurgle. It beat Freddy. He shoved the door open, and entered.

The man had moved, but he still had his face towards the floor. He made no sign that he had heard the door open, but as Freddy ran to him he shouted out.

"All right! I'll tell you! Damn you! Let go! Let go, you hear? I'm telling you! Can I speak while I'm being choked? . . . A house on Thetford Heath—West of Thetford—that's where they've taken her! Now go and follow her! It's an empty house, and p'r'aps the caretaker will give you a little souvenir. . . ."

Now Freddy's heart thumped. Thetford Heath! An empty house west of Thetford! So that was where she was!

And then the man on the floor burst out into fierce laughter. It was so fierce that Freddy instinctively drew back a step, and stared at him.

"And now you've gone, you damned fool," he shrieked, "I'll tell you something else. Thought you could get the better of me, did you? Well, go to Thetford! Enjoy yourself there! You won't find anything! Because it doesn't happen to be Thetford, Mr. Clergyman, but Holt! Ha, ha! You thought you could get the better of me, eh? Thought that, did you? Ha, ha, ha! Ha, ha—"

The hideous laughter ended in a gurgle. The form rose suddenly to a kneeling position, its eyes opened, and it stared straight into the eyes of Freddy. For the first time Freddy saw the forehead. It had a deep gash in it. Then the form sank back, and the fussy old man who had joined the 5.18 at Norwich lay very still indeed.

21

The Race to Holt

In an armchair belonging to some unknown person, with a dead man at his feet, and a storm raging outside, Freddy Reeve sat down to smoke a cigarette. Even though time pressed, he felt that he needed it.

"Just three minutes," he murmured. "Just three!"

He had a big job before him, and he wanted to be prepared for it, both mentally and physically. He was feeling a little dizzy, and it was necessary to steady his mind and his person. Had there been a drink handy he would not have waited for an invitation from his unknown host. There was no drink, however, and he had to content himself with gratitude that his silver cigarette-case, at any rate, was dry. For a full minute he smoked without attempting to ponder. "Every moment I am getting better and better," he informed himself, with the determination of Couéism. Then he began to think. His effort was to simplify his thoughts, and to form the wisest plan of action from the results.

It was easy now to piece together what had happened in this cottage—in this very room in which he sat. The five rascals had foregathered there. It was their place of reunion before completing their journey. Here they had made their final plans, and had perhaps been on the point of starting for Holt when the clergyman had turned up.

The clergyman's story fitted into the picture, although there were still a few blanks. Possibly he had lurked round the cottage while the conspirators were gathered together; possibly he had contrived to open the window, and to listen there. But all these details did not matter. They led to the obvious development, whatever they were, that the clergyman had confronted the kidnappers, or been caught by them—that four of them had departed with the girl, and that the fifth, who now lay dead on the floor, had been deputed to watch over him.

The clergyman had been knocked out. He had been wily, however, and had managed to turn the tables on his jailer after the others had left, and to wrest information out of him. Then there would have been a bit of a fight, during which the clergyman received a wound on his hand—hence the blood upon it—and the jailer had been crashed to the ground. The fellow had hit something as he fell the last time, and Freddy himself had turned up just as the clergyman was leaving.

"But why didn't the clergyman trust me," wondered Freddy, "if he were fighting Lydia Leveridge's battle?" Another thought followed swiftly on the heels of this one: "What reason had he to trust anybody—any more than I had, myself?"

No, it didn't quite fit. Freddy felt that he deserved to be trusted! Still, taking a wide view of the position, he realised that the clergyman's own mind must have been in some confusion, and that behind his apparent calmness he must have been struggling to pierce mists just as Freddy was himself. He, like Freddy, had been through a rough time. He, like Freddy, was not anxious to take any unnecessary chances. Miss Leveridge herself had told Freddy not to interfere, and if the clergyman was Miss Leveridge's ally, he may have known her reasons and have approved of them.

Well, the trust could come later. Meanwhile it was clear that the clergyman had gone to notify the police, and that the police would shortly turn up. Would the clergyman be with them? No! He would be on his way to Thetford—following a false clue!

By an amazing chance, Freddy himself possessed the right clue. He could wait for the police, and set them on the track, or he could follow the track himself. . . .

The idea of waiting for the police grew more and more distasteful. Perhaps they would be some while yet. Perhaps, when they came, they would disbelieve him. Perhaps they wouldn't turn up at all, but would accompany the clergyman to Thetford. Who was this clergyman, by the way? A detective in disguise? Probably.

"No, I'm dashed if I'll wait!" exclaimed Freddy, jumping up suddenly. "I'll go off this moment, and leave a note!"

Then another problem presented itself. He had no bicycle. How was he going to make the journey to Holt?

"Confound it!" he muttered. "That's finished it!"

Had it? No, not necessarily. There might be another bicycle somewhere. In an outbuilding or a shed. Anyway, he would go out and have a look.

Before leaving the room he bent down and examined the prone figure closely. There was no doubt about it; the fellow was stone dead. The heart was silent. No tremour disturbed that complete sleep. "Poor devil," thought Freddy. "P'r'aps his parents were crooks before him, and he didn't know any better!" He lifted a hand and let it drop. Immediately afterwards he wished he had not done so. The limp descent of the lifeless hand, and the little thud it made as it struck the carpet, gave him the most unpleasant moment he had encountered in this unpleasant cottage. He had created a memory that would take some quelling.

He hurried from the room, left the cottage by the front door, and walked round into a little yard. The rain had

156 J. Jefferson Farjeon

abated in violence, but it still fell steadily. Across the yard was a wooden building. He opened the door, and for once a welcome sight met his eyes. The dim outline of a car.

"By Jove!" he cried. "The Citroen!"

He was as delighted as a child, for not only did the car solve his immediate problem, but it provided another definite link in the chain of events. This, obviously, was the conveyance in which the clergyman had received his lift to Aylsham. It had been left here for the ultimate use of the man who now lay dead in the cottage, while the rest of the party had completed the journey to Holt in the red car.

Freddy was among the millions who could drive. In less than two minutes he had started the engine, ascertained that the car was in perfect working order, and had backed it out into the lane. Then he returned to the cottage and wrote a hurried, explanatory note, leaving it prominently on a chair.

Only one thing detained him now—his ignorance of the way to Holt. Of course, on reaching Holt he would be even more ignorant of the way to the empty house in which the final chapter of his adventure was to be laid; but sufficient for the moment was the evil thereof, and that later puzzle would have to be worked out when it duly presented itself.

"Holt! Holt!" muttered Freddy, back in the car. "Why the devil don't I know my map better?"

A voice answered him out of the darkness.

"Excuse me, mister," said the voice, "but could yew give me a lift?"

Freddy swung round in his seat. It was the workman.

The meeting was a surprise to both of them. The workman wondered why Freddy had not got farther, while Freddy wondered how the workman had got so far. Each waited vaguely for the other to explain.

"By Jove—you gave me a start," said Freddy, breaking the unprofitable silence. "How did you manage to get here so soon?"

"Met a man with a Ford," replied the workman, "but 'e turned off a mile back." He drew closer, and stared at Freddy. "'Ave yew caught 'em?"

"Not yet."

"Where be my bike?"

"It's gone for the police."

"It be 'aving a rare night out, that bike! I see yew got a car now."

"Yes, but it's no good to me unless you can tell me the way to Holt."

"'Olt?" repeated the workman. "Didn't that bit o' paper say 'Aylsham'?"

"It did," answered Freddy. "But they've moved on."

"Oh! 'Ave they?"

"Yes—"

"To 'Olt?"

"Yes."

"And yew be goin' after 'em?"

"Of course, I'm going after them! And be quick, please! Which is my road?"

"To 'Olt?"

"Yes," said Freddy, patiently. "For the Lord's sake, old chap, get a move on!"

"That'll be through Blickling."

"Well, which is the road to Blickling?"

"And then yew'll 'ave to go through Saxthorpe an' Edgefield."

"Right! I've got the names. How do I start?"

"What part of 'Olt?"

"Heavens, does that matter?" snapped Freddy, exasperated. Then, all at once, he realised that it did matter very much. "I've got to try and find an empty house three miles from Holt," he added.

"'Ow be yew goin' to do it?" queried the workman.

"Perhaps I'll find somebody in Holt more helpful than you are!" retorted Freddy.

The workman remained unruffled.

"P'r'aps, sir, yew'll find me in 'Olt," he observed, "if yew'll give me that lift I'm askin' for."

"What! Do you mean you'll come with me?" exclaimed Freddy.

"Well, I'd like to get to 'Olt," said the workman.

"Jump in, jump in!" cried Freddy, shedding his exasperation in the joy of obtaining an ally. "This is a stroke of luck! Why, you may be able to help me find that empty house I mentioned!"

"We'll 'ave a try, sir," answered the workman, as he got into the car. "Keep straight on fer a bit. I'll tell yew when to turn. I used to live at 'Olt."

"Oh, you don't live there now, then?" asked Freddy, as he started the car.

"No, sir," said the workman.

"Where do you live?"

"Aylsham."

Freddy found himself oddly affected by this information. He did not speak for several seconds. He was rather annoyed to discover that he was becoming emotional.

"I think you're rather a good chap," he said, presently.

"Left 'ere," replied the workman.

"I said, I thought you were rather a good chap," repeated Freddy, as he turned left.

"Go on," retorted the workman, uncomfortably.

Then a longer silence fell upon them, while the Citroen slid through the slush of the dark and dripping lanes.

Many miles ahead, another car was slipping through the lanes. It was a dark red car, an Armstrong-Siddeley, and in it were five people. The eyes of four of the people were open, but the eyes of the fifth were closed, and though the fifth was bound and gagged, and could move neither hand nor foot, her heart fluttered with strange triumph. For soon she would be where she had set her soul on being— and what happened after that was in God's hands.

22

THE HOUSE ON THE HEATH

Midnight was striking as the Citroen wound its way across an isolated heath west of Holt. Ahead, to the left of the sodden road, was a dark clump of foliage, and behind it rose the dark shape of a portion of a tall house. In the daylight the foliage looked untidy and unkempt, but its outline glimpsed at night still retained some memory of original culture, suggesting a human haven amid the wildness of the heath. Even before the dark shape of the house had been discerned against the torn night-sky, Freddy sensed that a house would be there.

"Is this it?" whispered Freddy.

"Ay, 'tis the one I'm thinkin' on," replied the workman. "It's been empty these five year, that I know."

So had half-a-dozen others to which the painstaking workman had directed Freddy. Theirs had been a strange, haphazard search. But an odd sensation, expressed in a queer tightening of his muscles and a more audible beating of his heart, told Freddy that at last they were nearing their objective, and that the God Chance was smiling momentarily upon them. It might be an ironical smile. They certainly had been led the devil of a dance, and there was no promise, even now, that the final measure would be harmonious; indeed, that grim dark outline looked forbidding enough, and rather suggested discord! But the outline was none the less welcome to Freddy, who longed for something concrete to get his teeth into, and whether Chance was smiling kindly or ironically made no difference to Freddy's determination.

"I'm going to stop here," he whispered to his companion, as they neared a small clump of bushes. "We don't want them to hear us approach."

"Tha's right," agreed the workman. "Like as not they got a gun."

It was an unpleasant but highly probable suggestion. In fact, Freddy knew they had a gun. Possibly the very weapon that had covered him in the road before Aylsham was covering him now from one of the upper, unseen windows of the house. As the thought came to him he turned off the road onto the stubbly green and crunched as quietly as was possible to the protective bushes. They were on the left of the road, as was the house itself, but the bushes were close, whereas the house lay considerably farther back.

"We'll leave her here," murmured Freddy, switching off the lights. "Mark the spot, old chap. When we come back, we may be in a hurry!"

"Tha's right," agreed the workman again. "Like as not."

Now they left the car in the pleasant protection of the clump, while they themselves crept out into the open and began to cross the ragged flatness that lay between them and the house. Their carpet was coarse grass. Low bushes grew out of it haphazard and patternless. The grass said to the scrubby bushes, "Let me alone! Can't you see I'm trying to be respectable, and that I'm leading to a gentleman's house?" The scrubby bushes replied, "Don't talk nonsense! This is a wild heath, where you can't do such things. If you want to be prim you must go nearer a town!" And, meanwhile, little pools and sodden patches squelched and gurgled at the amusing discourse, playing a separate game of their own.

The dark house was now only fifty yards away. Behind the two men who cautiously approached it was the road they had left, and on their right was a narrower road which forked into the broader way at a point beyond where they had turned off. The narrow road was the route from the house to the wide road, the route along which their car would have travelled if they had not left it under the clump of bushes.

Fifty yards—forty yards—thirty yards. As the house grew nearer, the encircling foliage grew taller. But an iron gate made a gap in the foliage, and through this gap could now be seen the lower portion of the building.

"Car bin along 'ere, sir," reported the workman abruptly.

He had been scanning the narrow road for signs. But Freddy did not answer him. He had been scanning the iron gate, and something far more interesting than car tracks had caught his eye. Something small and white—a little white knot—that winked up moistly from a ditch near one of the gate-posts.

He dived forward and stooped. Now the little white knot was in his hand, and his heart thumped tumultuously against his ribs. For the little white knot was a lady's handkerchief, and when he undid the knot he found a piece of paper inside. Eagerly he scanned it for writing. There was none. Disappointment succeeded elation.

The disappointment was only momentary, however. True, there was no writing on the paper, but he knew the paper, just the same! It was the same kind of paper as that which he and the workman had found in the road before Aylsham, and which had given them the name of the town. He produced the first piece of paper from his pocket, to make sure. Yes! Not a doubt of it! Then his heart gave another leap. Each piece had an edge that was torn. He fitted these edges together, and they completed a whole.

"Ay, car bin along 'ere," repeated the workman. "See they marks?"

"You're right, old chap," Freddy whispered back. "A car has been along here—the car we've been looking for!"

"'Ow do yew know that?" enquired the workman.

"Look," answered Freddy.

The workman looked. He was quite an intelligent workman. His brain did not work tremendously fast, but he had a habit of getting there. Why, hadn't he got to Holt? We are not just enough to our workmen. If we gave them a little more time, and ourselves a little more time to watch them utilizing our gift, we should make some illuminating discoveries.

"Well, I be blowed!" murmured the workman. He was true Norfolk, but workmen are blowed in every county. "That gel—she be a smart 'un!"

"She's more than smart," muttered Freddy. "She's—wonderful!"

The workman glanced at Freddy. *He'd* had a girl once, and *she'd* been wonderful—even though she had gone off with the blacksmith's son.

"Well, sir—wot be next?" queried the workman.

"Why, we're going to get into that house, of course," said Freddy.

"Ay, but 'ow?"

"Somehow."

"Ay, but 'ow some'ow?"

Then Freddy became practical.

"What's wrong with the gate, to start with?" he suggested.

The workman became more practical. He tried the gate, and found that it opened. Beyond it lay a negated, overgrown driveway leading to a neglected, overgrown porch.

"Come on!" whispered Freddy.

"Ay, but wot's goin' tew 'appen when we get there?" the workman whispered back.

It was a pertinent question. Freddy considered it.

"I expect that'll depend on what we find when we get there," he answered. "If any of the doors are as obliging as this gate, or if we spot an open window that we can get to—in we go, eh?"

"Ay," mumbled the workman, after a moment's hesitation, "tha's right."

The iron gate proved friendly. It was not only open for them, but it opened without a groan or a squeak; and they saw to it themselves that it closed without a clang. Inside the neglected, dripping grounds they paused. The front of the house was in darkness. No light glimmered from any window. That did not prove, however, that eyes were not watching them. You can watch better from a dark room than from an illuminated one.

As this thought came to Freddy he seized the workman's arm and drew him to the side of the driveway.

In the protection of tangled bushes they crept towards the house. Now the protective foliage came to an end, and the house was immediately before them.

"Stay here a moment," whispered Freddy.

He slipped quickly to the porch, but was back again in five seconds.

"Door no good," he murmured. "And no windows open on this side. Let's slip round to the back."

"Ay," answered the workman. He might have been snugly tucked up in bed at this moment. "Tha's right. Mind out there bean't no dog!"

During the next two minutes, they completed their survey of the house. It looked impregnable. A faint light glowed behind one of the back windows, high up, and a water-pipe had possibilities. A journey up the water-pipe, however, would end at a small window where there was no light, and which was closed.

"If only that window were open," muttered Freddy.

"Yew could never climb that," replied the workman.

"Couldn't I!" retorted Freddy. "I'd have a shot!"

"Mebbe," said the workman, "but it bean't open."

This undeniable fact did not bring them any nearer a solution of their problem. The workman got a brainwave.

"'Ow'd it be," he suggested, "fer one of us tew 'oller like 'e was dyin', and then when they come runnin' out, fer t'other tew slip in?"

"Not a bad idea," replied Freddy, "but I think they'd smell a rat."

The workman tried again.

"'Ow'd it be," he said, "tew throw a stone at one o' t'winders, an' break it?"

"That might be possible, if we did it in a thunder clap," answered Freddy, "but the thunder's stopped, and the noise would be sure to bring them along."

"Tha's right."

"No, we'll have to invent some reason for ringing the bell. The trouble is, they've seen me and would recognise me—"

"But they ain't seen *me*," interposed the workman. "'Ow'd it be fer me tew ring the bell, say I lorst me way, an' ask fer a night's lodgin'?"

"By Jove—that's an idea," exclaimed Freddy, and then cursed himself the next moment. He had raised his voice more than he meant to. "Yes—that *is* an idea," he whispered. "They've no reason to suspect you—excepting that they're liable to suspect everybody!"

"Night like this, sir, any'un might lose 'is way," the workman pointed out.

"Quite correct," nodded Freddy, grabbing at straws. "But they'd never let you in."

"Mebbe not, sir. But yew'd be nigh—an' the door'd be open. It might 'elp tew know 'oo opened it."

"Right again!"

"If 'twas a little 'un, we might jump on 'im an' break 'is neck afore 'e could say nothin'. Or if 'twas a big 'un, 'ow'd it be tew faint? If I was tew faint, they'd 'ave tew take me in."

"You know, you really are a bit of a sport," murmured Freddy. "I'm not sure that I've any right, dragging you in like this."

"Yew bean't draggin' me in," returned the workman, solemnly. "I'm *'ere!*"

And then, as though he feared sentiment, he suddenly slipped round the wall and made for the porch.

Freddy followed him. He did not know whether the plan was a wise one or not. One side of him wanted to discuss the scheme further, the other wanted impatiently to get on with it. After all, they couldn't stand here talking all night! Heaven knew what horrible things might be happening at this moment behind these dark and silent walls—or up in that little back room where the light faintly glimmered!

Yes—better let the workman get on with the job. . . . Meanwhile, Freddy would crouch behind a bush, and watch events. If the workman got into trouble . . .

"Good Lord—he's rung already!" thought Freddy.

The bell sent its incongruous music through the night. The workman stood, a dark shadow, in the porch. Reality was rushing fast towards them.

"Now, don't forget," reflected Freddy grimly, selecting his bush, "if that fellow gets into danger, you've got to go and get him out of it!"

The absurdity of the reflection! Of course, the workman was in danger! So was he, Freddy Reeve, in danger! And so was the girl for whom all this danger was being endured. . . .

The bell rang out a second time. The shadow in porch remained motionless. Suppose nobody came?

Hallo! Somebody was coming! A light appeared in the hall. It glimmered behind the almost opaque glass of the door. And now the door was being opened . . . just a crack . . .

"Who's there?"

The question came in a short, sharp bark. It brought with it a queer, instantaneous vision. A vision of an agitated old woman, trying to escape from a pugnacious cockney bloke at Liverpool-street station. Liverpool-street station! Did it exist? Had it really been the 5.18, that civilized, iron creature of iron habits, that had brought Freddy to this bush! . . .

"Lost me way, ma'am," mumbled the shadow in the porch.

"Well, you'd better go and find it again," retorted the sharp voice from within.

Freddy expected that the crack would diminish and the door would close. The opposite happened. The crack widened abruptly, as the workman tottered forward heavily.

"Feelin' a bit faint, like," he murmured.

Now the door was nearly wide open. For an instant Freddy dimly glimpsed a flickering hall, with the figure of the workman lurching into it, and an old woman retreating a step. Then the door was banged to, and he saw no more.

Dead silence succeeded that fleeting episode. The silence became unnerving. Freddy slipped forward from his bush, and made for the door. He had no definite plan, but the one thing he could not do was to remain inactive any longer.

He did not reach the door, however. A sound brought him to a sudden standstill. The sharp, decisive crack of a pistol.

23

On the Brink

"No, don't move, my young friend," said a voice behind Freddy. "That is, unless you wish to share the fate of your companion who has just gone inside."

It was the voice of the large and expansive gentleman, and for a moment Freddy Reeve was paralysed. Then, as the situation dawned upon him, his mind suddenly woke up and became amazingly cool. Freddy hardly recognised his mind. It was quite unlike itself. The very hopelessness of the situation, the very horror of it, seemed to have transformed his brain into a new instrument, an instrument which was dedicated to the extermination of the equally cool individual who was standing behind him with a revolver directed at his back.

"You really think we are terrible fools, don't you?" went on the bland voice. "I'm afraid we return the compliment. You see, if only you hadn't been a fool you would have completed your journey to Cromer, and would have buried your head in your pillow instead of in other people's business."

"I'm quite satisfied," said Freddy.

"Well, that, again, is mutual," observed the large gentleman. "Though perhaps, in your case, I can't quite see any cause for satisfaction. You see, my friend, you have only about five more minutes of life left to you. But then, after all, life is a very troublesome possession, isn't it?"

"Oh, and how am I going to die?" enquired Freddy.

What was the matter with him? He did not feel in the least afraid. He couldn't quite understand it. Perhaps one never felt afraid when the time actually came?

"I can't say, at the moment," responded the large gentleman. "It depends entirely upon you, you see. If you move before I tell you to, or make any trouble after I tell you to move, you will share the experience of your—er—labour candidate. Where did you pick him up, by the way? He certainly wasn't on the train!"

"But if I don't move before you tell me to?" asked Freddy.

"Oh, if you're good, then I daresay I can arrange a nice little motor accident for you," said the large gentleman, genially. "You will be found at the foot of a hill about a mile from here, with an overturned Citroen on top of you."

"I should think that would take some arrangement," suggested Freddy.

"It will. But then I'm rather good at arranging things. Perhaps you're beginning to make that rather late discovery?"

"And perhaps *you'll* make some discoveries rather late, before we've finished with each other," interposed Freddy.

"Come, come," reproved the large gentleman, "that doesn't sound like a good little boy talking!"

"You might tell me what I will gain by being a good little boy," suggested Freddy. "Why, for instance, shouldn't I wheel round suddenly, and get that bullet? If I'm to die anyway? It would be quicker."

The large gentleman smiled. Freddy could not see the smile, but he felt it.

"I'll tell you," he replied, "although I expect, in your heart, you already know what I am going to tell you. Life is a horrible business, but we always cling to it. Even if it's only a matter of five minutes, we still cling to it. Five minutes—three hundred seconds! Each second may produce the miracle that will give us—another five minutes, eh? Or let me put it more blatantly. Wait, and you are still alive. Turn round now, and you will certainly be dead in an instant. Would you care to try it?" He paused. Freddy remained immovable, his eyes on the door ahead of him, his mind on the pistol behind him. "But delay the instant—give me the five minutes that I require to arrange our little accident—and, well, anything may happen in that time, may it not? Your wits will be working hard. I may make a false move, or stumble. That, my young friend, is why it may pay you to be a good little boy."

"You're quite right," said Freddy. "I'll hang on to the odd chance. It may come off, you know. But grant one request to the good little boy, will you?"

"I must know it first."

"Stop calling me 'my young friend.' It irritates me peculiarly. I may be young, but I am certainly not your friend. I am your enemy. At this moment, and during all eternity. I regard you as a foul and putrid thing, who ought to be stripped in the presence of virginity and burned in the fires of its innocence." Of course, it was nonsense, but Freddy could not help himself. "You are a skunk. You deserve to be tarred and feathered. So, you see, it naturally annoys me to be called your friend, and if I am annoyed I may forget to be a good little boy—"

"And get my bullet?"

"Exactly. And I assume that, like myself, you also prefer the motor accident."

"And why do you assume I should prefer the motor accident?" enquired the large gentleman, rather ominously.

"Don't be an ass," retorted Freddy. "If you didn't, why would you go to the trouble of arranging it? I expect you've got a pretty large number of murders on your books, and the more you can give the appearance of suicide, the longer you will live to add to the list."

"Upon my soul, you talk quite well, if not quite wisely," said the large gentleman. "I think I'd like to hear you talk a little more. Tell me, where—actually—do *you* come in, in all this?"

"What do you mean?"

"Oh, we might as well be frank, in our last moments. Don't you think so? Are you a detective—like the unfortunate commercial traveller who fell out of the train, poor fellow, in the tunnel just before Ipswich? And like the clergyman who irritated me so in the next compartment— and who is now, by the way, lying dead or unconscious on a cottage floor? I mention these little matters," went on the speaker, while Freddy's heart gave a little bound, for *he* knew that the clergyman was not lying on the cottage floor, and he knew that the large gentleman did not share his knowledge, "I mention these matters just to show you that we don't do things by halves. But you haven't answered my question. Are you a detective?"

"What do I gain by answering it?" demanded Freddy.

"Nothing."

"Then you must make a bargain with me."

"Of course, you are in a splendid position to bargain," murmured the large gentleman, and all at once Freddy felt something hard and cold pressing into the small of his back. "Still—before I give the order to march—what would be the bargain?"

"Well, just as a matter of curiosity, I *should* like to know why you kidnapped Miss Leveridge? It must be a pretty big motive to do a dirty trick like that!"

"Amazing, the ignorance of some people!" exclaimed the large gentleman, accentuating his amazement by an extra pressure of the hard, cold thing in Freddy's back.

"Miss Leveridge is the daughter, you should know, of Sir Henry Leveridge. Sir Henry Leveridge, you should also know, is an exceedingly rich man. And you would also know, if you read your newspapers as thoroughly as I do, that Sir Henry has been exceedingly indignant through the press lately at what he calls the apathy of the police. He has pointed out on several occasions—am I boring you?—"

"Only with your revolver," said Freddy. "Go on."

"Really, I'm almost sorry I've got to kill you," chuckled the large gentleman. "Still, even humorists must die. As I was saying, Sir Henry Leveridge has pointed out that there has been a good deal of kidnapping lately—notably one little girl—Rose Terrence, I think the name was—who is still in the hands of her captors. 'If ever a daughter of mine were kidnapped,' he wrote, only a week ago, 'I should be so distracted that I would not wait for the police to move, but would pay any sum the blackguards demanded from me!'" The large gentleman paused. "So, naturally," he concluded, almost deprecatingly, "when a few society paragraphs mentioned that Miss Lydia Leveridge was Sheringham on a certain date, by the 5.18 from Liverpool-street station—when her photograph was published—and when it was discovered that she was travelling alone—well, what could the poor kidnappers do but gather up these pleasant little crumbs? The motive? Oh, yes—it's quite big, as you suggest. I think it is to be fixed at £50,000."

"By Jove—what blackguards!" murmured Freddy.

"Come, come!" exclaimed the large gentleman. "Do you value her at less?"

Freddy did not answer. He valued her at more. But something had suddenly risen to his throat—emotion does not always choose the right moment—and he was struggling to quell his desire to swing round and deal the speaker one good blow in the face before meeting extinction.

"And, now, *your* side of the bargain," said the large gentleman. "Are *you* a detective?"

"Never mind," muttered Freddy, shortly.

"I don't," smiled the large gentleman, "for I can see you're not a detective. You lack what authors describe as the steely quality! This means that I must look out for myself, because you amateurs are as troublesome as novices at poker!" And now, all at once, the hard, cold thing in Freddy's back bored into him so sharply that it hurt. "Forward, march," said the large gentleman, quietly.

Freddy obeyed. There was nothing else to do. He expected to be taken to the gate, and was surprised when he found himself being driven in the opposite direction.

"I thought it was to be a motor accident," he remarked.

"It is," nodded the large gentleman, "but the actual tragedy will occur in the back garden."

"I don't follow you."

"No, you precede me," chuckled the large gentleman.

"Very witty! But, don't forget, you said humorists die."

"No, I don't forget. In the end, we must all die. Humorists and solemn owls alike. Life would lose most of its strain if we realised that death was not an avoidable issue, but was merely a matter of a date."

"And this is my date?"

"I'm afraid so. Now round to the left a little."

"You haven't thought that it may be yours?"

"Oh, yes, I have. But I'm giving you the preference. Now round this tree."

"Where are you taking me?"

"My dear young—enemy!" The large gentleman corrected himself amiably. "Why be impatient to see an unpleasant sight?"

"Oh—just natural curiosity, I expect."

"Well, it will be satisfied in a moment. Only a few steps more. Here we are. . . . Halt!"

Freddy stopped. Indeed, had he walked on, he would have walked over a precipice. Ahead of him was a deep, scarred pit, an excavation of the past that had fulfilled its original purpose, and was now to be used for one not in the original design.

One little shove, and over a man would go, landing at the bottom with a broken neck. . . . And then, presumably, the man would be picked up, and carted to a motor-car. . . .

Behind them, like a frowning shadow, was the back of the tall house. As he had passed round it, Freddy had glanced upwards, and had seen the dim light still gleaming faintly, and also the closed window at the upper end of the water-pipe. He wondered whether anybody were at the window with the light? Whether the eyes that had recently looked into his across a pretty dinner-table were looking at him now—looking at him with fear, and sympathy—and understanding! Understanding! Yes—if she were looking, and understanding . . .

"You know—all this is new to me," said Freddy, with odd simplicity. He supposed it was his voice. It gave him a queer sort of pleasure to find that he could still use it. Soon the voice that was Freddy's would be lost in the chaos of eternity. There would be plenty of other voices like it, but the voice itself would be gone, like a snuffed light, since the instruments that produced the voice could never be reassembled. . . . "Are you really serious?"

"Yes, I am really serious," replied the large gentleman, and a note Freddy had not remarked before was behind his words. "Killing is not the pleasantest part of the game. In this case, however, it is sheer self-preservation. Or—am I wrong?"

"No—you're damn right," answered Freddy, and prepared to twist his body round and hurl it at his captor.

His captor was waiting for the movement. He was quite ready for it. But he was not ready for a broken bottle that suddenly came hurtling down upon his head.

He started violently, shouting with the pain of that impact. His hands shot up, and the revolver slipped down. A moment later Freddy's arms had gripped him frenziedly, and had hurled him into space.

24

Up the Water-Pipe

Freddy stood on the edge of the precipice, numbed. Somewhere in that black hole below him lay a man with whom he had spoken only a few seconds ago, and who had expected that, at this moment, he himself would be staring down at—Freddy! Yes, Freddy ought to be there! He, not the large gentleman, should be stretched out in oblivion, his little span completed, his insignificant song sung. Yet here he was, free to continue his span, to go on with his song, and to hold still to the sweet hope of immortality!

Then the numbness passed, lifting from him like a bad cloud, and reaction followed. He was free, and he must make use of his freedom! Turning swiftly, and wrenching his thoughts as well as his body from the depths, he stared at two objects on the ground before him. One was the dropped revolver. He stooped and seized it greedily. The other was the broken bottle.

It was this bottle that had saved his life. Where had it come from? Why, from the house, obviously! But from what part of the house, and who could have thrown it?

Now he raised his eyes and stared at the house. The dim light still glimmered from the high-up window. As he stared, a shadow appeared on the blind; a shadow, it seemed, of a small head. But then, as the shadow vanished, another window caught and held his attention. It was the window to which the water-pipe ascended—and it was open!

"By Jove!" thought Freddy. "So *that's* where it came from!"

A second thought swiftly followed. The window had not been open a couple of minutes earlier. Whoever had opened it had only just done so!

He gazed at the window, searching for some sign of the person behind it. No one was visible. Surely this was odd? If the person were a friend, there could be no object in concealment. If it were an enemy, why had the bottle been thrown? Well, it was profitless to propound questions. The thing to do was to find answers. And the answer to this question lay at the upper end of the water-pipe!

Freddy was a good climber. The water-pipe was a thick water-pipe. These facts, to which were added the substance of a stout vine, assisted Freddy on his way; but as he neared the open window, which yawned down on him like a dark query, he had to cling tightly to retain his hold, and once, when a bit of the vine gave way, he nearly fell. If anybody had thrust a head out of the window at that moment, it would have been a very simple matter to have sent Freddy down to the ground far more swiftly than he had ascended.

Now the window was immediately above him. The gap between the window and the end of the water-pipe was greater than he had imagined. He seized a rotting vine that formed an insecure link, and it tore away in his grasp, but the momentary support of the vine assisted him to grip the ledge, and, after pausing for a few seconds, for his strength was giving out, he managed to raise himself to the ledge's level. Here he paused again for another little breather. He must have presented a strange sight to anybody in the room. But at first he thought the room was empty. Then, as his eyes grew more accustomed to the dimness, he made out a form on the floor. It was the workman.

Freddy was in the room in a bound.

"Damn them!" he muttered, bending over the prone figure. "What have they done to you?"

"Get 'un on the 'ead—tha's the spot—get 'un on the 'ead," mumbled the workman without moving. "Now, then—let 'er go!"

"You threw that bottle, did you?" asked Freddy, quickly.

"Even if yew miss 'un, 'twill make a noise," murmured the workman. "Bang on the boko! Tha's good! Bang on the boko!" There was a dull stain on the carpet, suggesting delirium, but suddenly the workman moved his head and peered at Freddy.

"'Allo," he said. "Where did yew come from?"

"The water-pipe," answered Freddy, in a low voice. "Look here, old chap, are you badly hurt?"

"Water-pipe!" said the workman. "'E could never climb that. Not possible! Still—'e want tew try—now, if I can run and get tew the window. . . ."

Very gently, Freddy shook the delirious figure. The workman closed his eyes, and opened them again.

"'Allo!" he said.

"Splendid! Stick it!" smiled Freddy, encouragingly. "How are you feeling?"

"I be dead," responded the workman, solemnly. "Tha's wot I be. Dead. Ay, but I give 'em the slip fer a bit. Got tew open the winder, see? Tha's right. Waterpipe." He frowned, shook his head, and rambled on again. "Ay, but yew can't do it, sir! Too thin! 'Oo could?"

He closed his eyes once more, and seemed to fall asleep. His sudden silence gave Freddy a nasty shock. But a hasty examination told him that the man was still alive, and that probably all he needed was a doctor.

"Seems rotten, old chap," he muttered, "but I'm afraid I'll have to leave you for a bit. Back as soon as I can, though."

He ran to the door. It was locked on the passage side. Freddy swore. . . .

Standing by the door, he did a bit of reconstruction. This was what must have happened. The workman had evidently dodged that first shot, or at least had not been brought down by it. He had raced to this room, and had either been shot here again, or had succumbed to the effects of the original shot. Then they had locked him in, and he had managed to crawl to the window, open it, and throw the bottle out. Afterwards, he had presumably fainted off again. . . .

Right. So much for that. But what were the other inmates of the house doing meanwhile? Where were they *now?* Waiting for the large gentleman to return to them? Searching for him in the grounds? Or—

Freddy's forehead became suddenly wet as another idea flashed into his mind. Suppose, the alarm having been raised, they were now preparing to depart again? Suppose they were carrying Lydia Leveridge to another spot—while he remained impotently locked in this room! The thought sent him speeding to the window. He would have to negotiate the water-pipe again! That was, if—

A soft step sounded in the passage. Quick as a flash, Freddy was back again by the door, whipping his revolver from his pocket. The step paused outside. The key was turned.

"Now for it!" thought Freddy.

The door opened inwards. As it swung towards him, he kept behind it, his revolver gripped firmly in his hand. He was in no two minds about the revolver. If necessary he was going to use it, and without any preliminary argument.

Now the door was open wide. The person outside was entering.

"Hands up—*and sharp!*" cried Freddy, springing from his concealment.

A quick gasp answered him, and from one of the raised hands flashed a ruby ring.

"God!" Freddy almost sobbed, and caught the girl as she swayed.

From the floor came the workman's mutter,

"Yew can't climb that water-pipe, sir. Too thin! Never do it!"

25

ROSE

Joy and terror tread on each other's heels. While you are experiencing the one, the other may be waiting for you round the corner. A few minutes ago Freddy Reeve had been standing on the brink of a dark pit with, by all the laws of logic, one second between him and Eternity; but the laws of logic had slipped aside, Eternity had missed him, and here he was with a girl clasped in his arms, her heart close to his, hair touching his cheek. No, not a girl! *The* girl! The girl who had caught his careless eye in a dingy London terminus, who had turned a holiday train into a train of mad adventure, and whom he had sought through rain and storm and darkness!

"I don't understand it," thought the simple part of Freddy. "I simply don't understand it."

The girl did not understand it, either. The sight of Freddy had turned her own world topsy-turvy, and had caused her to yield, for the first time, to her weakness. In a sudden confusion below she had managed to give her jailers the slip; now she was confused and breathless. . . . But she was the first to recover. Freddy felt her body stiffen and grow tense against his, and a moment later she had conquered herself and had sprung away from him.

"What's happening?" she panted.

"I don't know," he answered. "All I know is that I've found you, and that I'm going to get you out of here!"

"No—not yet!"

She was speaking to him, but he realised that he was receiving only half of her attention. The other half was out in the passage.

She was listening intently. From below came muffled noises, but they told no story to Freddy's confused mind. What was happening? she had asked. Freddy had no notion. Out of his confusion, however—out of its glory and fears and urgency—he strove to be constructive.

"Yes, I'm going to get you out of here *now,*" he said. "There's not a moment to lose!"

"Corse, 'e *might* do it," murmured the workman from the floor. "'E's a slippy sort o' chap. . . . An' we've got tew save the gel, don't yew see?"

The workman's voice, inexplicable as it must have been to the girl, seemed to pierce the wall of her numbness. She might have stared at him, asked who he was, and how he had got there. Instead, she used his words as a springboard for the next idea. She turned suddenly to Freddy, and her eyes were alive with a kind of pleading necessity. In their need they sent fierce little darts rough him, darts that pricked him further into her service; but he longed to see the eyes smiling and serene, and wondered if he would ever see them so.

"I'm not the only one you've got to save!" she whispered tensely. "We can't talk now. Later. But there's another—a little girl—I must get her—I *must!*"

Something flashed into Freddy's mind. A little girl. Hadn't he heard something about a little girl . . . why, yes! Rose Terrence! The large gentleman had mentioned her. . . .

"Help me find her!" the girl said. "I'll go then—but not before!"

The noises below became more distinct. A door slammed. Someone was issuing a sharp order. . . . Rose Terrence! Yes, of course. But what had Lydia Leveridge to do with Rose Terrence? . . .

"God!" exclaimed Freddy, in a sudden blaze of light. "You've come here for her—let yourself be kidnapped so you could find her—"

"Quick! Quick!" pleaded the girl. "For heaven's sake!"

Then Freddy's mind moved. It seemed as though it had never moved so fast or so clearly before. Bad things were happening down below. Dangerous things. He must not let this girl run into those bad and dangerous things. Nor must he leave the workman at their mercy. Good chap, that workman—good chap! Get him a new bicycle some day. . . . And Rose Terrence. He must get Rose Terrence! Rose Terrence meant the world to Lydia Leveridge, who had run into all this danger for the child. Yes, but how had she. . . . Well, no time for that now! What were the three things he had to do? Oh, yes! Just stick to those three things for the moment. . . . The girl—the workman—Rose— "What are you doing?" exclaimed the girl.

"Don't interfere, or I'll crack up!" replied Freddy, at the door. "I'm not good at this sort of game, but just obey me and we'll be all right!"

She sprang to him, and caught hold of his shoulders. Her lips were close to his.

"I've got to find that child!" she cried.

"Yes, you're *going* to find her," answered Freddy, struggling against the intoxication of the moment. "Rose Terrence. I know." Her grip on his shoulders loosened, and she stared at him. "You see, I know more than you think. You can trust me. And then—that chap down there. We owe him something, too. We've got to think of him, as well as Rose Terrence."

"But—do you know where she is?" gasped the girl.

"Yes," replied Freddy. "I've *seen* her!" He seized the door-knob. "Look here—while I'm gone, go to that fellow on the floor. Let him see you. Let him touch you. Let him know we've *done* it, eh? He needs a bit of comfort!"

The next instant Freddy was out of the room.

The room with the light—the room where he had seen that small face! He knew the position. On the next floor, and then two rooms farther along the passage. Right at the end. P'r'aps there was a second staircase somewhere. A back staircase. By Jove, yes! . . . just along there. . . .

So the whole thing was a frame-up! Lydia Leveridge had allowed herself to be kidnapped in order that she could find out where Rose Terrence was. And those other two— the fellow in the brown suit, and the clergyman—must have been detectives who were to try to follow her, and form the connecting chain between her and the world of security she was voluntarily leaving. . . . Dash those noises below! They were getting louder. . . . And, of course, she didn't want Freddy to interfere because, if he prevented her from being kidnapped, or did anything to scare the kidnappers, the whole plan would fall to the ground. . . . Ah, here he was! Top of the back stairs. Now which way? To the right, of course. . . . Jolly plucky girl, Miss Leveridge. And jolly plucky fellow, her father, writing to the papers like that, and baiting the trap! No, but was he plucky? Had he any right to let his daughter run into such danger? . . . And then, those rings! What about those rings? . . .

The noises below were ascending. Ahead was a door, to the right of the passage. It was the third door, the only door under which a streak of light gleamed. . . . Probably the clergyman had been afraid to trust Freddy, too, lest he should make a muddle of things. . . . Yes, but here he

was—he, Freddy—at the door, and where was the clergyman? Where was the man in the brown suit? Where was
the whole blessed police force? He, Freddy Reeve, he and
a common workman—*they'd* pulled it off. . . .

During all this confused thinking, thinking which he
tried to avoid but which came rushing at him like a suddenly released flood, his body was responding to all the needs
of the moment. He had reached this door without pause,
and his hand was now on the knob, turning it. He could
do no more than turn it, however. The door was locked.

"Well, of course, it would be," thought Freddy. "I'll
have to smash it in, that's all."

Freddy had reached the mood that towers above circumstances, and he was going to save Rose Terrence if he
had to smash in fifty doors.

"Damn!" he muttered, the next instant.

The noises were now definitely approaching him. Feet
were hurrying in his direction. The play wasn't over yet.
Something would happen in a few seconds at this door!

He steeled himself. Then, all at once, he relaxed, or
rather passed into a new kind of tension. Madness to stay
by this door! He had to get the door *open!* Probably the
person who was approaching had come for that very purpose, too. Well—why not let him do it?

There was an angle at the end of the passage. In a flash,
Freddy had dived round it. He was not a moment too soon.
A figure came hurrying into view. It was the horsy man,
the man with the too-compelling eyes.

The eyes were not fixed on Freddy, however, as they
had been during those distressing moments in the train.
They were fixed on the door with the crack of light under
it. With fierce joy Freddy noticed that the man had a key
in his hand. The key made sweet, metallic music in the
lock. It turned. The door was thrust open. . . .

"Hands up," said Freddy. "And, by God, I mean it!" The horsy man stopped abruptly, as though he had already been shot.

"I shoot when I say three," said Freddy. "One—two—" The hands went up.

"Get in," said Freddy. "Get in, and then lie down flat on the floor. Face downwards."

He had left his place of concealment now, and was pressing his revolver into the horsy man's back. The operation gave him a fiendish satisfaction. Peaceful, law-abiding Freddy Reeve was enjoying the unchristian business of making another man suffer. This same revolver, not long ago, had been pressed into his own back!

"What the devil—!" snarled the horsy man, fuming.

He was like a volcano, longing to throw off lava. But a lid had descended upon him.

"Flat on the floor, d'you hear?" roared Freddy. His hand shook. The trigger was nearly pulled in the tension of the moment. *"Face downwards!"*

The horsy man obeyed. And from a little bed across the room, a small, white-faced girl stared at her visitors in sobbing terror.

Three seconds later, Freddy had the child in his arms. Or, rather, in one arm. The other never ceased pointing towards the man spread-eagled on the floor. In another three seconds, the door of the room had been closed again, and locked, and the man on the floor had the room to himself.

Reaction set in as Freddy hurried along the passage with his precious, warm bundle. The child was quietly crying. Suddenly, to his profound astonishment, Freddy found that he was crying, too. "Good Lord! What are we blubbering about?" he asked. "Everything's all right now!"

The child clung to him tighter.

"Listen, Rose!" he whispered, comfortingly. "You see, I know your name, even if you don't know mine. I'm taking you now to a great friend of yours, so you needn't worry any more. It's really she who's saved you, not me—but you'll hear all about it presently."

"Who is it?" the child asked, through her tears.

"Miss Lydia Leveridge," answered Freddy.

"Who's that?" said the child.

Who was *that?* Freddy's mind refused to admit the question. It had grappled with all the questions it could manage.

Now they were down the back stairs, and he was listening to the room in which he had left Miss Leveridge and the workman. Thank heaven, the passage was clear! But as he reached the door a fresh sound fell upon his ears. Somebody was running up the main staircase towards them.

There was no time to lose. He would be powerless to use his revolver unless he set the child down, and he could not set the child down in the passage. He sped to the door. It was open.

"Miss Leveridge!" he cried.

Something shot out at him and struck him on the forehead. With the child in his arms he was unable to retaliate. The next moment the child was seized from his arms and a second blow, this time on his chin, turned the world black.

26

GRIM COMPANY

Few people seek oblivion, but there is this to be said for it. It wipes out trouble. For a number of seconds Freddy Reeve had no trouble in the world, becoming as great as William the Conqueror, Canute, and the First Man. But the oblivion that blessed him was merely one of those temporary glimpses of ultimate peace, and he soon returned from its velvet security into the less kindly consciousness. While William the Conqueror, Canute, and the First Man remained great in their dust, the flesh of Freddy struggled back to its battle against crumbling and resumed its necessary agonies.

He struggled back slowly. At first he did not want to come back at all. It was much more restful down here on the ground, where there were no riddles and responsibility. Why not stay here, drifting on this pleasant black tide? It was soft and comfortable, even though the tide was speckled with disturbing points of gold that pricked and worried and tantalised. Soft and comfortable . . . soft . . . yes, by Jove, *soft!* And surely not the softness of the sea—or of a hard floor? Because . . . of course, he was on a floor! Somebody had hit him. Had hit him a hammering blow. And he had fallen to the ground. And now here he was, opening his eyes, and the ground beneath him ought to be *hard!* Yet it wasn't! It was soft. Soft like a large sack filled with sand. Perhaps he had fallen on a sack?

He groped with his hand, still disliking the idea of exertion. His hand told him that he was not lying on a sack. It told him that he was lying on a body. . . .

Activity returned galvanically to the dazed man. He scrambled to his feet, and then turned to regard the body he had been lying on. It was the workman's body, but whereas formerly he had regarded it with pity, now he regarded it with horror.

"Hallo, old chap!" he muttered foolishly. "How are you?"

It was a grimly ridiculous question. Merely a device to frustrate reality. It was quite obvious how the workman was. The workman was dead.

Freddy knelt down by the prone figure. A dull mark on the face had not been there before. The workman must have received some fresh wound . . . yes, and the body was in a different spot, too! As Freddy visualised the scene conjured up by these two circumstances—the circumstance of the fresh wound and the altered position of the body—his heart became cold with hate. He was almost awed by the sudden intensity of his own anger and the new impulses set up within him; for the scene he visualised was a brutal one. It was of a sudden attack upon this room during his own temporary absence, of the overpowering of the girl, and of the battering of an already wounded workman who was struggling to the girl's assistance. After that, Freddy had received his own quietus, the child had been snatched from him, the villain had fled. . . .

Yes, he had fled, but he could not have got very far yet. Even if he had got far, he must be found, and "Paid" must be put to his account.

Freddy stared at the silent form of the workman, and his soul groaned. "*I* brought you to this!" he thought.

All he could see was his own responsibility, but had he been in a mood to delve he would have seen further. Our fates are formed by our own characters, not by the chance adventures we meet along the road, and though it was Freddy who had offered this adventure to the workman, it was the workman's own spirit that had accepted it and that had brought him to his heroic end.

He turned to the door. It was closed. He ran to open it. It was locked.

Obviously, the door would be locked! But the obviousness of the imprisonment did not make it any the easier to bear. He turned from the door to the window, and here another disappointment met him. To climb up the water-pipe had been difficult enough; to climb down it would be impossible. The vine that had formed a feeble connecting link between the top of the pipe and the window had been torn away, and was now hanging uselessly, out of reach. Freddy was imprisoned with a dead man, and saw no possible means of escape.

He had been in many unenviable positions since the 5.18 had steamed out of Liverpool-street station, and once had been on the very brink of eternity, but no position had left him more blank than this. Even on the brink of eternity he had been face to face with his adversary, and his mind had been working incessantly. Now there seemed nothing for his mind to grip on to. He tried to batter the door down. The sound of his blows echoed mockingly through the house. He went again to the window, and confirmed its hopelessness as a means of exit. All he could do was to wait, while a dead man who had saved his life lay accusingly before his eyes.

What was happening outside the locked door? He listened, but all was silence. Had the rascals flown, or were they still in the house? What sounds would his ears have recorded if they had not been cheated during his period of insensibility? The silence was not proof of either alternative, but the conviction grew in Freddy that a flight had been accomplished, and that he and the dead man were alone in the house. Would not a flight be logical? For all the rascals knew, others might be following Freddy to the house. And, if they were still here, surely some sound would intrude upon the stillness—a footstep, a door closing, a whisper, an exclamation!

Suddenly, as he listened, his nerves grew tense. The silence had been broken at last. Somewhere above him, a banging had started.

He tried to locate it. It was not immediately above. On the next floor, a room or two away. . . . Yes, of course! The horsy man! Freddy had left him locked in a room, and he had the key in his pocket!

"By Jove!" he thought. "If they don't smash that door in, they'll come for the key—and they'll get a warm reception!"

He put his hand into his pocket. The key met his fingers comfortingly. Splendid! Splendid! He had one up on them, anyway. Of course, they would get the key in the end, but he'd make 'em fight for it. . . .

"No, I'm damned if they'll get this key!" he muttered suddenly. "I'm damned if they will!"

He took the key from his pocket, walked to the window, and threw it out. It sailed through the darkness, as a broken bottle had sailed that night before it, and ended down the pit. Had Freddy known it, he might have drawn some ironic satisfaction from the fact that he had hit the large and expansive gentleman again, although the large and expansive gentleman was beyond caring by now whether anybody hit him or whether he was left in peace. It will be remembered that he had joined the august company of William the Conqueror, Canute, and the First Man.

But even Freddy's more modest satisfaction was short-lived. The key had scarcely disappeared before a crash above indicated that the key would not be required. The door had been broken down.

"Damn!" thought Freddy. "Now what?"

Silence followed. Three minutes went by. Then a door banged, and a few seconds later the engine of a car began to purr outside. At the window once more Freddy craned his neck, but he was on the wrong side of the house to see anything, and he could merely picture the departing car in his mind—picture it with its inmates, two of them bound or drugged.

In a sudden frenzy, he flung himself at the door again. The door took no notice. "What's the good of attending to you?" it seemed to say. "Really, some people never learn!" The door that had been forced above was an older door, and there had been more than one weary man to force it.

Beaten, Freddy left the door, and sat down beside the workman. While struggling for something constructive to do, it occurred to him that he had not examined the workman thoroughly to make sure that he was dead. Suppose he wasn't dead? Suppose, after all . . .

He knelt down beside the body, almost in a panic, and opened the shirt. It was a cheap shirt, but it was not a dirty shirt. The fellow had had some self-respect. Freddy applied his ear to the rather thin chest and listened for heart beats. The tiniest voice within that silent frame would have whispered the message, "He is alive." But there was no voice. A watch had stopped that could not be re-wound.

A bit of broken mirror suggested another test. He placed it close to the workman's mouth. The mirror remained bright and unclouded. Yes, the workman was undoubtedly dead. And this confirmation of his original impression was almost a relief. If the workman had not been dead, but dying, a fresh problem would have presented itself. That, at least, was spared!

The minutes slipped by. Freddy struggled against a hopeless apathy that began to settle upon him. Partly to dispel the apathy, and partly because hope springs eternally in the human breast, he had periodic spasms of abortive activity. He renewed his fruitless onslaught against the door; he climbed as far as he dared out of the window, and then climbed back again since a broken neck would assist nobody; he shouted. But nothing happened. The house mocked at his efforts, while the minutes went on slipping by.

But, all at once, something did happen. The house that had appeared as dead and as silent as the work man on the floor began to rustle with little sounds. At first Freddy did not believe the sounds. He thought they were creations of his mind; for just as your eyes can hatch a sight that is not present, so your ears can hatch a sound that does not exist. These little sounds, surely, were mere echoes of desire! But soon he realized that, even when you are in a highly strung, imaginative mood, reality can enter. These little sounds were *real!* That soft pad-pad—some foot had caused it. That queer slither—a shoulder against a wall? That rhythmic intrusion on the silence, dividing it into small portions without any coherent contribution to the portions—might that be breathing? Breathing half-suppressed, but beating its hushed measure because Life insisted that it should even against all caution! Yes—it *was* breathing! And Freddy held his own breath as he suddenly realised that the breathing was taking place right outside his door.

"Now for it," thought Freddy, steeling himself.

For instinct told him that in a few seconds the handle would be tried, and the key turned, and the door slowly opened. . . .

Ah! He was right. The knob moved and revolved. Then it moved and revolved back again. Then, with just the tiniest squeak, the key was turned, and the little bit of metal that had denied Freddy freedom had slipped back into its socket. Then the knob revolved again, and the door slowly opened.

Freddy longed for his pistol, but that, of course, had been taken from him. Still, a fist could be useful, and especially so when backed by such ire as was in Freddy's soul.

"God, he's going to get it!" thought Freddy.

The door was now open wide enough for the visitor to enter. It became motionless again. The visitor, still unrevealed, was staring in. Behind the door, Freddy waited.

He waited an eternity; then something gave way in him and he could wait no longer. He pulled the door wide with a quick tug. Before him stood the man in the dark brown suit.

27

The Man in Brown

"Put your hands up," said the man in the brown if suit.

The request did not ease the situation.

"Why?" demanded Freddy, struggling to remain intelligent through his stupefaction.

"The reason's staring you in the face," replied the man in the brown suit.

The reason was a revolver.

"Well, the reason's not good enough," answered Freddy. "Shoot, if you want to."

"Suppose I do?"

"Then I'll go to Kingdom Come."

"That would be a pity."

"You bet it would. But I've nearly been there before this evening, so I'm getting used to the feeling. By the way, why aren't *you* in Kingdom Come? I thought you were shoved out of a train in a tunnel?"

The man in the brown suit frowned.

"Oh—so you know about that?" he enquired. "Tell me a few more things you know."

"Why should I?" retorted Freddy.

"Is there any reason why you shouldn't?" asked the other.

Freddy considered the question, watching his cross-examiner carefully, as he himself was being watched. Why shouldn't he? After all, this fellow was supposed to be a detective, according to the large and expansive gentleman. But, if that were true, why was Freddy being threatened by the law? And how the devil had the law escaped a cracked skull?

"I'm waiting," said the man in the brown suit.

"So am I," responded Freddy. "You see, there are questions to ask on both sides."

"Only I happen to have the advantage of you."

"That's admitted. Just the same, I *would* love to know why you're not dead, Mr. Biddock?"

The frown increased.

"Oh, so you know about that, also?" murmured the man in the brown suit.

"Yes. And I know you're supposed to be a detective," exclaimed Freddy, "and that you're supposed to be a friend of Miss Lydia Leveridge. But whether you really are or not I can't decide, with that confounded pistol aimed at my face!"

"Miss Leveridge," said the man in the brown suit, and now he looked at Freddy very intently indeed. "And how do *you* stand in regard to Miss Leveridge? Are you supposed to be her friend?"

"No. Not supposed to be. I *am!*"

"Is that why you're here?"

"I don't make a habit of visiting empty houses at night for fun. Look here! Are you under the impression that I'm one of these blasted kidnappers, and is *that* why you're threatening to shoot me?"

"If you are one of the blasted kidnappers, I'm under the impression that I shall shoot you—"

"Then, for the Lord's sake, don't play the giddy goat any longer," interposed Freddy, "because I'm on your side, and Miss Leveridge's side—"

"And on *his* side?" enquired the man in the brown suit, pointing to the body on the floor.

Freddy did not answer for an instant. He had momentarily forgotten all about the dead workman, and the sudden reference to him brought him up like a cold douche. He turned and regarded the silent form, then faced his interrogator again.

"Yes, and on his side," he answered, quietly. "If there's any more shooting to be done, believe me, I'd like a hand in it."

The man in the brown suit seemed impressed by Freddy's tone. All at once, he slipped his revolver back into his pocket.

"I'll take a chance on you," he said. "Let's have your story double-quick, and then, if there's time, I'll tell you mine."

"I'm not sure that there's time for either," answered Freddy. "How about taking each other for granted and letting the details go? We're not helping Miss Leveridge by standing here chatting."

"You're right," agreed the man in the brown suit. "If my head weren't splitting I'd be spry enough. What's the position here?"

"The position is that they've taken her away again."

"What's that?" exclaimed the other. "She's been here, then?"

"Of course! Didn't you know?"

"How should I? I followed a clue, but it was only a chance one. Just before I was shoved out of the train I got a bit of paper out of that rascal's pocket. It had this address scrawled upon it. So this really *is* the place, eh?"

"It is," said Freddy, "but now we've got to find another place. This poor chap on the ground here helped me to track the blackguards, and then he got killed in the fuss. As I say, they've now gone off again—"

"Taking Miss Leveridge with them?"

"Not only Miss Leveridge, but a child—"

"A child!" cried the man in the brown suit, interrupting again. "By Jove—the child was here, too?

Freddy nodded, and something rose to his throat. He had held the child in his arms. . . .

"I say, let's be going," he muttered. "Get a move on, eh?"

"Where shall we move to?" enquired the man in the brown suit. "I'm ready to follow any useful suggestion."

But Freddy had no suggestion. He had no notion whether the fugitives had gone north, south, east or west, and it suddenly dawned upon him that good intentions alone are not sufficient in this world. To continue the chase he needed a skilled brain to add to his own, and it was impossible for the skilled brain to function unless it had a clear knowledge of all that had happened. Freddy spent the next two minutes, therefore, in giving his new companion a brief and hasty account of all that had happened. The detective listened shrewdly, and at the conclusion of the narrative he pondered silently for several seconds. Then he said,

"The principal points we've got to take into account and deal with, then, are these. First, that poor fellow there." He looked towards the workman. "He is beyond our help, unfortunately, but of course this new crime will have to be reported—and it gives us, I think, an additional incentive to go on full tilt with this business."

"By God, it does!" agreed Freddy, fervently. "He was a great chap! I'd hang on for his sake, even if there were nothing else!"

"Second, there's Barlow."

"Who's Barlow?" demanded Freddy.

"The man *you* killed. Don't worry. You were justified in law as well as in fact. We don't hang people for defending themselves. Still, that's got to be reported, too." He paused, as a thought entered his mind. "If he *is* dead?"

"Good Lord—I never thought of that!" exclaimed Freddy. "But—he must be!"

"Well, we'll make sure. Third, Riggs. That's the chap you left in the cottage. At least, I imagine it must be, from your description. It was wise of you to leave that note. It may prove immensely useful."

"If anybody finds it," interposed Freddy.

"I think somebody's bound to find it," answered the detective. "I can hardly believe that your clergyman would have failed to return to the cottage after going to the police station. You were waiting there, you see. Yes, he'd undoubtedly return, or send someone. And either he or that someone would read the note, and follow you here."

"But no one has followed me here," Freddy pointed out.

"Someone's probably trying to find you at this moment," retorted the detective. "Don't forget your directions were necessarily vague. And don't forget, also, that before the note was found, the police at Aylsham had probably started on a fruitless journey to Thetford Heath. That had to be stopped, if possible. Your note involved a rather elaborate alteration in plans." He paused, and stared out of the window towards the spot where the man named Barlow lay. But Freddy knew he was not thinking of Barlow at that moment. He was trying to visualise events that had occurred earlier at Aylsham. "How's this?" the detective went on. "By the way, my name's Trant. What's yours?"

"Reeve," said Freddy. "But, for God's sake, go on! Aren't we wasting time?"

"We haven't wasted a second," answered Trant, definitely. "The people who waste time are those who run before they know where they're running to. A slow start is better than a false start. We had to learn each other, didn't we? To know how we stood with each other? And now we've got to work out a puzzle, haven't we?"

"Yes, of course. You're quite right," admitted Freddy. "But, somehow—standing here chatting like this gets on my nerves." And then he burst out, impulsively, "Those skunks! Why, at this very moment, they may be doing terrible things! And Miss Leveridge—she's waiting and hoping—"

"Don't get emotional," advised the detective, curtly. "*That's* waste of time, if you like. When I got shoved out of the train I didn't get emotional. I just said to myself, 'Is this it? Shall I be dead in a second? Well, I'll soon know.' And when I found I wasn't dead, but my head was full of splitting lights—you may like to know it still is—I said, 'Keep steady. Don't go off the handle. Stay and think. If you howl, you may upset everything.' I didn't even rush to a police-station when I crawled out of the tunnel. I couldn't trust my mind —it was playing tricks—and the whole position was too vague. There were enough of us on the job, too—one false move, and we'd scare our quarry, and never find out what we were trying to find out. . . . By Jove, my head was going round. Still is." Again he stopped speaking for a moment, and Freddy looked at him anxiously. For the first time he realised what the detective had gone through, and the iron control he had exercised to keep himself from "going off the handle," as he expressed it. Certain little attitudes of the detective became clearer to Freddy, too, as he listened. Trant was an ill man. He was thinking and acting under difficulties. No good trying to hurry him. Trant himself realised this. So, now, did Freddy, as the detective ran on: "No. I decided that it would be best to let matters proceed, and to follow my one clue. The paper I'd taken from Jarvis." That, concluded Freddy, would be the cockney bloke. "I'd go to the address it mentioned. So I found a doctor, and he patched me up, and I borrowed the doctor's motor-bike. God, it was a ride! Damned inconvenient, that storm! . . . Well, here I am. And now that's off my chest. Half a moment."

He sat down abruptly. He closed his eyes. But, as Freddy reached him, he opened his eyes again, and smiled.

"Don't worry. But just remember we're not quite two men. About one-and-a-half. Or perhaps only one, eh? You've been through a bit yourself."

"Yes, but I'm all right," said Freddy, quickly. "Would you like to sit quietly for a bit, while I have a look round?"

"What would you look round for?" asked Trant. "Oh— the relief party. Well, we'll do that together in a minute. But first let me finish my bit of reconstruction. How's this, for what happened at Aylsham? Clergyman sends police to Thetford Heath, returns to cottage, finds your note, and comes on here. No. He'd have to go back and tell the police first, wouldn't he? Yes. He goes back and tells the police. But the party has started. That means there are two jobs to be done—to stop the party, and to come on here. Stop the party first, eh, and then come on here? No. Too important to come on here. So there's a division of work. Some go to stop the party, some come on here. No—here's a likelier notion! Clergyman wouldn't go back to the cottage alone. He'd take a policeman or two with him. Yes—that's it. At least two people read your note. Back goes one to try to stop the police party, and to bring 'em to Holt instead of Thetford, while the other comes here direct. Something like that, anyway. So we can look out for assistance from two sources—from the person or persons who came direct from the cottage, and from the diverted police party. If this isn't clear, blame my head."

Now, then, he went on, "what happens here, meanwhile? You give our quarry a scare. They say to themselves, 'Things getting too hot here. We can deal with this annoying young man, and we have killed his companion'—that is, the workman—'but others will probably follow'—quite right, they will—'so we must do a flit.' Right. They flit. How? By car! The car you chased. Red. Something to know that. Where? To Thetford Heath?"

"Why, of course!" cried Freddy.

"No—not 'of course,'" responded Trant. "If they'd had a place at Thetford Heath, would Riggs have mentioned it at all? No reason why he should. He could mention anywhere. He wouldn't give away one of their haunts, even if it *wasn't* being used at the moment. No, not Thetford Heath. Anywhere in the whole world but Thetford Heath. You say your car is parked somewhere near here?"

"Yes, by some bushes," answered Freddy.

"Funny I didn't see it. Wonder if it's still there? We'll get along. But first let's have a look at Barlow. It's possible we may learn something from Barlow."

"You mean, you don't think he's dead?"

"He probably is dead. But a dead man's pockets can sometimes speak. Come on."

He rose. But Freddy found a sudden disinclination to leave. A sense of desertion entered into him, and for an instant he could not account for it. Then he realised that the reason lay stretched out on the floor.

"What about him?" he muttered, glancing at the workman.

Trant turned, and now he, also, stared at the workman.

"Believe me, Mr. Reeve, I'm not forgetting him," he said, quietly. "We're going to avenge him, aren't we?" Suddenly he knelt down by the workman's side, studying the immobile face. He studied it for quite awhile, and once he touched the lifeless arm. Then he rose, and remarked, as he walked to the door,

"All the brave men in this world aren't detectives."

28

In the Pit

The moon was rising. An edge of it slipped out of a great black cloud as Freddy and the detective entered the passage, and doors grew out of the dimness illuminated by the new pale light. The atmosphere was definitely ghostly. Freddy could not believe that he had set out on a holiday, and that others who had set out with him had received no similar interference with their plans. In joyous peace they had fallen asleep. In joyous delight they would wake up, and go down to the beach with bathing towels. The big wave that broke over them and knocked them down would form their great adventure. Adventure! What did they know of it? What had Freddy himself ever known of it? The 5.18 had opened his eyes to the meaning of fear, to the coldness of death—and to the warmth of life. Yes, with all its terrors and its risks, he would not have exchanged his adventure for the big wave and the mouthful of salt water! Before long, *he* might be lying somewhere, as others near him at this moment were lying, with a bullet in him, or with a broken skull. But, if it had to be, there would be something splendid in it, something warm that defied the cold. He would be no more dead, in spirit, than was the workman. The workman's body was stiff, but his soul had joined the ranks of glorious memories—and perhaps, if Freddy died, somebody would remember him, too. . . .

"Steady, you're getting ridiculous," warned the prosaic side of him. It was odd, how he could not help thinking of that workman. . . .

"Feeling all right?" queried Trant.

"Eh? Yes, of course!" answered Freddy, quickly. *"I'm* not the invalid. I say—what about these doors?"

"Just what I was thinking," said the detective. "I've not been all over the house yet."

"P'r'aps we'd better do it now?" suggested Freddy.

"No p'r'aps about it," responded the detective. "I was in the middle of the job when I came upon you."

They spent five minutes opening doors. It was an uncanny occupation. Every door held its little throb, its little expectation, its little disappointment or relief, according to how you looked at it. The doors of cupboards were the worst. A room, at root, is friendly. A cupboard is not. It is a tamed servant, serving us darkly. If it can revert to the black deeds of original windowless spaces it is only too pleased to do so. It will conspire with your own dressing-gown to give you a shock. Certainly, the cupboards in this gloomy house were nasty matters, and one under the stairs, divided by a couple of descending steps, was particularly unpleasant. It was on two levels, the front part forming the upper level, and the back part the lower. The back part had a dark angle, too, that required a deep breath to poke your head round.

Then there was one door, not of a cupboard this time but of a room, that was locked.

"We'll have to break this down," said the detective.

"Of course," nodded Freddy.

They smashed through it. A chair lost a leg in the process. The room was empty, like all the rest. The detective smiled.

"Clever devils, aren't they?" he said. "Out to waste our time, eh?"

"Looks like it," replied Freddy. "Well—what next?"

"Barlow next," answered the detective. "The house has told us nothing. Perhaps the grounds will."

They left the house. Twenty thousand years ago, Freddy had entered it up a water-pipe. As he looked at the water-pipe he wondered how he had done it. The reason, of course, had been the incentive inside. If the face is beautiful enough, you can jump from one skyscraper to another, or dive into a shark's mouth!

"This the direction?" asked the detective.

"Yes," said Freddy. "A few yards farther on. By that tree."

The moonlight made it an easy journey. They stopped where the moonlight ended in a pool of black windows. Somewhere in that pool lay Barlow.

"How are we going to get down?" enquired Freddy.

"Not the way *he* went," replied the detective. "I expect we'll find a spot if we move round a bit."

The ground sloped gently downwards on either side of them, and following the right-hand slope round the edge of the precipice they came shortly to a negotiable path. The moon illuminated the first portion, and the detective's torch illuminated the rest. The path turned and twisted, and ended in a large, stony pit. . . .

"I don't see him," muttered Freddy.

"Over there," said the detective, moving his spotlight.

"Yes—so he is," murmured Freddy; and added, despite himself, "Poor devil!"

"Don't see it," grunted the detective, as he walked towards the huddled form. "But for a fluke, you'd have been where he is—and *as* he is!"

"Yes, I know," replied Freddy. "Still . . ."

What he meant, but could not express, was that we are all poor devils, when we can get away from ourselves and look at ourselves. Poor devils doing our best or our worst, and moving very little this way or that from the impulses that were chained to us at birth. Blind, helpless devils, immensely confident, immensely self-opinionated, and immensely impotent.

"I'm not hard-hearted," said the detective, bending down, "but there are some things you can't forgive, you know."

"Daresay you're right," replied Freddy.

"I know I'm right," retorted the detective. "Crimes against women and children . . . and then, that workman! Don't you want to carry on for *him?*"

The bigness slipped from Freddy's soul, and the human littleness re-entered.

"You bet, I do!" he said. "I'm ready to do murder myself for that chap!"

"Not to mention Miss Leveridge? And that innocent little kiddie—"

"Shut up!" interrupted Freddy. "I'll hit, when you do!"

There was a silence. The detective was feeling about the body.

"Quite dead, I suppose?" queried Freddy, watching him.

"Quite," nodded the detective. "If any punishment's coming to him, it's out of our hands. Can't find any revolver on him."

"No, he dropped that before I—before I pitched him over."

"Oh, yes, so you said. And then the revolver was taken from you?"

"Yes."

"That's a pity. One each would have been useful. Hallo—here's something bulky." There was a pause. The detective was drawing something from the hip-pocket. "Case. Letter-case." Another pause. "By Jove!" murmured the detective, with a low whistle. "Small fortune here. Notes."

"How much?" enquired Freddy.

"It seems to run into thousands," replied the detective. "Pound notes—five-pound notes—hundred-pound notes. Some of the spoils, eh? Some they haven't been able to use yet."

"How do you mean?"

"Why, you can't cash hundred pound-notes too easily when the numbers are known and are being watched out for. I'll wager there was some language flying around when one of their victims sent along these! Still, all of 'em aren't big ones—and, anyhow, they always find ways in the end. What *I'm* thinking of is this. Are this fellow's cronies going to let all this stuff go?"

"I don't quite understand you," said Freddy. "They've *let* it go, haven't they?"

"Temporarily. But—wait a minute. Let me think." The detective closed his eyes, then opened them again. "Doesn't it occur to you that, at first, they may have thought Barlow was joining them in their get-away? And that, when they find he doesn't turn up, some one or other may come back and look for him?"

"Knowing we're here?"

"Knowing we've *been* here," corrected Trant. "But what should *keep* us here—excepting for the very knowledge we've just hit upon—the knowledge of something that may bring them back?"

"I see what you mean," nodded Freddy. "You detectives know how to work things out. But, look here—haven't they got something more important to do than to return for this money?"

"You evidently don't realise how much the money is," replied Trant, with a grim smile. "There are some five-hundreds here, as well. The price of a wife or a sweetheart, eh—or a mother? Or, again, of silence! Anyhow, here they are, and I reckon that, honestly come by, you could turn them into not far short of ten thousand pounds. That's worth a risk, isn't it, to folk who live by risks? Yes—I'm willing to wager someone will come back for these—"

"But they don't know they're here, in this pit," expostulated Freddy.

"No. They may not know anything, beyond the fact that Barlow is missing, and that the money is on him. On the other hand, they may know more than we give them credit for. We can't get entirely inside their minds, and my idea is that our friends are going to try to carry out two jobs before sunrise—the safe removal of Miss Leveridge and Rose Terrence to another place, and the regaining of this wad of notes. Which means," he added, thoughtfully, "that you and I will have to part company."

"Don't see why," grunted Freddy. "Shouldn't we stick together?"

"I'd like nothing better than to stick together," admitted Trant. "I've played a lone hand as long as I appreciate. But one of us has got to try to follow them and if we both go, who's to give them a welcome if some others of them come sneaking back?"

The logic of this was dismally apparent. Freddy, also, had had quite enough of his own company during the past few hours; moreover, he was beginning to realise that his brain was not strictly designed for detective work. Still, he wasn't in a mood to argue with a brain that obviously *was* so designed, so he murmured "Right-o," and asked for explicit orders.

"I think I'd better stay," answered Trant, after a few moments' thought. "Fact is, I'm still a bit groggy, and I don't know if I can last out another journey unless I look after myself for a bit first. Yes, but, after all, what about you?" he interrupted himself, abruptly.

"Fit as a fiddle," retorted Freddy. "Not a Strad, perhaps, but good enough to scrape a tune."

"Well, you're game, I'll say that, Mr. Reeve. Then it's agreed I stay here, while you go out and try to pick up the threads. You can use my motor-bike, if you like. You'll find it outside, fifty yards along the hedge. To the right. And I've a notion you'll find your car gone. Study the road marks. You may pick up tracks that way. Ask anybody you meet, provided you're lucky enough to meet anybody, if they can give you any news. Failing all else—and you probably will fail—get into Holt, and notify the police. Here—here's my card. This'll help you." He shoved a little piece of paste-board at Freddy. "Tell 'em quickly what's up, and then follow their advice. They ought to get into touch with Aylsham and Thetford, provided they've not already done so. My own view is that this is a dash for the coast. Probably Cromerwards—but, look here, are you taking all this in?"

"Every word," replied Freddy. "Forge ahead. I want all the points you can give me. Why Cromerwards?"

"Well, it's marshy towards the west, and if they struck the dikes at Blakeney and Cley they'd have the devil of a journey out to the sea, but at Sheringham or Cromer they could easily find a boat, and as likely as not they've got a friend in need hanging around there. Still, of course, this is only a guess. Put the idea up to the superintendent, and let him judge."

"Right," nodded Freddy. "Anything more?"

"Yes. You might get them to send a man or two here, if they can spare 'em. Only they must come cautiously—don't want them scaring the birds away if they're hopping back for the pickings!"

"I'll emphasise that. What else?"

"This," said the detective.

He held out his revolver. Freddy shook his head.

"Rot!" he exclaimed. "That's one order I'm *not* obeying!"

"Why not?"

"You may need it."

"So may you."

"All right," said Freddy. "I'll give you another reason. You're an iller man—and a better man—than I am."

"Without admitting the last part," returned the detective, "I'll now give you *my* reason. I'm not thinking of you, or of me. I'm thinking of—" He paused for an instant. "—of Miss Leveridge, and that little kid. They're better than both of us, eh? And it'd be preferable to lose this darned money in a scrap than to lose *them*, wouldn't it?"

"Confound you!" muttered Freddy, holding out his hand. "You do me every time, don't you?"

29

RIDERS THROUGH THE NIGHT

As the detective had predicted, the Citroen was no longer in its snug retreat, and Freddy had to embark on the next stage of his amazing journey on the motor-bike. It was his fourth conveyance since he had boarded the 5.18. He had begun the adventure in a train, had continued it on a push-bike, completed the third stage in a car, and was now ending it on a motorcycle. Would this last stage, he wondered, prove as eventful as those that had preceded it?

Despite Trant's dissertation on the situation, Freddy left the lonely house with only the vaguest idea as to what lay ahead of him. He was equally disturbed in regard to what lay behind him. Indeed, had he allowed himself to dwell too deeply on the predicament of a sorely fatigued and unarmed man who was liable at any moment to be set upon, he might have weakened in his resolve to go forward, and he might have gone ack. For this very reason he refused to dwell deeply on the past, but fixed his mind firmly on the future.

"Anyway," he reflected, "there's precious little chance that I shall pick up any clues if I waste time poking around here. I'll make straight for Holt—and I'll see that someone returns here to keep Trant company."

He did spend a few dutiful minutes "poking around." He searched for tracks and for clues that might have been provided by Miss Leveridge's further ingenuity, but he found no tracks that he could identify, in spite of the kindly moonlight, and evidently Miss Leveridge had failed this time to leave any guidance behind her.

"Well, that's that!" grunted Freddy. "Now for Holt. I hope to heaven the superintendent will be a reasonable and helpful sort of fellow!"

It took him a few minutes to find the direct Holt road. When he turned into it he let the engine have all it could stand. He had barely eaten up a mile, however, before he abruptly slackened speed. A figure was standing by the roadside.

"I want your machine," said the figure, coolly. "Stop, or I'll fire."

So he had established contact with the enemy already! Good! Now for it!

He swerved and ducked. No bullet came. Perhaps that was because he was slackening his speed. A moment later he had contrived to steer into a deep shadow, jump off his machine, and stoop behind it. Now his own revolver was brought into action.

"Put *your* hands up," cried Freddy, "or, by Jove, *I'll* fire!"

But no bullet came from Freddy's pistol, either. The figure now clearly silhouetted in a pool of moonlight was that of the clergyman.

And now Freddy saw something else as well—something that at first had escaped him. It was another motor-bike. The machine was lying in a ditch, and the clergyman's clothes were eloquently the worse for wear.

"Well, I'm damned!" murmured Freddy.

"You will be, if you stay gaping any longer," replied the clergyman, suddenly darting forward. "We'll take our mutual surprise for granted, and postpone exclamations, if you don't mind. Take me behind you double quick, and go where I say."

Freddy was not in a trustful mood. If a frog had hopped across the road he would not have accepted its harmless intentions without question. Nevertheless, there was something in the clergyman's tone that warned him against delay. And, after all, the clergyman was all right—wasn't he?

"Jump on," barked Freddy. "Which direction?"

"Left," answered the clergyman. "And all out!"

Freddy obeyed. As the motor-bike shot forward again like a joyous, noisy school-boy released from control, he felt the clergyman's hand against his back. For a moment he thought it was a revolver point. "Here, don't get jumpy!" he reproved himself. "Your passenger's an ally!"

They swung round to the left. Freddy discovered that he would not make a bad dirt-track racer. Ahead ran a narrow, straight road. The machine devoured it.

"Now where?" asked Freddy, as they came to a fork.

"Right," answered the clergyman.

The machine performed another miracle.

"Questions permitted?" enquired Freddy, without slackening.

"Certainly," responded the clergyman, "provided they don't interfere with efficiency. I'd like to ask a few myself. But yours first."

"Then whom are we following?"

"Miss Leveridge."

Freddy's heart leaped. So did the motor-cycle. Something definite, at last—something *definite!* No, not some thing! *The* thing! Look here—were they going to save her, after all? And was he, Freddy, really going to assist in the saving? . . .

"We'd better not get killed," came the clergyman's voice.

"They'd better try!" answered Freddy, ridiculously.

"They probably will, before we're much older. But, meanwhile, must *you* try?"

"Me?"

"Yes. Are we doing three hundred or four, do you think?"

"Oh, I see," grinned Freddy. "Well, we're in a hurry, aren't we?"

"The biggest hurry it's possible to conceive."

"Well, then—"

"I retract. You're right. Only you'll have to stop at the next fork, so I can look for marks. . . . No, no, don't stop! Just slacken. I'm banking on Sheringham, but it may be Cley."

Freddy slackened.

"To the right!" cried the clergyman, fixing his eyes on the road.

The bike leaped forward again.

"How did you find them?" asked Freddy.

"It was when we were trying to find *you*," answered the clergyman.

"You got my note, then, at Aylsham?"

"Yes. I returned to the cottage with a bobby after sending a party off to Thetford. If we're saving the situation, it's undoubtedly due to you. I sent the policeman back to headquarters to make a report, and cut across to Holt myself. Reported there. We weren't lucky for awhile. . . . To the left here, I should say. . . . Hey, don't shave trees like that! . . . And I followed two or three false scents. It wasn't till we were joined by some of the Aylsham police that we struck gold."

"You mean, you saw them?"

"Yes. The red car."

"Sure of it?"

"I recognised the driver. It was a rather horsy-looking individual who boarded the train at Norwich. You remember?"

"Of course, I remember!" muttered Freddy.

"When we heard the car coming we lay low, on the chance, but the wretched thing turned off before it reached us. I just had time to spot the colour of the car—and the face of the driver—and it was gone. Direction of Norwich. Of course, we followed."

He paused for an instant. Freddy did not. Their lane ran straight, and he was making the most of it. Soon, it would bend and twist again. . . .

Away to the left, beyond a little dip in the land, shimmered the line of the sea. It sent a salty breath across the marshes. Freddy turned his head to glance at the eerie scene, while the clergyman turned his head to listen.

"Keep on," said the clergyman. "I've a hunch we're right."

"I'm keeping on," answered Freddy. "You're clever if *you* can!" Odd, that he could joke! He had seen death, and might soon see it again. The next few minutes might bring him within sight of eternal glory or eternal despair. Dazzling gold, or blasting blackness. Yet he could jest! Quite, quite inexplicable! "Well, go on. Never mind me. You followed. What then?"

"Then I changed my mind," continued the clergyman. "I was behind—on my motor-bike—and just as I was about to put on speed to catch up with the police car, and pass it if I could . . . steady! . . . that's a pond! . . . I heard another car starting up. Can't say exactly what it was that made me so curious. Sixth sense, perhaps. But I'd been delayed a bit, and it occurred to me that this car was starting off in the devil of a hurry, and that its occupants might easily have imagined that I was well out of the way by now. My mind doesn't always jump to the right conclusion, you know, but sometimes it does—and jumps *fast!* I turned round, and in half-a-minute I found myself running straight for our old friend, the Citroen!"

"The Citroen!" cried Freddy. "Is *that* the car we're chasing now?"

"It is," answered the clergyman, grimly. "I knew it at once, as, you'll recall, I had travelled in it to Aylsham. And I knew the little cockney chap who was driving it. You get the idea, I expect? A blind! Red car is taking the hounds off the track. The real hare is the Citroen! And you and I, my friend, are after the real hare."

"I see," muttered Freddy. "Yes, I get the idea. What happened when you—"

"Slow up a bit," interrupted the clergyman. "We're coming to another turn. I say—look over across that flat stretch there—no, not directly towards the sea, more to the right. Towards Sheringham and Cromer. See anything?"

"You bet!" replied Freddy. Some miles away, a little silver beetle was running smoothly along a straight white line. The moon was generous to pursuers tonight, and ruthless on the pursued. "The Citroen!"

"I think so."

"I'm sure so!"

Behind Freddy's back, the clergyman smiled. He read in Freddy's conviction the intense desire to be convinced. Still, he would have wagered himself that it was the Citroen. And since it was on the Sheringham road, and its occupants did not know—yet—that they were being pursued, there was a sporting chance of an interesting encounter before very long.

"Left," said the clergyman.

"Right," responded Freddy, unconscious this time of humour. "I say, can you go on? What happened when you spotted the Citroen, and made for it?"

"The obvious," said the clergyman, grimly. "I came upon them too suddenly; they had a shot at me, killed a tyre, and sent me into the ditch where you found me."

"I see," murmured Freddy, reflectively. "I see." Then, suddenly, "Yes, but look here! That couldn't have been long before I came upon you!"

"No. It wasn't."

"Then—I don't understand! Why, they left the house long ago! I thought they were leagues away by now! Why on earth didn't they make off immediately? All at once he gave an exclamation. "By Jove—*got* it! They were hanging around somewhere waiting for that other chap to join them—the chap I killed!"

There was a short silence. The Citroen was no longer in sight for they had now dropped to the lower land themselves and had lost the sweeping view from the hills; but they were gaining on it. Then the clergyman said, quietly,

"So you've *killed* one of them? It's got as far as that?"

Freddy nodded gravely. "Yes—it's got as far as that. It was the elderly stout fellow—Barlow, didn't you say his name was? It was in the grounds of the house. He was just about to shove me over into a pit, but I managed to turn the tables on him—thanks to the workman."

"The workman?"

"Oh, of course, you've not met him. Chap I borrowed the push-bike from. He'd got into the house, you see, and managed to chuck a bottle at Barlow from a window just at the right moment."

"Then I hope I do meet him!"

A shadow passed over Freddy's face. "Afraid that's impossible," he answered. "They—they got back on him afterwards. At least, it wasn't exactly getting back on him, because if my theory's correct, they never knew that Barlow had been killed."

"Then how did the workman get killed?" asked the clergyman. "This is an even worse business than I imagined."

"Yes, it's pretty bad," agreed Freddy, "and I keep on forgetting that you don't know all of it. You must forgive me if I ramble a bit. Funny thing, but my head feels a bit light. I say, are we still going right, do you think?"

"Yes. Keep on. I know this coast road, and at this rate we'll soon be in Sheringham. You were telling me how the workman was killed?"

"Well, it was like this. I say, I believe we must be gaining! He joined up with me—real trump, that chap. If I get too sentimental or sloppy, jab me in the back. As I told you, he got in the house first, through a trick, spotted the trouble in the garden, and shied the bottle. He'd been winged even before that, but not quite outed. But when I got in afterwards—"

"How did you do that?"

"Water-pipe. Where was I? Oh, yes. I climbed into the room where he was, and it was after Miss Leveridge had joined us—she evidently managed to escape somehow—and after I'd found the kid—oh, but do you know about her?"

The clergyman did not reply at once. Something seemed to be happening to him, though Freddy was merely conscious of the silence. Then the clergyman said,

"Yes—I know about her. So—you found her, too? Well?"

"I was just bringing the kid to Miss Leveridge when somebody hit me and sent me to sleep. It was when I woke up that I found they'd sent the workman to sleep, also—for good."

There was a quiet tenseness in the clergyman's voice as he commented,

"Do you know, I think the people we're chasing are going to deserve all we're going to give them."

"Carried unanimously. Thank God, we've got a pistol each. Just the same," added Freddy, "I'm not sure but that one murder per night is about my limit. I think Barlow's enough to have on my mind at the moment."

"Don't worry," said the clergyman. "You've helped the world quite a bit by ridding it of Barlow. But how did you know his name was Barlow?"

"*You* told me, didn't you?"

"So you said a few moments ago. But I didn't tell you."

"Oh, no—of course," exclaimed Freddy, remembering. "It was Trant—"

"Trant!" cried the clergyman. "*Trant?*"

"Yes. Brown suit. One who was chucked out of the train."

"Good God!" murmured the clergyman. "How did *he* turn up?"

"Through having a pretty tough head, I should imagine," replied Freddy. "Heaven looked after him when he fell out into the tunnel. He turned up on the very bike you and I are riding now. But for him, I'd still be locked up in that house."

"Yes—that sounds like Trant!" muttered the clergyman. "He'd do it somehow! But where is he now?"

"He stayed behind."

"Why?"

"Two reasons. . . . Sorry—that was rather a sharp turn. Am I still right?"

"Yes. There's Sheringham right ahead. What were the two reasons?"

"One, he was groggy. I tell you, Trant's another white man. Two, he wanted to hang around in case anyone came back."

"If I know Trant, he had some solid reason for thinking someone'd come back," observed the clergyman. "Why *should* anyone come back? Let's hear Trant's reason!"

"This is the reason. We had a look at the body of that chap Barlow—and found a large wad of money on it."

"How much?"

"Pretty well all their savings, I should think. Trant said something about ten thousand."

"Ten thousand," repeated the clergyman. "Yes—that's worth going back for. Trant was right. Things are being knitted up, aren't they? The rascals waited for Barlow, who was to join them, and who had the cash. Barlow didn't arrive—for a reason *we* know, but *they* didn't know. When they couldn't wait any longer, they fled. One car went towards Norwich, to put us off the scent—and the police are chasing that. The other car is going along the coast— and *we're* chasing that! All quite clear, isn't it?"

"No. It isn't clear why they didn't go back to the house to find Barlow when he didn't join them."

"But that's clear, too. By that time the police were swarming around. They had Miss Leveridge and the child to deal with. Why, if they'd gone back, they might have run right into the police's arms, for all they knew—or else have led them straight to that ten thousand pounds! . . . Steady now for a bit. We're just getting into Sheringham. Slow down at the next corner, please. We'll probably have to stop."

A minute later they reached the outskirts of the town. The town itself lay mainly on their left. Had the Citroen turned into the town, or kept straight on?

"Afraid we'll have to stop," murmured the clergyman. "But get ready to go on again at once. I'm going to look for marks."

While the clergyman searched the road, Freddy stood beside the bike, ready for an instant resumption of the journey. He was not kept waiting long. Almost immediately, his companion returned to him.

"Straight on," he ordered. "They've gone on towards Cromer."

"How on earth can you tell?" asked Freddy.

"Defect in one of the back tyres," replied the clergyman. "I made a note of it at Holt. It shows quite clearly. Now, then—full steam ahead!"

Sheringham—Cromer! The two names suddenly flashed into Freddy's mind from a new angle. Or, rather, from their old angle. Two holiday resorts, to one of which Miss Leveridge had been travelling, while he had been travelling to the other! Well, Miss Leveridge had just completed her journey, and when Freddy reached Cromer, he would have completed his. But it did not look as though either of them were stopping!

They proceeded in silence. The road between Sheringham and Cromer is full of charm. It passes pleasant golf-courses, winds round pretty corners, and embraces amiable ruins and a couple of attractive villages. The happy aspects of the road were missed on this night ride, however, since each mile shortened security and brought conflict nearer. Freddy paid no attention to the ruins that slept in the moonlight waiting for some poet or leisured philosopher to awaken them. He did not notice West and East Runton as he ran through them. The disappointment of Sheringham—for he had counted on overtaking the Citroen by then—was causing him now to concentrate wholly on his job. Any further delay would not be due to Freddy Reeve!

"There's Cromer church," said the clergyman, as they topped a little hill and saw Cromer down beyond.

The sea was now close on their left. Ahead lay the tall church tower, almost unnatural in its clearness; below stretched the pier. And beneath roofs that became visible lay many sleepers who had journeyed with them on the 5.18. One sleeper awoke as the motorbike chugged by. "There ought to be a law against motor-cycling at night," he thought, darkly and unreasonably. He would have been astonished had he realised that his indignation was directed against two recent fellow-passengers.

They entered Cromer. Cromer is like a little, narrow maze. Every road seems to lead to every other road, yet until you are in the central square which is fathered by the church itself, each road is blind to its neighbour. You go round corners, and find you are almost at the spot where you began. You turn up a by-way, and discover yourself angling back to your starting point. Only the coast-line itself is definite, and the town straggles right to the coast and does not even permit the sea-road to continue uninterrupted along it. Thus, to resume the interrupted sea-road beyond the town, you have to negotiate the maze and wind your way in and out of it.

Somewhere in the maze, two engines were throbbing. One was the engine of a Citroen, the other of a motor-cycle. The Citroen was at the farther end, and the sound of the motor-cycle seemed to startle it into sudden action. Perhaps it had been conscious of the motorcycle before, or perhaps this was its first knowledge of it. The motor-cycle itself had taken a wrong turning, and was nearly coming to grief round a hairpin bend that swung unreasonably round a sea-wall.

"What's the matter?" barked the clergyman, as Freddy swerved and slackened.

"Mind out!" exclaimed Freddy.

They struck a seat that stood on the edge of the sea-wall. Next morning, a local official noted the mark with indignation, and blamed a small boy for the damage. But, several hours before this unjust accusation, the real cause of the trouble was examining the damage to a motor-cycle, which was far more important.

"Nothing vital, is it?" asked the clergyman, anxiously.

"No—something's jammed—soon have it right," replied Freddy.

"The sooner the better," muttered the clergyman.

The sound of the Citroen's engine grew fainter. The clergyman strove to remain patient. The two minutes he

had to wait seemed like twenty. Even two minutes can lose
a race.

Now they were off again. They wound out of Cromer.
At the farther end, a night stroller paused and stared at
them.

"Seen a car?" cried the clergyman.

"Ay," replied the yokel.

"Know which way she went?"

"Ay."

"Which way?"

"Same way."

"What do you mean?"

"Same way yew be goin'."

"Idiot!" rasped the clergyman. "You don't know which
way we're going! Did you see whether they turned to the
left along the sea-road, or whether they went inland?"

"No, I didn't see, but they went to Norwich."

"How do you know?"

"They asked me th' way, that's 'ow I know. 'Which way
to Norwich?' they asks me. 'Up the 'ill,' I tells 'em. Norwich."

"Then it's up the hill for us," said Freddy.

"No, it's round the coast road," retorted the clergyman.
"Those chaps know their way around here like a book!
Why would they ask the way to Norwich, unless it were to
put us off the track?"

At the spot where the roads divided, the clergyman
proved his case by the tyre-marks. They continued along the
coast road. Round more bends, up more hills, round more
bends, and down more hills. Down past another church,
from the churchyard of which quiet ghosts watched them
and recalled how they, in the ignorance of solidarity, also
used to rush and hurry and fret the days away; by poppies
and cornflowers, their sombre night shades silvered by the

moon; by the haunts of fishermen and the houses of those they served; by a big building that rose like a great windowed shadow on the edge of the cliff.

"Overstrand Hotel," murmured the clergyman, as they raced by. And added, incongruously, "The last time I came by here I was in flannels."

This was the last irrelevant remark made on that journey. From a spot some way ahead came the hum of the Citroen. It was the voice of the little silver beetle, and the voice grew louder every moment.

"We're catching 'em," muttered the clergyman.

Freddy did not reply. He knew it. The cycle shot forward dizzily. The silver beetle came into view. A moment later it was out of sight again, for the road bent and twisted continually, but when it came into view again, the distance between them had materially lessened.

"Keep it up," said the clergyman.

Freddy kept it up. The beetle was now beginning to show its emotion. It was behaving oddly, swerving from side to side to save a few inches when the road curved this way or that. It looked literally as though it were attempting to shake off its pursuer.

"Gone again!" murmured the clergyman. Then, a few moments later, "There she is. . . . Gone again! Heavens, what a road!"

Now they came to a great sweeping bend. They expected to see the Citroen again. It had vanished!

"Good Lord!" gasped Freddy.

"Right!" bawled the clergyman. "Right! Right!"

Just in time, Freddy saw the opening. He swung round into it, the machine tottering and straightening itself like a little steamer in a storm; they shot down a hill, under a little bridge, up a hill beyond, and on into narrowing lanes. The road seemed to be aiding them now, closing in on all sides, and impeding escape. It grew rougher, as well as narrower. The Citroen had erred in hoping to give its pursuers the slip and to find this a channel to safety.

They rounded the last bend of the chase. Ahead, almost within a stone's throw, was the Citroen. Freddy gave a final spurt, while the clergyman raised his revolver. It was levelled at the little window at the back of the car.

"Don't fire!" shouted Freddy suddenly. "You may hit Miss Leveridge."

"Miss Leveridge isn't there," replied the clergyman.

The next moment, his bullet had shattered the glass of the window to bits.

30

AT BAY

Freddy Reeve was to young to have been through the war, but he now experienced a little taste of it. He discovered what it was like to be in the midst of bullets, and to wonder when one of the bullets would be in the middle of him. The splintering of the little window in the back of the Citroen was the start of the battle.

A bullet came winging back from the car. It was very wide. The next shot came from Freddy's own revolver, though he did not remember raising his weapon or firing. Freddy's shot, also, went wide. After that various bullets spat into the night air, but they spat in a queer meaningless fashion, and none of them found a human mark. The whole thing was like an absurd game, yet a game that could change to reality at any instant. That was the unpleasant thrill in it.

This sense of playing a game was increased by the absence of Reality from the car itself. Had Miss Leveridge and Rose been there, every move would have been significant; and events, as well as aims, would have been directed by a simple, compelling emotion. The absence of the two girls, however, complicated the psychology of the situation, substituting irritation and anger for a more reasonable and comprehensible incentive.

After all, why were they all potting at each other? Wasn't the whole thing utterly senseless? Perhaps sheer funk and self-preservation were at work, demonstrating their dangerous nonsense because there had been no opportunity for preliminary negotiation! Yes, that must be it, decided Freddy, while he ducked into a shadow and raised his revolver to shoot out of it.

He found he was covering the cockney. The cockney was standing, hot and dazed, by the car. The fellow's spirit seemed to be wavering—or perhaps he had no more bullets? Freddy had a couple more. He could kill the cockney with one of them as easily as he could knock a box of matches off a mantelpiece.

But could he? He found he couldn't. And when he heard the clergyman murmur, out of another shadow, "Don't shoot," the injunction was quite unnecessary. The clergyman was covering the other late occupant of the car—the old woman. When Freddy had first come upon these two, bickering at the station and apparently at daggers drawn, he had little realised that before the next sunrise the pair of them would be standing shoulder to shoulder, fighting for their lives—against *him!*

From this moment, Freddy's mind began to clear. All that had happened before had been jumble. Now, clarity returned. The battle had been won—heaven knew how!—and the victors were in a position to dictate terms.

"Drop your revolvers, both of you," said the clergyman, quietly.

"Wot's the use?" growled the cockney.

"Do as I say."

"There's nothink more in 'em!"

"Do as I say!"

The revolvers slipped to the ground.

"Good. Now put up your hands."

"Wastin' time, ain't it?"

"I can see you have got an idea into your head that I am not serious," said the clergyman. "It will save your life, if you think it worth saving—a disputable point, I admit—if you now get it into your head that I am serious, and that I shall shoot you if you disobey a single order, or fail to answer a single question. You talk about wasting time. I don't want to waste any. That is why I tell you now, for once only, that I shall repeat no future order, nor shall I ask any question twice. You will obey me instantly, or you get a bullet. And your companion, too. Is that clear?"

Four hands went up.

"Thank you. Now, then. Where are your captives? Sharp!"

"Norwich," replied the cockney.

"You mean they were in the other car?"

"Corse they was. Mugs you were ter foller us—"

"I think we will decide whether we were mugs or not. Why didn't you go to Norwich, also?"

"Ter put you orf the track. Like we've done."

"Who *has* gone to Norwich?"

"The boss."

"Our horsy-faced friend?"

"Let 'im 'ear yer say it!"

"I hope he will hear me say even less complimentary things. What is his name?"

"Smith."

"Thank you. And what is his real name?"

"That is 'is real name."

"It is not his real name. And your captives have not been taken to Norwich. You've had your chance. Unless I get truthful answers to these two questions in the next ten seconds, you'll be shot like a dog."

"Oh, for gracious sake, let's get it over!" exclaimed the woman, bursting out suddenly. "His name's Chisholme, if you want to know. William Chisholme. And I wish to God I'd never met him!"

"Chisholme," repeated the clergyman. "So that's who he is! I've often wondered. And he's gone to Norwich?"

"Yes."

"Alone?"

"Yes."

The cockney spat, and gave it up.

"Why did he go alone?"

"He expects to join us."

"I see. And where does he expect to join you?"

"At Horsey."

"Fool!" muttered the cockney.

"Fool yourself!" retorted the woman. "What's the use? We're cornered, aren't we?" She turned to the clergyman again. "Yes, that was the idea. But it went wrong. And now you've got it."

"No, not all of it. There was another. Barlow. What about him?"

"P'r'aps you knows more abart 'im than we do," snapped the cockney.

"Is he joining you, too?"

"He was to have joined us, but he never did. So we couldn't wait any longer—"

"You were right," said the clergyman, turning to Freddy. "It was waiting for Barlow that caused the delay."

"Yes, but where's Miss Leveridge?" cried Freddy. "God! What does all the rest matter? What have you done with her?"

He flung the words at the cockney, but the woman answered.

"Oh, I'll tell you. She's still at the house—"

"What!" cried Freddy, in astonishment.

"Steady," murmured the clergyman. "Don't lower your gun." He turned to the woman. "Go on. Let's hear it. And double quick!"

"Well, I'm telling you, aren't I?" retorted the woman, irritably. "She's at the house still. So's the child. They're locked up in a cellar—you get there through the cupboard under the hall stairs—and there they were to stay until we got what we were after."

Freddy's hand shook, and the woman eyed his revolver apprehensively.

"Are you telling us that those two girls are locked in a cellar at this moment?" he cried.

"You've ears," grunted the woman. "Chisholme's got the key."

"Left there alone—perhaps to starve?"

"There's bound to be food there," interposed the clergyman. He spoke calmly, but beneath his calmness he was no less moved than Freddy. "Kidnappers cheat themselves if they kill their victims."

"Of course, there's food there," said the woman, scornfully. "Enough for a week! Think we're fools?"

"Come on! Let's get back!" exclaimed Freddy.

"We'll start as soon as we can," replied the clergyman, "but there are a few details to settle here first. We've got to get these people to the nearest police station. And we've got to arrange to have Chisholme met at Horsey. By the way, as Chisholme was your boss, I suppose he was also your financier? Your treasurer, eh? Carried all the funds?"

"Oh, shut up," snapped the cockney. "You make me sick!"

The woman, however, was more communicative.

"Shut up yourself!" she cried, raspingly. "Do you want to raise their tempers and be killed? What I say is, when you know you're done—let it go! You might as well tell straight out what'll be dragged out of you, even if you don't! Besides, what's it matter who was treasurer?"

"I'm still waiting to know," remarked the clergyman.

"All right. Chisholme was the boss, but Barlow was the treasurer—as you call him. It was because he was bringing along the funds that we waited for him so long. You see, we thought he might be quitting for good. Oh, I don't expect I'm telling you anything you don't know," she added shrewdly. "I expect you know a bit more about Barlow than you're saying. Do you?"

"I'm asking questions, not answering them," replied the clergyman. "Is there any rope in your car?"

"You may find some."

"Then stand aside. No—keep your hands up. You know what will happen the moment they come down."

They found a useful length of rope. It was evidently a part of their equipment. Two minutes later, the cockney and the woman were securely bound, and deposited on the floor of the car.

"What next?" asked Freddy, anxiously. "Straight back to Holt, eh, and drop 'em on the way?"

"You needn't stop to drop them, if you want to stick to your motor-bike," answered the clergyman. "In fact, I think you'd better get back there as fast as you can. Here, take this flash torch. You may need it in that cellar. I'll be right on your heels, remember."

"Right!" cried Freddy, and sprang to the machine. But, all at once, he paused, and his face fell.

"The key to the cellar!" he exclaimed.

"If Chisholme reaches Horsey, he'll be met there, and the key will be taken from him," replied the clergyman. "But Trant's theory was that Chisholme would return to the house. I agree with Trant."

"Mightn't he be caught already?" suggested Freddy.

"That's also a possibility," agreed the clergyman. "But, somehow, I think Chisholme will give them the slip. And, if he does—"

"Well, then, *we'll* have to catch him, instead," said Freddy. "I reckon we can!"

"I reckon we'll try," nodded the clergyman. "But it's going to be a race."

"It is," answered Freddy. "We'll win it!"

31

THE TRAP

The man in the brown suit, otherwise known as Trant, sat
on a little grassy mound and waited. He had been waiting,
it seemed, for an eternity, but there was nothing else to
do. He could not quit until his mission had been accomplished, or until someone came to relieve him, and apparently nobody was coming to relieve him. This disturbed
him, although he took the position philosophically. It
also surprised him. The arrangement had been that Freddy
Reeve should obtain reinforcements from Holt. He could
not believe that Freddy Reeve would deliberately ignore so
obvious a necessity.

"For it is a necessity," thought Trant, soberly. "I'm not
at all sure how long I'm going to last out."

He felt very groggy. Even the most hardened man cannot fall out of a train without experiencing some effects.
His mind was not as clear as it had been. The clouds were
rolling up again. When the enemy returned—*if* the enemy
returned!—he would not be in the fittest condition for the
meeting.

"Wonder what the time is?" he reflected.

His watch had been smashed several hours earlier
during his tumble into the tunnel. As he stared ahead of
him, however, the sky began to answer his question. Above
a clump of trees towards the east was a vague greyness. It

crept slowly upwards and outwards, advancing fan-shaped against the night. Saving for its promise it was scarcely preferable to the night, for it was cheerless and cold, revealing rather than illuminating man's misery. Ghosts that had been comfortably hidden now flitted faintly, like trapped phantoms. The clump of trees that had slept in the blackness shivered fretfully in this uncouth awakening. A bird, surprisingly close, made a clucking sound in its sleep. Gods and little insects! was it time to get up?

"Sunrise soon," murmured Trant. "Jove—wouldn't a cup of tea go to the spot?"

He watched the expanding grey patch above the tree clump. Then something stirred again. The bird once more? . . . No, not the bird this time!

Abruptly, Trant stiffened. His instincts were alert, and they told him that the thing that had stirred did not belong to the winged fraternity. They told him, also, that the stirring thing was not friendly. No sensitive night animal, suddenly startled, could have been more surely informed through its sixth sense that trouble was on the way.

Well, Trant expected trouble. That was what he was here for. And he was prepared for it; he had not entirely wasted his waiting hours. But one thing puzzled him. He had not heard any car approaching. Had he, perhaps, been asleep without knowing it?

Then the solution dawned upon him. The obvious solution. When enemies approach, they do not invite noise. True, this particular enemy did not expect there would be anybody here to be roused by noise, but he was not one to take undue risks, and he was a cunning customer. Trant maybe, was the last person in the world the enemy expected to find at the silent house to which he had returned; he had returned, nevertheless, primed to meet Trant, or anybody else, and the car he had returned in had evidently been vacated some way off, at a sufficient distance to render inaudible the sound of its engine.

Well, cunning could be met by cunning—as the enemy would find out!

"If only my head were clear!" chafed Trant.

That was the one weakness of his position. His buzzing head. His plans were laid, and well laid. If only he could keep steady . . .

A twig snapped. Hallo—there was one of his plans going west already! The enemy was not approaching by the front gate, but through a hedge. The hedge was very close. Confound it! Trant slipped from his grassy seat, and crouched by a bush.

A minute went by. Then a voice, scarcely more than a whisper, came through the opaque greyness.

"Barlow!"

Another minute went by. The whisper came again.

"Barlow!"

Now the enemy advanced once more. A vague bulk suddenly appeared not ten yards away, and was lost again a moment later. The enemy was creeping towards the house.

Trant stood motionless. He let the enemy reach the house. He heard the very faint sound of a key. Then he slipped swiftly after. He got to the porch just as the front door closed.

That didn't matter. It was all according to plan. Barlow was not in the house, and the enemy would soon come out again, and start searching the grounds. There was nothing else in the house to detain him. . . .

"At least," reflected Trant, "I don't suppose there is."

He waited outside. He was used to waiting by now. The enemy was remaining a long time inside! Or perhaps it only *seemed* long? Nuisance, having no watch. When your head's throbbing, you can't reckon time. But, surely, the enemy ought to be out of the house by this? What on earth was he doing? . . .

"Idiot!" grunted Trant, suddenly. "You know, this head of yours is going to lose you the game, if you're not careful!"

The *back* door, of course! The enemy would probably emerge from there! Trant had decided that he would keep both the back and the front under observation, yet here he was sticking only to the porch, like a fool! Self-anger merged into the throbbing. Quietly he hurried round the building. . . . Yes—there was the fellow! Poking around the back garden, sticking his nose into sheds and out-buildings. . . .

Ah, now he was near the pit! Trant's heart beat a little faster. From the security of the shadows he watched the enemy grope about, as a big-game hunter might watch some large animal for which he had dug a hole. The pit, of course, was not covered up as the hole would have been, but the bait was there. Human bait—golden bait—

"Hallo! *Now* what's he doing!" thought Trant.

The enemy appeared to be giving up the hunt. He had reached the edge of the pit, glanced down vaguely, and was now moving away again. Moving towards Trant!

"This won't do!" decided Trant.

You do not want to meet the tiger that has refused to drop into your hole! On the contrary, you must try to divert him back again. All this trouble for nothing? All this devising? And the world beginning to dance about, and turn black. . . .

If the enemy reached Trant, there was no hope. The enemy would be armed. Trant was weaponless. Even if the enemy were not armed—a ridiculous assumption in this case—he would still be strong, while Trant was weak. Therefore, the enemy must not reach Trant.

It was the instinct of self-preservation, as well as the instinct of preserving his plan, that caused Trant suddenly to stoop and find a stone. If he had not found the stone, the enemy would have been on him in a matter of seconds. The stone, however, altered the course of events. Trant did not throw the stone at the enemy. That would merely have delayed the advance for an instant, while betraying Trant's presence and whereabouts. Instead, he threw the stone into the air, so that it sailed over the enemy's head. It was a fairly big stone, and the enemy was not directly facing the thrower. It fell, as intended, into the pit, landing with a swish and a crackle. The enemy swung round.

"Good!" thought Trant. "One to me!"

He was justified in his jubilation. After pausing for an instant, the enemy went quickly back to the edge of the pit, and now looked down more intently. The floor was half-concealed, and still in deep shadow. He peered down for a long while, and as he peered something bright gleamed in his hand.

"Barlow!" called the enemy.

Silence.

"Who's there?"

Silence again. Then the enemy began to walk round the edge of the pit.

There was only one way down. Reaching it, the enemy paused, and peered. He repeated his enquiry, but the dead cannot answer, and only his own voice came back to him. "Hell!" he muttered, and began to descend.

His legs disappeared, his body, his head. Trant slipped from his shadow, and crept towards the spot. He drew as near as he could without the risk of being seen, and waited, crouched on the ground, with his ear cocked. In his mind he visualised that descent, trying to time it. He visualised the cautious figure climbing down, pausing every now and again to stare round and try to pierce the darkness below, revolver firmly gripped and ready for instant action. He visualised the last stage of the descent, the arrival at the bottom, the poking around . . . until . . .

"*God!*"

Trant held his breath. The picture he was visualising became suddenly more vivid, for now he was no longer guessing. That sharp exclamation from below betrayed the point that had been reached. Yet it was only with difficulty that the crouching man at the top of the pit resisted the temptation to confirm his conviction, and to add the evidence of his eyes. Trant had been through a lot. He had suffered acutely; was still suffering. In his weakness, he was bitten with a desire to watch someone else's agony and dismay—he wanted his fill of it! But discipline prevailed. He did not move. In a few moments he would provide further dismay. Meanwhile, he must go on waiting for just a little longer.

The figure below, having made its gruesome discovery, was now examining Barlow's body. Again, Trant visualised. Two hands—hands with the guilt of blood upon them, and waiting to be handcuffed—would be feeling about the body, groping in pockets, touching a wallet, and opening it. But the wallet would be empty, saving for a half-sheet of paper, on which, if a match were struck, or an electric torch switched on, or if it were taken to a corner of the pit where the grey light just penetrated, could be read this message:—

"You are beaten! You are covered at this moment by four pistols. If you wish to leave this pit alive, you will call up to those who are now watching you, and you will tell them where your two captives are, and you will stay below, still covered every moment, until they have proved your truth. Then, only, shall you have a run for your money. Otherwise, you will be shot like a rat in a trap. You have five minutes."

This was what Chisholme found in the wallet of Barlow, instead of some thousands of pounds.

32

THE BATTLE ON THE BRINK

Five minutes! And four revolvers covering him! Chisholme, the blackmailer, looked upwards from his black hole, and experienced for the first time the sensation of those he had so often trapped himself. Now, *he* was the one against the many. Previously, it had always been the other way round, and he had been among the many against the one! Yes, but his own victims had usually been released, when a price had been paid for them, or at worst had succumbed to some swift "accident." There would be no release for him. His price was too high! And his exit from the world of toil would not even resemble an accident. It would be a deliberate, minutely-planned exit, planned for the protection of Society, with all the shame and publicity attached to it, and the agony of the waiting . . . the waiting . . .

He looked upwards, but all he saw were figures of imagination. Though the light was gradually increasing? it was still vague and deceptive, and had four men with revolvers actually been covering Chisholme, they could easily have remained invisible among the shadowy foliage of the high ground above the pit, or among the trees. So, spurred by these unpleasant imaginary folk, Chisholme imagined folk even less pleasant—a judge in a black cap, a jailer, a prison chaplain, and another figure more dark and forbidding still, the figure that would send him speeding into eternity.

"Well, wouldn't bullets be better?" thought Chisholme.

Trant, crouching above, was praying that such a thought would not enter Chisholme's mind. It was to prevent the thought that he had suggested giving Chisholme a run for his money. Now Chisholme reviewed that run, and its meagre possibilities.

A precious chance he would have! *He* had never shown any mercy. Then why should he expect mercy? Why should he even expect to be given a run at all, since he had broken his own word over and over again? Set a thief to catch a thief—tell a lie to catch a liar—these obvious truisms damned his prospects. No, there would be no hope for him, even if he did provide the information that was required of him!

Then why provide the information? If he were going to die, it should be in as large a company as possible—and, incidentally, in the pleasantest fashion of death. Bullets were pleasanter than the hangman's rope. . . . And his own bullet might be the pleasantest bullet! He could ensure a neat, quick job of it.

But, though Chisholme was not a physical coward, the idea of hastening his own end did not appeal to him. There was something *small* about it-—and even a blackmailer, odd as it may seem, can have his vanity, and can parade his actions before some queer tribunal. Therefore Chisholme decided not to kill himself, but to send his defiance forth, and then—to wait.

He raised his revolver, and fired it upwards into space. That was his answer. Then he drew to the side of the pit, and counted the seconds.

The seconds slipped by. They became minutes. The tension was almost unbearable. It was as unbearable to the man at the top of the pit as to the man at the bottom.

An idea came to Chisholme. It was not born out of any definite plan of self-preservation, because he already regarded himself as theoretically dead though he still had to go through the agony of it. It was born of the twist in his character, the defiance that was in his soul, the refusal of one born graceless to conform to grace, even on the threshold. He lit a cigarette, gave one quick puff, then held it away from him at arm's length. Keeping to the shadows, he walked slowly to the body of Barlow, lowered the cigarette to the dead man's mouth, and fixed it there.

Then he moved away. It was based upon an old trick, and would not be likely to draw more than one bullet. Still, even that one would be amusing, and would form a good final entertainment. Meanwhile, as a gesture of contempt against the universe, the spectacle of a dead man smoking had its points.

More minutes flew by. The cigarette dropped, and fell from the dead man's mouth. "That's the signal," reflected Chisholme, superstitiously. "Now the bullets'll come." But none did come. An amazingly long five minutes!

"This is more than five minutes!" was Chisholme's next coherent thought.

It was a thought that struggled through perspiration. Chisholme's forehead was very moist by now. Even though he was cheating the hangman, he was experiencing some of the agony he was attempting to evade. . . . More time went by. Five minutes? Hell! More like ten—or twenty!

"God!" gasped Chisholme, almost hysterically.

For a new thought had come to him. A thought that bore a little breath of life. *Were* four revolvers directed at him? Had he been going through all this for nothing? That note—it might have been written an hour ago! They did not know for certain that he would return! Something might easily have occurred to lead his pursuers away from this spot, to give up their original plan, and try another. They might have waited for him, and then departed. Or they might have departed, to return again. Now Chisholme was suddenly alive and active again, and was speeding for the path of escape.

He paused once. He recalled that sound in the pit—the sound that had directed him to it. Still, the cause of this might have been some small animal. It proved nothing. Whereas the absence of any offensive movement proved a lot!

Beaten, was he? Not a bit! Life was still his, the game was still his, and the prey was still his! And he'd see that the ten thousand pounds the police had taken from Barlow's body was made up to him! He would tack it on to the price of Miss Leveridge and Rose Terrence!

Now he was half-way up the path. His spirits rose even faster than his body. Not one of the four revolvers was trying to prevent his escape! Had they been directed upon him, would they have remained silent? He laughed softly. What a fool he had been! But it had been a tricky business, quite the trickiest in his recollection, and after the night he had been through perhaps he could be forgiven for a little bungling. Even Napoleon blundered once!

Three-quarters of the way up! Above, the dim outline of the pit's edge. Only a few seconds more . . . now a leap . . . and over the top. . . .

Two arms wound round him. For an instant, he became a limp and helpless thing. He had imagined himself alone, and now—this octopus! But a second later, as he found himself toppling backwards, the instinct of self-preservation reasserted itself, and he hurled himself into the surprising contest with all his strength. At first his strength merely played a negative part. It kept him stationary. The thing that had attacked him had used the weapon of surprise, and he was in a nasty position. But soon it became apparent that surprise was the attacker's only weapon, that there was no knife or revolver to back it up, nor even great physical strength. The attacker could wriggle and kick,

but could not hold. Chisholme, making this pleasant discovery, shoved his great body forward and upward, edged
himself round, and then, with a sharp jerk and a twist,
rolled his attacker beneath him.

"Got you, eh?" he gasped, pausing for a moment, but
keeping his vice-like hold on the other's throat.

Trant looked up at him. The world was becoming very
dim. Rather soft, but with a great throbbing, and something pricking somewhere. . . .

"By God—so it's you, you little rat, is it?" hissed
Chisholme. "This is the last time you'll be at my heels!"

The world became a little more understandable.

"Hallo, Chisholme," gasped the man in the brown suit.
"I guessed it was you."

"Did you? Well, now you know!"

"Yes. Now I know."

"And do you know what's going to happen next?"

Trant struggled against a desire to close his eyes and
have done with everything.

"Yes, I can guess that, too," he murmured. "I'm going
down into the pit. And you'll be hanged. And may God
forgive us both."

"Hey!" roared Chisholme.

For the man beneath him, as though suddenly inspired
by the very name of God, had given a great heave, and
had sent Chisholme sprawling. For an instant Chisholme
found his head pressed backwards over the pit's edge. One
instant more, and the end would come. But, as suddenly
as it had come, his adversary's strength departed, and the
grip relaxed. Trant slipped limply to the side, and lay on
the ground, a huddled heap.

"Your trick, Chisholme," he murmured. "Get it over."

Trant's eyes closed. Chisholme stared at him. Just one
little shove, and the trick would be his without dispute.
He laid his hand upon the body. What a fool this fellow

had been to hang on to his heels! About to kill the fool, Chisholme discovered the necessity of hardening his heart for the job.

"Oh, hell!" he cried, suddenly. "I can't wait here!"

He seized Trant's limp form. Then something struck him on the back of his head. And Chisholme's form became even limper than Trant's.

33

THE CIRCLE OF TIME

Trant opened his eyes. He found Freddy Reeve, with a revolver in his hand, staring at him. The world was full of miracles.

"Afraid I've done for him," muttered Freddy.

Trant did not reply. After such an experience as he had been through, one cannot be conversational all in a moment. But he managed to shift his position so that he was a little farther away from the edge of the pit, and to sit up slowly, while the world grew gradually closer again.

"Feeling pretty groggy, eh?" asked Freddy.

Trant nodded. He was feeling exceedingly groggy, and even yet did not trust his voice.

"Well, so am I," said Freddy. "Killing's not in my usual line."

"It was him or me," Trant now managed to say.

"I know it was," replied Freddy. "I don't think I could have shot him in cold blood like that, otherwise."

"Perhaps it's as well," murmured Trant. "You've probably saved a lot of bother. But I wish I'd made him speak before he died."

"What do you mean?"

"I was trying to get him to say where—"

"Miss Leveridge was?" interposed Freddy, and Trant nodded.

"Well, you needn't worry about that any more."

"What!" gasped Trant. "You've *found* them?"

"I know where they are, and I'll have found them in a minute," said Freddy. "They're *here.*"

"Here?" gasped Trant. His mind raced. Emotionally, he was midway between joy and disgust. Joy, since success was at hand; disgust, because he had failed to divine the solution himself. "How do you know?" he asked.

"Too long a story to tell you all of it now," replied Freddy, falling on to his knees beside the prone figure of Chisholme, "but, briefly, we chased a couple of the gang to the world's end, and got the information out of them at the point of the pistol. They're here, man. *Here!* Been here all the while! And thank heaven this chap did return, as you said he would, because he's got the key! Pretty rotten work, going through a dead man's pockets, but it's got to be done. Anyway, I've done worse than this to-night to save Miss Leveridge and, if necessary, I'm ready to go on doing it!"

Trant, regaining his breath, watched him curiously.

"You think a lot of Miss Leveridge?" he queried.

"Don't *you?*" asked Freddy.

"Of Miss Leveridge? Well, perhaps not quite so much at this moment as you do." Freddy's groping hand paused at this astonishing assertion. "You see," went on Trant, "the girl you're helping isn't Miss Leveridge at all."

"What?" cried Freddy.

"Miss Leveridge is in Sheringham," replied Trant.

Of course, the man was raving! Freddy continued with his search. It was more important to find a key than to listen to the ravings of a man whose mind was being unhinged.

"She went there by car," said Trant.

"I say—try to pull yourself together," urged Freddy, seriously. "Miss Leveridge took her seat in the 5.18—"

"And, just before the 5.18 started, she left it again—and somebody else slipped into her seat. Somebody dressed like her, and who had even been photographed purposely as Miss Leveridge in the morning's papers. *That's* the lady you are interested in, Mr. Reeve—not Miss Leveridge!"

"But why—?" began Freddy, blankly.

"—should she have done this? Why should she have travelled on the 5.18 as Miss Leveridge for the express purpose of being kidnapped? Go on with whatever you're doing, and I'll tell you." Freddy began fumbling about the dead man's pockets again, in bewildered haste. "The whole thing was a plot to trap the kidnappers. Sir Henry Leveridge's letters to the papers were the bait. They directed attention to his daughter. The press paragraphs directed attention to his daughter's plans, and to the train she was travelling to Sheringham by—alone. But it was never Miss Leveridge's intention to travel in the train. . . . I suppose you're looking for a key? Try his hip pocket. . . . It was this other girl's intention to travel in her place."

"Why?" demanded Freddy, still groping.

"Well, she hoped that if she were kidnapped herself she would be taken to the place where Rose Terrence was hidden, and Rose Terrence happened to be her sister. Pretty plucky girl, Miss Terrence, don't you think?"

Freddy did not reply. He had found the key, and he preferred his actions to speak for him.

"Wait! Half-a-second!" muttered Trant, as Freddy sprang towards the house. "Can you give me a hand?"

"You're in no condition to move," replied Freddy, stopping.

"I'm not dead yet," retorted Trant.

He rose, with Freddy's assistance. Soon, he hoped, his most urgent requirements—peace and a bed—would be satisfied, but meanwhile one had to plod on while ability remained.

"Where do we go?" he asked.

"That cupboard under the stairs," answered Freddy. "Remember it?"

"So that's the spot," murmured Trant. "I'm losing my sixth sense!"

They hastened to the house. The back door was open. Chisholme had left it so. Groping their way quickly through the passages, they made for the cupboard, threw the door open, and entered it. Freddy looked around anxiously. He had a momentary fear that, even now, they were being duped. Certainly, the first rapid glance did not reveal anything. But when they had descended to the lower level of the cupboard at the back, they found what they were searching for round the dark angle. A key-hole was in the wall. The key from Chisholme's pocket fitted it.

"Thank God!" murmured Freddy.

The wall swung open, and they passed into a black passage leading to descending stairs. Freddy blessed the flash lamp the clergyman had given him. At the foot of the stairs was another door, and this gave Freddy a second nasty moment. No key to this door was needed, however. It was merely bolted on the outside.

They shot the bolts and flung the door open. They found themselves in a small chamber. In a corner was a wooden case, upon which was a candle, and sitting near the case, staring towards them with startled eyes, were the child and the girl who meant more than all the rest of the world to Freddy Reeve.

"Miss Terrence!" he cried.

She jumped from her chair, and the startled look in her eyes changed to an expression of amazed relief. Then she swayed, and Freddy bounded forward to catch her. For a dizzy moment he held her to him. Then Trant's voice recalled him to earth. Trant had run to the child, but now he swung round swiftly.

"Someone's coming!" he rasped. "Look out!"

Footsteps were approaching along the passage. A man burst in upon them. It was the clergyman.

The effect of the clergyman's entrance into that gloomy chamber was astonishing and galvanic. Trant stared for an instant, then turned away and began to cry. Freddy, on the other hand, expressed his hysteria by laughing uncontrollably. But Miss Terrence flung herself out of his arms and into the arms of the clergyman, while the child ran forward shrieking joyously.

"Daddy!"

Freddy heard it, but it didn't stop him. He just went on laughing, and Trant went on crying. Laughter and tears often express the same emotion.

The sun was rising as a Citroen car to which the inmates had only a poetic right glided away from a house of grim nightmares. Driving it was a clergyman, with a small child snuggling in the seat beside him; behind were a young man in a Savile-row suit, although Savile-row might not have been proud to claim connection with so torn and bedraggled a garment, and the most beautiful girl in the world. Thus, at least, she would have been described by the young man in the Savile-row suit.

"Miss Terrence," murmured the young man, breaking a silence.

"Well?" replied the girl.

"There's one thing still on my mind," he said. "You're still wearing that ruby engagement ring."

She held out her finger, and regarded it reprovingly.

"So I am," she answered. "This ring was my one really bad mistake. It wasn't till I saw you staring at my ring-less finger in the train that I remembered Miss Leveridge would naturally have been wearing an engagement ring."

"Yes, she *was* wearing an engagement ring," nodded Freddy, "and that was why I stared. But hers was a diamond ring."

"And my ring, which I slipped from another finger, was a ruby one. Yes, I know. But I had to risk that. I couldn't hatch diamonds all in a moment."

"From another finger," repeated Freddy. "May I see which finger that ruby ring really belongs to, then?"

She removed it slowly to the third finger of her right hand. Her engagement finger was now bare.

"Thank you," said Freddy. "I like that ever so much better." Then he added, as an afterthought, "For the time being."

"What does that mean?" she enquired, and then flushed quickly. "No—I retract!"

"Too late," he retorted. "I'm going to tell you what it means. It means that, before long, I hope you and I may travel together on the 5.18 under happier conditions!"

There was a short silence. Then she replied, with a sudden little smile,

"Well, of course—it *might* be rather jolly!"

All at once, he found her hand in his. Did it mean gratitude—or more? He refused to enquire. Perhaps he was not in a condition to enquire. For the touch of a woman's hand can dissipate all problems in the magic of the moment, and can even banish spectres. With that warm hand in his, it was impossible to believe that death lay behind them, and lay ahead of them. It was impossible to believe that anything intrinsically bad could exist in the great adventure through the universe.

"Look!" whispered Freddy suddenly.

They were passing a grey-towered church. The low sun sent its shaft upon the clock, and turned time gold.

The time was 5.18.

Twelve hours ago . . . !

THOMAS KINDON

MURDER
IN THE
MOOR

THE SEVEN BLACK
CHESSMEN
John Huntingdon

MURDER
AT SEA

RICHARD CONNELL

THE MAY DAY MYSTERY

OCTAVUS ROY COHEN

Coachwhip Publications

CoachwhipBooks.com

Coachwhip Publications

CoachwhipBooks.com

THE STUDIO
MURDER MYSTERY
THE EDINGTONS

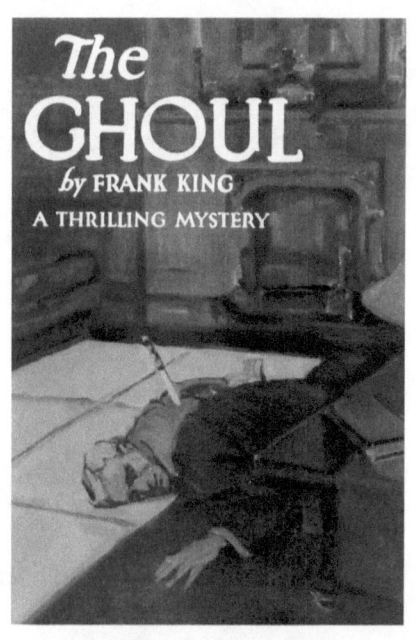

The
GHOUL
by FRANK KING
A THRILLING MYSTERY

CRY MURDER
EDITH HOWIE

NO FACE TO
MURDER
EDITH HOWIE

Coachwhip Publications

CoachwhipBooks.com

FULL CRASH DIVE

ALLAN R. BOSWORTH

GRIMM DEATH

LADY IN LILAC

SUSANNAH SHANE

MURDER IN THE WPA

ALEXANDER WILLIAMS

Coachwhip Publications

CoachwhipBooks.com

Coachwhip Publications

CoachwhipBooks.com

MURDER IN THE FAMILY

NICE PEOPLE MURDER

Mary Hastings Bradley

THE 13th GUEST by ARMITAGE TRAIL

MEDORA FIELD

WHO KILLED AUNT MAGGIE?

BLOOD ON HER SHOE

MEDORA FIELD

Coachwhip Publications

CoachwhipBooks.com

MURDER
À LA RICHELIEU
THE ADELAIDE ADAMS MYSTERIES
ANITA BLACKMON

MARIAN
GALLAGHER
SCOTT

TALL MAN WALKING
————————
THE ATTIC ROOM

THE CRIME,
THE PLACE,
AND THE GIRL

DOUGLAS AND
DOROTHY STAPLETON

CRIME IN
CORN-WEATHER

MARY MEIGS ATWATER

Coachwhip Publications

CoachwhipBooks.com

Coachwhip Publications

CoachwhipBooks.com

The
Hollow Tree
Mystery

MADELON ST. DENIS

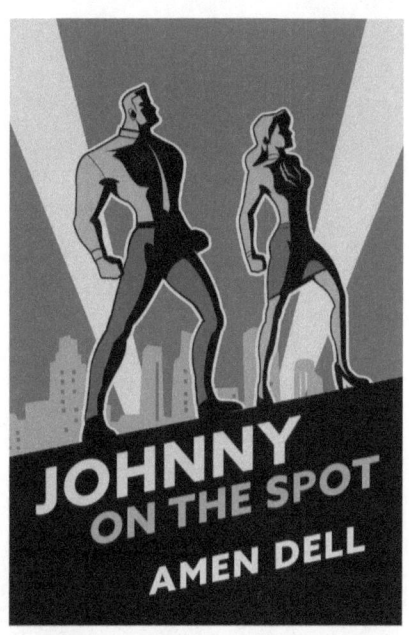

JOHNNY
ON THE SPOT

AMEN DELL

VULTURES
IN THE SKY
A HUGH RENNERT MYSTERY

TODD DOWNING

SAMUEL ROGERS

YOU'LL BE
SORRY!

YOU LEAVE
ME COLD!

Coachwhip Publications

CoachwhipBooks.com

www.ingramcontent.com/pod-product-compliance
Lightning Source LLC
Chambersburg PA
CBHW050406260626
47156CB00003B/888

* 9 7 8 1 6 1 6 4 6 6 1 0 7 *